THE
WEDDING
Shake-up

OTHER TITLES BY JJ KNIGHT

The Wedding Confession

Big Pickle

Hot Pickle

Spicy Pickle

Royal Pickle

Royal Rebel

Royal Escape

Tasty Mango

Tasty Pickle

Second Chance Santa

Single Dad on Top

Single Dad Plus One

THE WEDDING Shake-up

Wedding Meet Cute Series

USA TODAY BESTSELLING AUTHOR

JJ KNIGHT

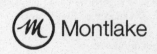
Montlake

Text copyright © 2023 JJ Knight
Excerpt from *The Wedding Confession*, copyright © 2023 by JJ Knight
All rights reserved.

Published by Montlake, Seattle

www.apub.com

Amazon, the Amazon logo, and Montlake are trademarks of Amazon.com, Inc., or its affiliates.

ISBN-13: 9781662512070 (paperback)
ISBN-13: 9781662512087 (digital)

Cover design by Hang Le
Cover image: © Colin Anderson Productions pty ltd / Getty;
© studioloco / Shutterstock; © Pogorelova Olga / Shutterstock;
© Billy333 / Shutterstock; © Chiociolla / Shutterstock

Printed in the United States of America

For Wesley.
I still remember the day
you decided to call me Mom.
It may have been a journey
for you to get to me,
but I will be your mother
for all the rest of my days.

Chapter 1

TILLIE

I can't scream. That would ruin everything.

I clutch my maid-of-honor bouquet as a black crab emerges from the brush line, uncomfortably close to our tiny beach wedding.

Its red eyes and charred legs give the impression that this oversize shellfish has recently surfaced from hell. A fat gray pincer reaches out and snaps a weed in its way.

My urge is to point, sound the alarm, possibly run.

But I can't be rash. It might scuttle the other direction, and I will have ruined the wedding for nothing.

The bride is my sister Ensley. She gazes adoringly at her groom, Drew, her veil fluttering in the breeze. It's a dewy-eyed moment. Drew slides the ring onto her finger and whispers, "I pledge you my love."

I shift my gaze back to the crab. It's paused, thank God. Hopefully, it's choosing its route wisely. *Go the other way!* Just in case, though, I scrunch my bare toes and bury them in the sand.

I told Ensley a beach wedding was a bad idea. Grit in your underwear. The ocean breeze melting your curls. The crab threat is the I-told-you-so moment baby sisters dream of.

But Drew and Ensley were involved in two wedding disasters in a row, including one where they got trapped in a shed together and completely missed their groomsman and bridesmaid duties.

So they chose La Jarra Island for their big day. A few guests, mostly family. Sunset wedding on the beach. Dinner. And *done*.

But now we have an uninvited crab. It darts several steps forward and back, as if trying to decide its next move.

Please leave us alone!

I glance to my right at our middle sister, Lila. Has she spotted the threat? But no, she's watching Ensley place the ring on Drew.

I may be the only one who's noticed.

I side-eye the guests. Drew's mother, Christy, is staring beyond the couple, her eyes wide. Okay, she's seen it, too.

She squeezes her mother's arm. Grandmother Forsythe probably thinks the gesture is about the sentimental moment. Christy rises slightly in her seat, alarmed. But she must also recognize what a fuss she's about to cause, because she sits again.

I'm with her. Until the crab comes our way for certain, we have to hold our chill.

But as the sun continues its descent, dimming the light a degree, another crab emerges from the brush. Then another. Then a bunch more!

It's a whole flock. School? Herd?

Nightmare. That's what it is. A nightmare of crabs.

The latecomers meet up with the leader, as if they are forming an attack brigade. My chest hitches as I try to control my breathing. I glance at Christy. She's covering her mouth with her hand.

The officiant raises his arms. "I now pronounce you man and wife. You may kiss the bride."

We've nearly made it. *Come on!* I want to watch this moment, but then the first crab moves forward. The others follow.

I can't suppress my squeal, causing Drew to hesitate while leaning toward Ensley for their kiss.

My older brother, Garrett, who stands behind Drew and faces the wrong way to see the invasion, jerks his head toward me and widens his eyes in a *what the hell* message.

But then everyone follows my gaze. I know the moment my sister Lila sees the crabs, because she has never been able to suppress a reaction to *anything*. A scream erupts from her that would make a horror movie director proud.

Drew's mother stumbles to her feet, followed by the rest of the guests. Grandmother Forsythe, who complained about how hard it is to walk in sand at her age, leaps onto a chair like a ten-year-old girl.

The crabs are startled by the flurry of movement and scatter. Some head back to the brush. Others scurry to the water. But a few confused ones end up racing toward our group.

Drew sweeps Ensley into his arms. Lila grabs little Rosie in her flower girl dress and lifts her onto her hip.

I want to crawl up the white arch, but I don't think it will hold my weight. "Why did you make us go barefoot?" I shout at my sister, high-stepping with my long skirt in my hands like I'm dancing a jig in fourth grade PE.

Garrett watches the panic with a shake of his head, picking up a chair and rushing the remaining crabs like he will crush them all in a mighty blow.

The officiant holds out his hands. "No, no, my friends. It's all right. These land crabs are native to La Jarra and are far more frightened of *you!*"

Like hell they are. They *charged*! Cries and screams leave the wedding scene in chaos, guests trying to stand two at a time on the wooden chairs, like Jack and Rose flailing on the door in the ocean water outside the *Titanic*.

Garrett raises his folded chair over his head. He refused to go barefoot and likely feels more confident in his steel-toed boots than the rest of us.

I notice a streak of green heading in our direction, and suddenly the chair is pulled from Garrett's grip and tossed aside.

"Tourists! You're the worst!"

It's a man, a stranger not from the wedding. He scoops up an over-size crab with both hands and rushes it to the ocean. Then he dashes back for another, his sandy hair ruffled, face red with exertion. In no time, all the remaining crabs are safely relocated to the water and disappear beneath the surface.

I drop the hem of my pale-blue cotton dress. Drew sets Ensley down. The officiant helps guests from their perches on wobbly chairs. There are several shaky laughs. More than one person presses a hand to their chest.

"We're all right," the officiant calls. "All we need is a kiss."

Drew nods, stepping close to Ensley as the wedding party resumes their positions. He tucks a loose bit of hair behind Ensley's ear. Her curls are falling. *I told her.*

I'm still breathing hard from the fright. Rosie sniffles on Lila's shoulder, startled by the commotion. I pat her back while Drew kisses Ensley and a sigh ripples through the guests.

The happy couple walks up the aisle between the chairs, and I turn to look for the man who saved the crabs. He's headed toward a circular beach bar with a thatched roof, his green surf shirt clinging to broad shoulders and powerful arms. He's barefoot and incredibly tan.

As soon as I'm down the aisle myself, I rush to catch up with him.

"Hey!" I call.

He stops and turns to look at me with the disdain I often sense between locals and tourists. Not that I travel a lot. I'm too poor for that.

But at the Atlanta bar where I mix drinks, we can always spot the out-of-towners. They're an easy mark for ridicule with their strange expressions and unexpected fashion choices, the perfect *us* versus *them*. No doubt this guy is going to complain about our wedding to his buds.

You should have seen those dumb tourists, he'll say. *Scared of a few local crabs.*

The urge to smooth things over is strong. "Thanks for helping. Sorry we got spooked."

He points at Garrett. "That punk was going to crush them. They're females with egg sacs." His accent is lilting and melodic. "The crabs are already losing their safe spaces. They're forced to cross the beach to deposit their eggs in the water."

My face contorts into a grimace as I picture an army of newborn red-eyed crabs. The babies can't possibly be cute. "Ewww."

His eyes blaze fire, hands fisted. "They're an important part of the ecosystem here."

I can't tear my gaze from his angry face, and parts of my body *start their engines.* I'm the worst about getting hot for passionate men.

But I can't handle being an ugly afterthought, even to a stranger. "That *punk* is my brother. And he was only protecting our sister, the bride."

He rolls right over it. "And that's why weddings shouldn't even happen out here. Especially not during breeding season."

Oh, this is getting good. "You'd cut out a million-dollar destination-wedding industry over a case of crabs?"

He stares at me for a moment, and I think my joke will crack his facade, but it doesn't. "If you can't handle the local wildlife, get off the beach."

I examine my fingernails like I'm completely unruffled by his yelling.

He stares me down, hands on his hips.

Dang. I want to tackle him. But I have to move on.

I glance at the wedding party, which is breaking up to head to the reception dinner. "I was trying to thank you, but you're damn crabby."

"You would be, too, if you knew anything about the island." His neck is as red as the invading crustaceans' eyeballs, and it's hard to leave him. But I have to go.

"Thanks, anyway." I attempt a jaunty twirl to head in the other direction, but end up kicking sand on his shorts.

He grimaces and dusts it off, muttering, "Tourists," before heading toward the bar.

Great. I couldn't have made a worse impression. Might as well put a finish on it.

As his form recedes down the beach, I call out, "I hope you get all the crabs you deserve!"

Chapter 2

GABE

I stomp through the sand back to my bar, flipping up the hinged section of the counter, and survey the empties in front of the customers.

Mostly tourists.

Can't live with 'em. Can't make a living without 'em.

But my friend Mendo is sitting there, too. And by the amused look on his face, he saw the whole thing.

"That's quite the fine lady you were talking to there." Mendo runs his palms over the shaved sides of his hair, his habit when people are looking at him. "You ask her out?"

"I don't date tourists." I point at a young couple and, at their nods, wash my hands and grab two clean hurricane glasses from the rack overhead.

"Right, you're a fighter, not a lover, no?" Mendo lifts his pint glass with a wink. "You are all brawn and scowl and women will not trifle with the likes of you."

"Mendo . . ." I cut off my growl. I have tourists to serve.

"Here is Gabe in his true form," Mendo tells the customers. "Strong, angry, tough. His exterior is as impenetrable as a conch shell, his heart as dried up as the husk of a coconut."

The couple next to him, snuggled close and most certainly honeymooners, look from Mendo to me to see how I will respond.

I sigh. Here we go. "Knock it off."

But I know my protest will have zero impact. Mendo loves telling wild tales to tourists. "Poor Gabe." He turns to the couple. "He once was in love with a woman not of La Jarra. She was beautiful and entrancing. Everyone who saw her fell for her instantly."

I dump ice into the glasses, shaking my head to dismiss the story. I will have no part in this.

The honeymoon couple is rapt, hanging on Mendo's every word.

He lifts his hand as if painting a picture for them. "She had long hair, black as night, that fell in ringlets. Her nose was as tiny as a pixie's, and her eyes were the cornflower blue of a perfect robin's egg."

Other patrons of the bar lean forward, trying to catch his words. He's good, making his La Jarra accent heavier for effect. He does boat tours and always hams it up for tips.

He continues his story. "This woman arrived one morning like dawn itself, wearing a dress as blue as the sea, her eyes on fire from the reflection of the rising sun."

I pull my hurricane mix from the fridge below the bar and measure out the red liquid. Another man holds up an empty pint glass, and I acknowledge him with a nod.

"Where was she from?" the first man asks.

"No one knows," Mendo says. "It was as if she was born of an ocean wave."

Mendo loves his details. I add rum to the drinks and give them a deep stir.

"What happened?" a woman asks.

"She walked along the beachfront, enchanting everyone who came her way. Men tossed flowers at her feet. Children danced around her like she was a fairy princess."

I drop a paper umbrella on the rim of each drink and set them in front of the young couple. Then I take the other man's empty pint glass and drop it in the sink, turning to grab a fresh one.

Mendo continues his story. "She had many admirers but would look at no one, casting only the smallest smile, until she reached this very bar. And there was our fair Gabriel, a fine picture of a man, making a rainbow-layered drink of his own invention."

The honeymoon woman slides the laminated cocktail menu closer to her. "Which one is that?"

Mendo shakes his head. "It's not on the menu. Only the locals know of it. It is his greatest achievement."

Now we're straying into infomercial territory. I fill the man's pint glass with beer.

Mendo stands in front of his stool, warming up to the story. "The woman from the ocean saw the sun strike the colors of the drink and sat right there." He points to a seat currently occupied by a middle-age woman in a flowered hat. She touches her windblown hair, flustered at the group's sudden attention.

"My lovely woman, you are as radiant as the sun yourself." Mendo lifts his glass to her, then resumes his story. "The goddess asked for the drink, and Gabe gave it to her, struck by her beauty, same as everyone else on this fair isle."

Fair isle. He's laying it on thick today.

"Did she like it?" the woman in the hat asks.

"Like it?" Mendo slaps the bar. "It was as though he'd given her a love potion. She lifted her gaze with those long eyelashes and instantly fell for Gabe."

This time the men reach for the cocktail menu. They've forgotten the drink isn't there.

"Did they start dating?" Honeymoon Lady's eyes are alight, as if she needs a good love story.

Mendo cuts the air with the flat of his hand. "Oh no, there is no mere dating with lovers like these. They danced in the sand to the music of the waves. The stars came out early to shine upon their happiness."

Good grief. I wipe my hands with a towel. Nobody's ordering anything at the moment. They're all listening.

Mendo takes a sip of his beer before continuing. "For long days and nights, they moved side by side. The goddess spent her time on the beach, never far from Gabe's bar. She brought him food, and when they had a moment to spare, they rowed out among the bioluminescent waters to gaze into the amazing future they planned together."

"What happened?" the flower-hat woman asks. She's invested.

"One night, Gabe rowed her out to one of the secret caves for a midnight swim. It hadn't occurred to him that his goddess never went in the water. When he stepped out onto the rocks in the darkness, he was only in waist-high waters, but the stones can be slippery with algae. When he reached for her, he lost his footing, tipping the boat. She went over the side."

Several gasps tell me that some of them believe she dies in this story. I rotate my hand to tell Mendo to speed it up. I can't have him bringing everyone down on one of my high-volume drink nights.

"The cave was dark, lit only by the blue glow of the plankton," Mendo says. "I know, because I run a secret tour of the caves that ordinary tourists can't visit."

Ah yes, the product-placement portion of the story. Honeymoon Man quickly asks, "Do you have a card?"

"I do." Mendo passes him a stack to share around.

And there it is. I wash the dirty glasses and set them in the dishwasher to be sanitized.

"What happened to the goddess?" the flower-hat woman asks.

Mendo watches the business cards move around the bar. "Gabe here heard only a splash and a swoosh. And the lady was gone. There was no sign of her in the cave. He looked all night and all morning. But when he brought his boat back out into the light, there were strange rainbow scales caught in the rope." Mendo meets the gaze of all his rapt listeners. "And he recalled seeing those same bright scales in his bathroom from time to time."

He sips his drink to let this information sink in. "He never heard from his goddess again." He slams his empty drink on the bar. "And so, no tourists for Gabe! No women at all. Not until his rainbow mermaid returns to him!"

The customers sit back, understanding they've been told a tall tale.

"I'd still like to try that drink, if it's real," says the flower-hat woman.

"Sure," I tell her. "It's called a mermaid sunrise."

"Sounds wonderful," she says.

I pull down a collins glass and set to layering it. Grenadine, juice, Midori mixed with vodka, then blue curaçao cut with water. The bright colors hold their positions, creating a rainbow effect.

I stab a pineapple chunk, a cherry, and then a green seahorse gummy candy and slide it into the glass. "Here you go."

"I love it," she says.

All the women look expectantly at their men, and soon I'm busily mixing a whole round of them. The evening is now above average in drink sales, and Mendo has two people waiting to talk with him about booking the secret cave.

All is well.

But as I go through the motions of mixing, pouring, and taking credit cards, my mind turns to the bridesmaid, with her ocean-colored dress and raven hair. Mendo used her to launch tonight's version of the story.

She's long gone, and it's unlikely I'll see her again.

I'm glad.

I do have a rule: no tourists in my personal life.

Not even if she is a beautiful, sassy, raven-haired goddess.

Chapter 3

Tillie

As the reception winds down, I feel more restless than tired.

When we get back to the condo, I hug my sister and brother good night. Despite my newfound fear of crabs, I walk along the shore in front of the condo complex, my sandals dangling from my fingers.

The beach is mostly quiet. The tourists have packed up for the evening. I'm guessing there are other places more suitable for locals. The waves roll in, frothing as they stretch along the sand. The moon is a crescent, reflecting on the water in a bright line.

The thatched-hut bar is still open, colored lights ringing the roof. A few people sit on stools, talking quietly. Maybe a nightcap will be good. I'm sure the green-shirt man is long gone. He's not among the patrons sitting along the circular counter.

As I choose an empty spot, there's a clink of glass from inside the bar. I assume that's the bartender, bent down to deal with barware or inventory.

I slide a laminated menu toward me, curious to see if there's anything I don't know how to make. Choosing a cocktail that tastes worse than the ones I mix myself is an occupational hazard as a bartender.

I scan the list, seeing nothing new, then spot a colorful layered drink in front of a woman a few chairs down.

She sees me looking. "It's not on the menu. Mendo told us all about it. It's called a mermaid sunrise." She gestures to a man on the opposite side of the circle peering down at his phone.

At his name, his face lifts, eyes bright against his dark skin. "Oh, hot damn," he says. "Gabe. Your goddess has returned."

Goddess?

And who is he talking to?

A head pops up from below the bar.

Then a green shirt.

Oh.

It's Crab Man.

He's the bartender. Gabe, apparently.

I freeze, wondering if I should leave.

Everyone's watching us, as if I've been the topic of conversation since the wedding a couple of hours earlier.

"Hey," I say.

Gabe's expression could scare off a shark. "You're back for more."

I see. We're picking up the fight right where we left off. "The wedding is over. The reception was only a dinner."

He dries a hurricane glass. "You aren't worried about attracting another case of crabs?"

Mendo laughs so hard, he chokes on his spit.

I scoot the menu away. "I figure I've already been exposed."

The woman with the colored drink taps her long fingernails on the bar. "Get her one of these on our tab. She looks like she could use it."

Gabe sizes me up. "It'll be on the house."

I don't want to insult the woman or her choice of drink, but that looks like a sugar bomb with the alcohol content of a Shirley Temple. "Maybe I'll just have a beer."

"You have to try it," the woman insists. "It's his own invention, created in honor of his great love, who turned out to be a mermaid."

Oh, the things I could say. I pinch my lips to keep my mouth shut. Gabe has the good sense to avoid commenting.

The woman realizes I'm not convinced. "And it's a love potion."

I drop my shoes to the sand at the base of the chair and set my clutch on my lap. This is definitely more entertaining than staring at the wall of my hotel room.

I nod at the woman. "You're right. If it's his tribute to his mermaid enchantress, created to make others fall in love, then I guess I can't pass it up."

Gabe heaves a sigh, shooting a dagger look at Mendo.

He shrugs. "Give the people what they want."

Gabe pulls a collins glass from the rack near his head and fills it with ice. Even if I'd rather not ingest something so sweet, I'm curious to watch his technique. Layered drinks aren't easy, especially with that many colors.

Red, orange, green, blue. The green and blue interest me the most. Midori shouldn't go above juice or below blue curaçao. The density is wrong. He must be cutting it with something.

The bar where I work doesn't encourage us to make drinks this complex. It's a hole-in-the-wall, catering to cheap well drinks and beer. Even a margarita machine is too far-fetched.

But my sister Ensley likes her fruity drinks, so I practice on her. We've all lived together outside Atlanta for the last two years.

Only when we return, Ensley will be gone. She's married now.

The thought sobers me. I still have Lila and little Rosie, of course. But it's hitting me. The big sister we've relied on for decades is officially somewhere else. We're on our own.

"Why the long face?" Mendo asks. "You're getting a free drink at a beautiful beach on the most glorious island in the world."

I straighten my expression. Maybe I've listened to a thousand sad tales from the other side of the bar for years, but I'm not about to become one.

"Post-wedding blues," a woman says, taking a sip of her drink. "Nothing like weddings and funerals to make you take stock of your life." She stirs absently as her gaze drifts to the ocean, and the various layers mix and swirl, spoiling the effect.

I glance at Gabe to see if he's noticed or cares, but he's carefully sinking the grenadine to the bottom of the glass. "Go light on the sugar," I say.

He raises an eyebrow, as if I've asked him to paint devil horns on the *Mona Lisa*.

"It *is* sweet," the woman says. "So watch out. It goes down like Kool-Aid."

"I like my drinks subtle," I say.

Gabe pauses. "This drink is about as subtle as a rainbow unicorn farting cotton candy."

"I'll take it, then," the woman says. She lists a little to one side, and I realize she's drunk. Normally I can spot them more easily than that.

Gabe makes eye contact with the man holding on to her.

The man nods. "I've got her."

"We're on our second honeymoon," the woman says. "I was knocked up the first time and kept puking."

Now I'm the one meeting Gabe's amused gaze. "Is that so?" I say in my perfect bartender blend of mild interest and an edge that doesn't encourage details.

Gabe deftly adds a juice mix to the middle, pineapple-orange, if I had to guess, then stirs a jigger of green Midori with a half shot of vodka. I knew it.

"I like this part," the woman says, leaning onto the bar.

Gabe holds a bar spoon over the drink, using the spiral handle to slowly ease the Midori mixture onto the juice to avoid mixing.

I can do it with a cherry. It's a spectacular trick and not nearly so lazy.

"Lazy?" Gabe's head snaps up.

Uh-oh. I said it out loud. This is one of my worst habits, sending thoughts that should be silent straight out of my mouth.

Everyone at the bar is looking at me.

I fold my hands together primly, as if I never meant to cause a fuss. "You can use a cherry to layer the liquors." Might as well double down. "It's a beginner's trick to use the bar spoon."

Gabe's face darkens like a cartoon character about to shoot smoke out of his ears. He pushes the glass toward me and slams the bottle of blue curaçao on the bar. "Show me."

"I need a cherry." I lift my eyebrow to drive the double entendre home.

The drunk woman does it for me. "Won't find many of those around here!" she cackles.

Gabe lifts a bowl from below the bar. It's piled high with cherries, all stemless.

I suppress my sigh. "I'll need one with a stem so I can hold it."

Gabe grunts and pulls out a jar of cherries and dumps a few on top of the others. These still have their stems.

"And I have sandy hands."

He drops a container of antibacterial wipes onto the bar. Damn, he's an angry one. But I knew that. He charged the wedding like a small-town sheriff about to bust some punk kids spray-painting the water tower.

I tug a wipe from the plastic jug and take my time cleaning my fingers. His eyes go as fiery as they did when I challenged him earlier.

I like this. I like it a lot. Poking bears is one of my favorite pastimes.

I pick up the bottle of blue curaçao like I'm going to dump it straight in and wait for his self-satisfied smirk. He thinks I'm stupid.

I speak to the patrons, who are all watching. "Of course, you can't simply pour blue curaçao on top of Midori and vodka. It's too heavy and will mix. Water, please? And a glass?"

He frowns. Ha. He thought he had me.

I stir the blue liquor with water in the glass. Then I use the cherry to slow the flow so the mixture lies neatly on top of the green. For an extra flourish, I quickly sink the cherry, making the color stream through the other layers in a streak of blue.

The bar patrons *ooooo* and clap.

Nice.

I smile at them, then turn to see Gabe's murderous look. Now I feel bad. I've shown him up in his own bar. I wouldn't like it if someone did that to me.

"A flourish on an already perfect drink," I say, pushing it toward the woman. "Just for fun."

Gabe grabs the bottle and the cherries and turns away.

I slide off the stool. Personal poking is fun. Professional one-up-manship is wrong. I know better. "I should go."

"Nuh-uh," Mendo says. "Things just got interesting." He turns to Gabe. "I've known you for nearly ten years. Nobody's improved upon your mermaid sunrise."

I hold up a hand. "It's all right. I have a slightly different skill set."

Gabe whirls around. "I thought you might be a bartender. Where?"

"Atlanta, Georgia."

"Oh." His angry demeanor falters.

The bear has feelings? Concerns? "Oh, what?"

"An American bar," he says.

I get it now. "What's wrong with American bars?"

"Nothing, if you like pale beer and watered-down cocktails."

The bar patrons let out the same *ooooo* you might hear at a wrestling match.

Apparently, I'm getting into a bar fight. Or, I suppose, a booze brawl?

"Who said anything about a brawl?" Gabe snaps.

Dang it. I did it again. Said my thoughts aloud.

Normally my bar is so noisy nobody notices.

Mendo bangs his fists on the counter in a steady rhythm. "Booze brawl! Booze brawl!"

The other patrons take up the chant.

Gabe holds up his hands, his ears red from his anger. Maybe smoke *will* come out. "We wouldn't want to embarrass the little lady. She's not familiar with island cocktails."

"Little lady!" I'm practically sputtering. "I could cocktail you under the table!"

"Whoooooo." The patrons turn to Gabe for his retort.

He shrugs. "If you want to do a drink challenge, we can." He wipes down a glass as if the whole idea is beneath his concern. But I know better. The redness has spread to his neck. He's mad.

"When?"

Gabe slams the glass on the bar with a thunk so hard I'm surprised it doesn't crack. "Right now is as good a time as any."

Mendo leans forward on his stool. "No, no, no. If we're doing a La Jarra versus USA bar brawl, we've got to do it right. Set a date. Promote it. Really pump it up."

Gabe's eyebrows draw together. "It doesn't have to be a big deal."

Wait. Is he nervous? "Afraid you'll lose?" I ask.

Another *ooooo* ripples around the bar.

Gabe stands opposite me, hovering over the counter until our faces are inches apart. His breath is warm and smells of cherries. He ate some. "I'd challenge you anywhere at any bar at any time."

The bar patrons erupt in cheers.

He's not going to scare me. "You're on."

I think fast. Drew and Ensley are headed to a tiny private island in the morning for their honeymoon. I don't have much scheduled because Lila has Rosie. Garrett and I are snorkeling at dawn, but then he has to fly back for work.

I'm pretty free, actually.

I move even closer to him to prove I'm not intimidated in the least. "Tomorrow afternoon?" Our faces are so close now that someone looking over from a distance would probably think we're kissing.

Gabe keeps the position a beat longer. Everyone holds their breath, waiting for his reply.

Finally, he steps back. He picks up a bottle of tequila, tossing it into the air with a perfect spin before neatly catching it in his palm.

Uh-oh. I hope I haven't been punked.

He aims the bottle at me. "Sure. Four o'clock?"

I nod. What have I gotten myself into? I don't have any bar gear. I'll have to use his.

But I can't back down.

"What are the rules?" I ask. "And the stakes?"

Gabe shrugs. "It was your idea."

Mendo stands. "I've got it. Three drinks. One for taste. One for presentation. And one wild card. I'll assemble some judges."

"I have to make sure I have the ingredients," I say. "I can't conjure the right liquor from nowhere."

"Come by in the morning," Gabe says. "We'll go over what you need. Anything I don't have, we can pick up at the wholesaler. I'll cover it."

"Okay. And the winner gets what?"

Mendo smiles. "The winner gets to run the bar with the loser as their lowly apprentice for the entire evening shift."

"It's a Saturday night," Gabe says. "I can't make her work that hard."

As if. I push away from the counter. "You've got what—twenty stools here? Try holding down a bar with *thirty* stools, four waitresses, and a roomful of tables."

He starts to open his mouth but I add, "And your barback doesn't show."

He closes it. "All right, then." He spins the bottle sideways on his palm. "Meet here at ten for a supply run. I'll let you get used to my setup. Then the booze brawl at four."

I tear my eyes from his fancy bottle work. "Make it eleven. I'm snorkeling in the morning."

"Done. And your name is . . ." He extends his hand for a shake.

"Tillie." I reach across the counter. When our skin meets, an electric charge flashes through my body. Yeah, that's no surprise.

Gabe is exactly the sort of man who gets under my skin.

Chapter 4

GABE

Mendo hangs around until the last customer closes out. He often does.

Tillie stayed only a few minutes past when we established the parameters of our booze brawl. She never even got a drink. Probably for the best. No point in tipping her off. I already know how she can dunk a cherry.

When I start latching the metal shutters that secure the bar, Mendo stands to lower the ones on his side. He's been uncharacteristically quiet since Tillie showed up and the challenge was made.

"So, Gabe Landers is having a drink war with a tourist."

I drop the last shutter, separating us. But I can still hear his laugh. I check all the locks and close down the register. When I duck beneath the back opening, he's there, watching the waves.

He turns, and his eyes glint from the lights of the condo property that backs the bar. "You have to admit, she's a looker."

I don't give him the satisfaction of a comment. It's not the first time Mendo has played matchmaker, or given me grief about women.

I shoulder my knapsack and scoop up my sandals. We have a long walk to the public parking lot half a mile up the beach.

Mendo falls into step beside me. "You sore I brought up the ocean goddess again?"

"I don't see why you always tell the story like I got ditched by some beautiful stranger."

"I'm telling the version of the story that sells drinks." He sidesteps close enough to ram his shoulder against mine. "Nobody buys from the man who loves 'em and leaves 'em. You, my friend, are a player."

I only grunt to that. Mendo adds the sales pitch to his story so he can justify telling it every time a cute girl glances my way. Sometimes the goddess is blonde and curvy. Other times, she's olive-skinned with sleek straight hair. Mendo can riff off anyone who walks up.

And give me hell in the process.

He shoves his phone into a jean pocket. "This new one's going to get you. I can see it."

"No chance."

"I saw that gleam in your eye."

"It's moot. She's a bartender. I'm a bartender. One of us will make better drinks than the other. Then she'll fly home, and we'll never see each other again."

Mendo shakes his head. "Nah. There's something to her. You agreed to the challenge. It's not like you."

"You've never set up a booze brawl before."

"You've never had eyes for another bartender."

Two crabs scuttle out of the brush to head toward the water, both females with heavy egg sacs attached to their undersides. We pause to avoid startling them.

"It's good publicity," I say.

"And it has nothing to do with the girl."

The crabs glide into the ocean, disappearing in the dark surf. "She could have been a dude."

"But she's not."

We start walking again. A bead of sweat rolls down my back. It's a haul down the beach, and the night temperatures don't drop much.

Mendo stares up at the waning moon. "You didn't think it was coincidental that she's from Atlanta?"

That turn of conversation gets my blood up. "It doesn't matter. It's pointless."

"I'm just saying, cozy up with her, maybe you get a free place to stay out of the deal if you want to go track down Anita."

"I've never said I wanted to do that."

"But you could."

I shake my head. "Not interested. My life is here. My mother is here."

Mendo sniffs. "It's an interesting coincidence that Tillie's from the same place, that's all."

My feet sink into the sand as we get to the damper part of the beach, closer to the marsh where the crabs live and breed.

"I'm sure a thousand tourists from Atlanta come through here, and I never know it."

"But this time you do."

"Irrelevant." My tone is harsh. I'm done with this line of talk.

We arrive at the lot, Mendo's junker Jeep and my motorcycle the only vehicles taking up spaces. I have a car for when I need to move inventory into the hut, but I prefer the freedom of the motorcycle for most things.

"See you tomorrow," Mendo says. "I have bookings all afternoon, but I'll head to the booze brawl the moment I get in."

I stop walking. "You aren't going to be there?"

He waves a hand at me. "You didn't consult me on the time. But I'll send judges, like I said. Morrie will do it. Chuck too. I'll find a third."

"We should get a girl. Otherwise, she'll think it's biased."

"I'll get two girls then. Anya and June."

"Okay."

"Don't worry about a thing. I'll put up flyers. I bet I can get Trubido to mention it on the radio."

"It's not going to be that big of a deal."

"It might."

"It's a beach hut. I can't even handle a big crowd."

"You'll have her to help. Don't knock it." He steps up into his Jeep with a wave.

I shove my helmet on while Mendo goes through his routine to get the engine to fire up. Then we're both circling out of the lot, Mendo heading to his house off the highway. I aim my bike toward my apartment on the edge of town.

Normally I take Saturday mornings to work out, run numbers, and check on my investments. I've been saving, but I'm not sure what for. The future seems a nebulous thing, fuzzy and far away.

But apparently, tomorrow morning I'm meeting up with a blue-eyed tourist from Atlanta, Georgia.

And there's no accounting for why the very thought of it makes my pulse race.

Chapter 5

TILLIE

Lila and Rosie are already up when I slide out of bed and start the coffee. My sister is one of those annoying morning people who begins the day with a bright, shiny personality and no need to slam caffeine to get there.

Little Rosie gets up at the butt-crack of dawn, as cherubic and giggly as a cartoon baby. The two of them have their routine, flowing in and out of cuddles, meals, diaper changes, and toy appreciation with a silent communication I envy.

Ensley and I have marveled at how Lila took so easily to motherhood, given our lack of a mother ourselves. Mom died only a few months after giving birth to me, and with Lila barely two years older, we don't have much example between the two of us.

We all have helped Lila with Rosie since she can't afford day care while working at a pizza joint. My role was critical back when Rosie was an infant. I could easily manage the three to six a.m. shift because I got home around then anyway.

But now she's sixteen months and sleeps through the night. And Ensley will be gone. We've been practicing a new pattern of work and childcare for the last month in preparation. Ensley's new house with Drew is deep in Atlanta, a good hour drive in traffic.

We're on our own, but Lila and I are firmly together on this. She's been through enough letdown and abandonment. We all have. Nothing would make me leave her while she needs me.

Lila pours juice into a sippy cup, Rosie on her hip. The baby has wrapped Lila's long pale hair around both fists. "I'd say I'm jealous of your snorkeling trip, but we both know it's a lie."

I stare at the coffee maker, willing it to work faster. "You never did like to swim."

"I'd be terrified in the ocean. What if there's a shark?"

I shrug. "What a way to go."

"Tillie!" She elbows me. "Don't talk like that."

The coffee begins to dribble into the carafe, so I shift it aside and put my mug in the flow. I'm not waiting for it to finish to get my fix.

"If I die in a shark attack, I leave you all my tiny bras for Rosie. I can't be the only flat-chested member of the James family."

Lila tugs on her pink T-shirt. "You'll be glad after nursing. Mine are down to my belly button."

"They are not."

"Are too."

Rosie sends up a wail, and Lila realizes she never passed her the juice cup. "Everyone wants to be the size of a fairy sprite," she says. "You don't even have to try."

We have this conversation a lot. I'm jealous of my sisters' ability to fill out a swimsuit. They hate that I can wear children's sizes in a pinch.

The mug is full, so I return the carafe to the machine and bring the sweet elixir to my face. Steam curls over my cheeks, and my nose is filled with the best smell in the world.

"Ahhhh." I breathe it in.

"You and your coffeegasms." Lila heads to the condo's living room space. She covers Rosie's eyes. "You're too young to see that."

I chuckle. Raised by three sisters, Rosie's got life on lock. She'll never go through what we did. We won't allow it.

And her deadbeat dad? Good riddance. We're everything she needs.

Garrett stumbles out of his room, his hair sticking up in every direction. "Did we really schedule an early-morning outing?"

I shift the coffee carafe off its perch and place another mug in its spot. "We were dumb."

"What time's my flight?"

"Noon."

He rubs his eyes. He's shirtless in low-slung shorts. And fit. Lila and I catch each other's gazes, eyebrows lifted. When did our brother become a *snack*? He's going to get snapped up soon, and then only Lila and I will be left as singles.

I finish my carafe-and-mug routine and pass him his coffee. "Have you been working out, Garrett?"

He glances down. "This last job has been more hands-on. Try moving steel beams for hours a day."

"Yuck." I sip my coffee.

Lila sets Rosie in her pack 'n play and joins us by the counter. "You dating anybody?"

He shrugs. "Here and there."

Garrett lives back in Alabama, where we grew up, so we don't see him as often now that all the sisters have moved to Atlanta.

Lila and I exchange glances again.

"Anybody we should know about?" she asks.

"Nope." He wanders out of the kitchen, bending down to tweak Rosie's ear before heading to his room. "See you in a minute."

"You better get dressed," Lila says. "You don't want to miss the boat."

I laugh. "Especially since we already got crabs."

She smiles. It's a good moment between siblings, even if we're missing Ensley. We're still at ease with each other.

"When will you be back?" she asks. "We'll have to drive Garrett to the airport by ten. Drew left us the rental car since they're taking a boat to the tiny island."

"Oh, right." I completely forgot about Garrett's flight when I made plans with Gabe. "Can you do it? I have a . . . thing." I know the moment the words are out of my mouth that I'm never going to get away with saying so little. This is my sister we're talking about.

"A thing. In a foreign country. Where you know no one." She leans her hip on the counter.

I sigh. Might as well get it all out. "I went back to that beach bar last night."

"I heard you come in late."

"I wasn't ready for the night to end."

Lila opens a loaf of bread. "The wedding get to you? It got to me."

"Because of Asshole?" Rosie's father is the worst.

She shrugs and pops the bread into the toaster. "Maybe."

"Don't be mooning over him. He made his choice."

"I know."

I pause, thinking maybe the change of subject means I don't have to bring up the bar challenge, but, of course, Lila doesn't let it go.

"So, what are you doing that keeps you from saying bye to Garrett?"

"Oh, I'll say bye." I sip more coffee, waiting to see if I can stop there.

"And then you'll be where?" Her toast pops out, only the barest gold. I like mine closer to burned.

"A liquor store."

She scrunches her nose. "Why? I don't like alcohol, and you only do it with Ensley."

"I might need a few things."

Lila opens a jar of grape jelly and spreads a thin layer on her toast. "Did the wedding drive you to drink?"

"No." I might as well lay it all out. "I somehow got roped into a cocktail challenge. I'm going up against a local bartender."

"Oh!" She holds her toast. "That sounds kind of fun. Is it at that beach bar? Rosie and I could go since it's all outdoors."

"It is. In the afternoon. The morning part is to get the liquor I need."

"How are you going to get the leftover bottles home?"

Always practical. "He's covering the cost. I assume he'll keep them."

"He?"

"The bartender at that bar. I think he owns it. Or runs it, at least."

"All this happened after the wedding?" She crunches into her toast.

I know better than to leave out the important part. If Lila shows up for the booze brawl, she'll recognize Gabe.

"He's the guy who came for the crabs."

"The green-shirt hero?"

I nod, my nose over the mug. The steam has cooled away, but it's still aromatic and calming.

"How did this happen exactly?"

I'm not sure how to explain it. The mermaid drink. The challenge that rose in me. The talk of crabs and cherries.

I'm saved by the baby. Rosie presses her face into the mesh side of the pack 'n play and lets out a howl that hits all of us straight in the heart.

Then Garrett comes out of his room in his swim trunks, a towel thrown over his shoulder. He sizes up my pajama shorts and tank. "What gives, lazybones?"

"I'm going!" I gulp the last of my coffee and rush for my bedroom. The rest of the story will have to wait until later. And time will be tight. We'll get back, hug Garrett, and I'll have to walk down the beach to the hut.

Maybe between now and then I can come up with an explanation that will make sense to Lila.

And to me.

Chapter 6

GABE

I don't get nervous about much.

I grew up on this island. There's nothing about life here that surprises me. Not crabs. Not hurricanes. Not my work or the people.

But as I stand in front of my locked-up hut waiting for Tillie to arrive, my stomach keeps clenching.

That pisses me off. I don't have any stakes in what happens at this cocktail challenge.

And she'll be gone in a few days no matter what. That's what tourists do. They come. Then they leave.

A dark-haired woman walks along the shore, watching the waves. My belly flips.

I want it to know that I mean business, so I say, "Stop it. I'm not putting up with this bullshit."

The woman down the beach turns toward me, and I realize it isn't Tillie. Her hair is too short, too flyaway.

But then a voice beside me asks, "Are you always so angry when you talk to yourself?"

Damn it.

I turn around to face her. "You always sneak up on people like that?"

She smirks. Her hair's damp from her snorkeling trip. The black ringlets are glossy and sleek. They fall past her bare shoulders. She wears a red tube top and cutoffs. I know I've stared too long when her smirk is joined by raised eyebrows.

"I just walked up," she says. "I can't help it if your *me* doesn't like your *myself* or your *I*."

This woman is exasperating. I have to focus on the task at hand. "Let's look in the bar and see if I've got what you need. If not, we can head to the wholesaler and pick up anything we're missing."

"So we're doing this thing?"

I've taken two steps toward the rear of the hut, but this makes me pause. "Do you want to back out? I don't think Mendo has put up the flyers."

Her chin lifts, like she's challenging me. "Are you chickening out?"

"Nope."

"Then I guess we're on."

Fine. I ignore how unnerved I feel by her and unlock the lower door to the hut. I duck under the metal shutters, not wanting to lift them and reveal that we're inside. Vacationers sometimes want morning drinks, and I'm not technically open until after lunch.

I flip on the lights since the hut is closed up and no sunlight can fill the place. Tillie has bent over to follow me inside. Once the door is closed, we're perfectly alone. No one would have any idea we're here.

She runs her delicate fingers over the rows of bottles shelved below the counter. The space is small, with no center island. The lower sections are filled with bottles, the sink, a dishwasher, and all the kegs for the taps. There are two short fridges. Glassware, napkins, bar towels, and other necessities go up high.

"This is a good setup for the space," she says.

"I like it."

She peers up at me. "Do you own it?"

"I rent this hut from the condo management. They outsourced it five years ago."

She pulls bottles and sets them on the counter. "Where do you pee?"

"That bottle you just touched."

She yelps and jerks her hand back. "Gabe! What the hell!"

I like that I got her. "Kidding. We can use the condo leasing office during the hours it's open. After that, you have to hold it."

"So I might have a long wait if I lose. Maybe I will hang on to an empty bottle."

I'm already picturing this and have to shake the image loose from my head. "Just because Mendo said there were stakes, doesn't mean we have to include stakes. No one has to work for anyone during tonight's run. It's a Saturday night. It's going to be crazy."

She stands up sharply. "So you *are* worried about losing."

"No."

Her gaze meets mine, and there it is again, that zip of attraction. Damn it.

"I think you are."

"If we have stakes, I get help either way. It's win-win for me. You lose a night of your vacation."

"True." She opens a drawer and extracts a bar spoon. "You work this by yourself? Every day? Every shift?"

"Always. This is my bar. If I don't work it, it's not open."

She rummages through the utensils. "I haven't thought through what I'm going to make."

"Me neither."

She sets a silver jigger on the counter and bumps the drawer closed with her hip. Her gaze fixes on my collection of glassware. "I think we should put on a real show."

"You mean like tossing bottles and the whole nine yards?"

Her gaze fixes on my face. "Do you do that normally? Juggle glasses and all?"

"No."

"You did last night."

"Why did you ask if you know I do?"

"Why did you lie if you know I saw you?"

Her hand is on her hip, and a lightning bolt charges through me.

"Can *you* juggle bottles?" I ask.

"I wouldn't dream of it."

She's exasperating. "Then why are we having this conversation?"

She laughs. "You're way too easy to rile. You seem tough, but you're a big pussycat."

"Is that what you consider a good time? Riling strangers?"

She elbows my arm, and despite how annoyed I feel, a flash of heat zips from her skin connecting with mine. This is maddening.

"We're not strangers," she says. "This is our third encounter. I know your name is Gabe. That you've worked this beach bar for five years, and that you love your crabs."

That again. "The joke is getting old."

"Nope. It will never get old. And besides, your temper is the first thing I knew about you."

"I was justifiably angry that your brother was going to crush the crabs."

"Right, right. Pity the poor dumb tourists afraid of getting their toes snapped off."

"The crabs are more afraid of you than you are of them."

"And when they got spooked, some of them ran right toward us!" Her blue eyes flash with anger and my body revs up at the sight of it. What is with my attraction to this impossible woman?

I turn away. "Back to the bottles."

"Right, I have to choose one to pee in." She turns a bottle of vodka so that the label faces her. "Any of them will do."

I assume this is a critique of my selection. "You're used to higher-end liquor?" I picture her in some stately wood-paneled bar, serving up shots of small-batch whiskey and thirty-year scotch.

"Hardly. It's a beer-swilling, tequila-shooting crowd."

Oh. "What are you looking for?" I wave at the collection of bottles on the counter.

"I'm waiting for them to speak to me."

"Your bottles talk to you in Atlanta? Because mine are the strong, silent type."

This gets a genuine smile out of her. "You're one hot mess." Then she claps her hand over her mouth like she didn't mean to say it. "Sorry."

I know she's only sparring with me, but her words cause that curl in my belly to wind more tightly. "Good. I like to keep my enemies close."

Now her grin is so wide that her eyes crinkle. "I think our rivalry is going to play well tonight. We just have to pick the drinks. Are you going to do the mermaid sunrise?"

"Sure. Are you going to layer? We could both do one."

"Love it. You could be the bright side, and I could go dark."

"Dark liquors?"

"Right. Shades of black and brown. I need one really dark one, though. We'll have to pick that up."

I spin more labels so they face out. "Okay, will that one be presentation or taste?"

"Oh, presentation for sure. For taste, I need a good whiskey."

"We can do that. And the wild card?"

"I don't know. What do you think?" She hops up on the bar, her bare feet swinging.

I focus in on her blue-tipped toes like I'm under a hypnotist's spell. Her legs are slender, a touch pink from being out in the sun. So are her shoulders.

Right. Because she's a tourist. Who will certainly be gone within a day or two.

I shake my foggy thoughts free. "Let's get some fresh fruits. Pineapple, coconuts we can use for cups. Things like that. We can brainstorm what to use them for at the farmers' market."

"I like that. Before we buy things, you sure you don't have a good whiskey?"

"I don't get much call for straight whiskey, but I can dig a little deeper to be sure."

I kneel in front of the bottles, Tillie's legs still swinging mere inches from my face.

I'm not going to obsess over them.

Really. I'm not.

Chapter 7

Tillie

Gabe is into me.

Not in any emotional way. I'm not looking for that, anyhow, certainly not with a stranger from another country. But his interest is as clear as his traitorous gaze that keeps taking me in.

So, this begs a question.

Do I want a fling during my vacation?

Maybe. Especially since we clash so spectacularly. It'll be hot, burn itself out, and then I go home.

Works for me.

Gabe bends low, moving bottles around, and I admire the way his blue shirt stretches over his back. The muscles in his shoulders shift and bulge.

Yeah. I'm into him.

And I've got some time on my hands.

Lila, Rosie, and I took two weeks off for La Jarra. We've never been anywhere and are too poor for trips like this. But Drew got us this condo and stocked the kitchen with groceries. So we're making the most of it.

We have a few excursions planned, ones that work with Rosie. Finding starfish. Petting turtles.

Mostly, we're hanging out on the beach.

The same beach as Gabe's bar.

I'm not opposed to mixing a little bartending with pleasure.

He emerges from the shelves. He works so hard to avoid looking at my legs that he bangs his head on the edge of the counter.

I reach out for him. "You okay?"

He nods, running his hand over his scalp. He hands me a bottle.

I set it aside. "Let me check. I don't want you saying I only won the bar brawl because you had a concussion."

"I'm fine."

"Bend down!" My voice means business.

He leans over, and my fingers part his hair, searching for a bump or a cut. "Does this hurt?" I ask, poking his head.

"No." His voice has a squeaky quality, and I realize I've pushed his face into my thighs.

I lift him away. "You'll live."

He staggers back like he can't get away fast enough. "Thanks. Will that whiskey do?"

I pick up the bottle and uncork the top. I give it a good sniff. "Maybe." I pick up the silver jigger and pour a shot.

It goes down like fire and charred caramel. I close my eyes to concentrate on the subtleties of the flavor so I can imagine what will pair well with it for the flavor competition.

"So?" Gabe asks.

"Mmmm. For sure." When I open my eyes, he's watching me with all the seriousness of a brain surgeon. "What?" I ask.

"Can you taste better with your eyes closed?"

"Don't you ever turn down the radio so you can concentrate when you drive?"

"Do you always answer a question with a completely unrelated question?"

I cap the bottle and hop down to wash out the jigger. "Okay, so the only thing I'm missing is a super black liqueur."

"You could use a coffee liqueur or black vodka."

I dry my hands on a bar towel. "Do you still have time for a shopping run?"

"Sure. You okay with riding a motorcycle?"

Ooooh. Sexy. "Sure."

The very idea of seeing the island through his eyes appeals to me. Today might be my only chance to test this thing between us. Once the bar challenge is over, it will be much more obvious if I keep showing up to talk to him.

Nope. It's all-or-nothing right now. Today. Until the evening shift is over. By then, we'll either have hit it off or not.

He picks up his keys from the counter and swings them around his finger. "You ready?"

"I think so."

Gabe ducks under the opening of the hut, and I follow him, waiting while he snaps a padlock on the latch.

We walk opposite the direction of my rental, where the parking lot is lined with bushes. Gabe's motorcycle stands in a space between the greenery and the building's back wall. Interesting. It's like he's hiding it.

"Trouble with the law?" I ask.

His face contorts with confusion for a minute. "Oh. You mean hiding the bike. Yeah. I only have loading-zone privileges. Normally I park a half mile away."

He opens the back attachment and passes me a spare helmet.

I shove it on my head. Helmet hair. Great. It's big, so I have to tighten the strap.

He dons his helmet and throws a leg over the bike. "You ride a motorcycle before?"

"Yes." I hop on and rest my feet on the passenger pegs. I'm not lying. Back when Ensley and I were sharing a car, I often caught a ride home with a bouncer named Horace. Zipping along the freeway on his bike was a feeling I could get into. I can't wait to do it across the island.

Horace's bike was an extra-wide hog with a backrest and a grip. Gabe's is lean and narrow. I'm going to have to hold on to him.

He glances back at me. "Hang on."

Here goes nothing. I wrap my arms around his waist. There's no lift in my seat to help me see over his shoulder, so I rest my helmet against his back.

Yeah, I could really get into this.

The bike roars to life, and I feel the rumble in my thighs. He taps my leg to let me know we're taking off, and then we're speeding onto the main road.

Now *this* is vacation. The condo complex falls behind us. To the left is nothing but trees and brush. I turn my head. At first, I see more rentals, but then the view opens up and there's the ocean, blue-green and endless.

The wind whips the loose ends of my hair and rushes along my exposed knees. The world sharpens like a prism splitting into color. Sky. Sand. Sea.

I feel open, like the world can finally sink in.

It's a moment I never want to end. Gabe is sturdy and strong. As we lean into a curve, the ocean air is suddenly saltier and tart, like I've bitten into the lime from the rim of a margarita. I grip him more tightly, the edges of his shirt flapping against my thighs.

Birds swoop alongside us, then wing out over the waves. The beach spreads out, endless and empty. Judging by the lack of buildings and the crumbled edges of the road, we must be riding through some less-used part of the island. I spot several chickens scratching about and wonder who they belong to.

Then civilization returns, storefronts and parking lots and brightly painted beach houses. We approach our first stoplight, and the roar of the motorcycle shifts down. I smell asphalt and industry.

Gabe turns his head. "You all right?" he calls out over the engine.

"I'm great!"

He points up the road. "The wholesaler is ahead."

Boo. But I look forward to the ride back.

The light turns green, and we roar through the intersection, past a strip of cozy shops, then a recessed line of businesses housing a Realtor, a tech repair company, and Joe's Wholesale Liquor.

When Gabe kills the engine, I pull off my helmet and fluff the hair on my scalp, hoping I don't look horrible.

He waits for me to swing off the bike, then puts both of our helmets away. "We'll grab the booze first, and then go down to the farmers' market."

Oh, right. We have two stops. I'm thrilled. This expedition is better than any tour. I get to see the real La Jarra.

The door jingles as we head inside. It's not as air-conditioned as a shop would be in Georgia, retaining the salty, clammy feeling of the outdoors.

The bald, gray-bearded man behind the counter lifts a hand in greeting as he checks out a woman with an entire cart filled with boxes.

"Hey, Joe!" Gabe calls.

Joe's eyes follow me even as he turns the credit card console around to the customer. I get the distinct sense that my arrival with Gabe is 100 percent strange.

"Liqueurs are over here," Gabe says. "We might have a different selection than you're used to. Not everything gets imported."

I scan the line of bottles for familiar names. "As long as I get a chance to adjust the ratios based on the flavor notes, it will be fine."

"The bar will be slow early afternoon, so you're welcome to hang out ahead of the challenge."

"I think I will." A thrill darts through me. I'm seriously into this man in a way I'm not used to. *Roll with it, Tillie. You already have a flight home. No chance for attachment.*

I pull two bottles off the shelf and hold them up in the direction of the windows to get a bead on their color. I go with the darker one.

I set the reject on the shelf. "This is good. You need anything yourself?"

"I should get more blue curaçao. I have a feeling we're going to be serving up a lot of rainbows."

"Good thinking. I might make a blue Hawaiian in a coconut for the wild card. If the judges' age skews upward, that will play to the Elvis crowd."

"I'm not sure Mendo knows anyone over the age of thirty," Gabe says.

"Oh, that's right. You'll probably know the judges." He'll have an advantage. But it doesn't matter. I don't have anything invested in winning or losing. Although it would be pretty fun to boss Gabe around in his own bar for a night.

Gabe snatches a blue bottle as we pass them. "Don't assume it will help me. Most of these people would be happy to see me subservient to a tourist."

Interesting. "How do the locals feel about tourists?"

"You're important to our economy. Like many Islands, we used to supply raw goods to big countries, but there is only so much land to produce it. Now we thrive on being a financial haven as well as a tourist destination."

"But how do locals *feel* about us?"

He hesitates, nodding at a passing customer. "I guess there's a sense that as more outsiders move here, the less La Jarra retains its culture."

That makes sense. "Do lots of people move here?"

"Not anymore. It's really hard to get residency. Now, resort jobs, those are easy to get a temporary work permit for. But not to stay."

We arrive at the checkout, where Joe is watching our every move. I plunk the bottle down. "Hi, Joe! I'm Tillie."

He sniffs, turning the bottle toward him. "Not your usual swill, Gabe."

Gabe shakes his head. "Glad you hold my bar in such high esteem."

Joe shrugs. "Must be the influence of the lady."

I grin at him. "I made him buy it."

"Mendo brought the flyer around already." Joe tilts his head toward the front window.

The sun shines through it, making it readable from the back, in reverse. I wander closer.

LA JARRA BOOZE BRAWL
LOCAL BARTENDER GABE LANDERS VS.
GEORGIA USA HOTTIE DRINKSLINGER
LOSER WORKS FOR THE WINNER ALL NIGHT LONG
COCKTAIL SPECIALS

It lists an address I assume is for the bar.

I turn to Gabe. "Georgia hottie drinkslinger?"

He sighs. "I didn't get to approve the flyers."

I shake my head. "I've been called worse."

Joe sniffs as he stuffs the bottles in a paper bag. "Don't let nobody disrespect her," he tells Gabe.

"I won't."

"Watch those hooligans."

"I will, Joe."

Gabe picks up the bottles and leads me outside.

"Hooligans?" I ask.

"We get rowdy tourists at times."

"You think you need to save me from the very element I've served daily since I was old enough to work?" Before, actually, but I don't plan to mention my fake-ID days.

"Nope," Gabe says. "I wouldn't dream of it. Probably you'll have to save me."

That's better. He stuffs the bottles in his little trunk, padding them with a bar towel.

And then we're off again.
The local and the Georgia hottie drinkslinger.
I like it.

Chapter 8

GABE

I really hope Tillie isn't insulted by Mendo's flyers. I could wring his neck. Hottie drinkslinger? He made it sound like it's a club where cocktail waitresses wear halter tops and booty shorts.

And he's putting the flyers where the locals go. We'll have people we know showing up. I prefer to work with strangers. That way if they annoy me, at least our relationship is short.

My hands tighten on the grips as we turn toward the metal structure where the farmers' market is set up. Tillie straightens behind me, trying to see over my shoulder.

Only when I've pulled my helmet off and heard the familiar "Gabriel, who's this?" do I realize I've made a grave mistake.

That's right. It's Saturday. The one day my mother sells her candles over here instead of by the cruise port.

Oh boy.

Her frizzy spiral curls, dyed black with stark white roots, pops over the top of a stall. Her broad face lights up when she sees the two of us on the motorcycle. She's on the opposite side of the wall. I can still get away.

Tillie swings her leg over the bike and pulls off her helmet.

Mom must be standing on tiptoe to get her whole head visible. "Gabriel? Who's this young woman?" Her lilting, melodic tone is a testament to all the blending of cultures that led to her deep roots on the island. Mine feel shallow in comparison.

Tillie's gaze meets mine. "Another friendly local like Joe?"

If only. "Something like that."

Mom remains on the wrong side of the aisle, so I simply wave at her and steer Tillie to the opposite corner of the covered pavilion. Pete's stand will be the best bet for coconuts and the other fruit, with the bonus of being on the end of the market farthest from my mother's candle booth.

But the crowd isn't heavy yet today, and Mom decides to leave her stall, moving with determination and purpose to the end of the row to get to us.

There's no getting around this.

"Mom's about to ambush us," I tell Tillie.

"Mom?" Tillie's expression freezes, like I've zapped her with a Taser.

I rub my jaw. "Yeah. She makes candles to sell to tourists."

Tillie tugs the top of her red tube top up, and the cutoff hems of her denim shorts down. She touches her hair.

Great, I've made her self-conscious.

"She's super easygoing," I say, even though it's a whopper of a lie.

Mom weaves through the stalls like a horse aiming for best in show, quick and determined.

Panic radiates off Tillie.

"I'll keep it short," I assure her.

"Maybe I should browse the market." Tillie slowly sidesteps away from me.

"Good luck," I say, but then it's too late. Mom has both arms around my neck, dragging my forehead down for a kiss. We rock back and forth, and I peer over her shoulder at the market's inhabitants, washing over with both belonging and embarrassment at how long it goes on.

She finally releases me and turns to Tillie. "Who's this?"

Tillie has made it several feet away, but she halts, her panicked eyes meeting mine.

"Mom, this is Tillie, a bartender from the States. We're having a cocktail challenge at the hut tonight and are shopping for some fruit."

Mom moves in to hug Tillie, but I take her arm and turn her away. "Mom. You don't want to leave your stall too long. The tour bus will drop off passengers any minute."

Mom plants her feet, then grips my chin so that I look her right in the eye. This is a common tactic, and those warm brown irises are so familiar to me that I could have painted them from memory. "Gabriel Adam Landers, are you tryin' to get rid of me?"

I spot Pete and his brother hiding smirks behind their hands. Yeah, she just used the middle name of a twenty-eight-year-old to scold me.

It's Tillie who steps up. "I'm afraid it's me who's got Gabe in a rush. He has to open his bar, but he graciously offered to bring me into town to grab a few things I need for the cocktail challenge."

Mom releases me to consider Tillie. She lifts a pair of silver-rimmed reading glasses from the chain around her neck, then extracts a folded piece of paper from her pocket and turns it around.

It's the flyer for the booze brawl. Great.

"Is this the girl from Georgia?" She peers at it. "The hottie drinkslinger?"

I let out a long rush of air. I purposefully left out the specific state Tillie's from when I introduced her.

Tillie may have tried to sneak off earlier, but now she's standing her ground. "It's a rather colorful description made by Gabe's friend." She lifts her chin. She's not letting anyone judge her, not even my mother.

Mom takes Tillie in. "I would have gone with 'spritely,' or maybe 'fairy goddess.'"

Tillie's shoulders relax. "I like those better."

There's another long appraisal, but Tillie is significantly less defensive. She and Mom seem to come to some understanding, and Mom tucks the flyer away. "What are you buyin'?"

"Some coconuts to use as cups. And pineapple." I take a step back to show Mom that we have to move on.

But Mom threads her arm through Tillie's. "Come with me to look at candles. I have one to bring good luck for the challenge."

And here we go. Mom's candles don't have regular scents like vanilla or lavender. They have purposes. And so many f-bombs.

Fuck cancer. Fuck bad bosses. Fuck your ex. I'm guessing the candle she's going to show Tillie is *Fuck bad juju.*

I draw in a breath. It will be fine. Tillie can handle it. And even if she doesn't, in a couple of days, Tillie will be gone and so will this Mother lode.

Pete sidles up. "You got yourself a lady?" He grins, showing a mouth of gold teeth.

"No. I have a rival in a cocktail challenge. I'm going to need ten coconuts, made for drinking. Can you do that for me?"

He nods. "You want 'em right now? That'll take a minute." He whistles at his brother. "Hey, Bodeen, start chopping." He turns back to me. "Ya want the water out of 'em?"

"Nah, you can keep that to sell. We're going to put our own drinks in them."

"For that booze brawl?"

Seems like everybody already knows about it. "Yeah."

He lifts his arms and looks out on the mostly empty stalls. "Official provider of the coconuts for the La Jarra booze brawl right here!"

I have a feeling we might get more business than we expect tonight. It's a Saturday, which may not mean much to the tourists, but for the locals, it's an evening out.

Pete spots Anya, a friend of mine and Mendo's. She's wearing a hot-pink bikini top with cutoffs and holds a stack of flyers. "Anya, over here!" he calls.

Anya hurries over. Like Pete and Bodeen, she's a mix of Jamaican and African, and can be fierce about her La Jarra pride. Her long black braids trail down her back, and when she sees me, she breaks out in a big smile. "Gabe! Gaber! Gaberooni!" She envelops me in a vanilla-scented hug. "Where's the Georgia babe?"

I release her. "With my mother."

Anya's eyes grow wide, her long fake lashes touching her stenciled brows. "Already? You settling down? Introducing her to your mama?"

"God, no. Mom hijacked her."

She watches me for a moment. "Of course. Can't imagine Gabe getting serious with no-body. No-body is good enough for Gabriel."

"Hey!" I reach out to yank a braid, same as I've done since kindergarten, but she predicts my move and swings her hair aside.

"Poor stone-man Gabe. Never goes soft." She shoves the stack of flyers at me. "Hold on to these. I'm going to spy."

I'm forced to accept the pages, already limp from the humidity. What does she mean, stone-man? I can have fun.

Bodeen elbows me as he lifts two perfectly cut and hollowed coconuts. "Like this?"

"Yeah," I say, tucking the papers under my elbow to accept them.

"Ya want all ten now?" Pete asks.

"Ten?" Bodeen crosses his arms over his narrow chest. "I ain't doin' all that."

Those two are always fighting. Bodeen is seventeen, and Pete barely a year older.

"I'll tell our mama," Pete says.

Bodeen scowls at his brother, then stomps back to their stall.

Pete takes one of the coconuts to inspect Bodeen's handiwork. "Not as smooth as I do it."

"It's fine," I say. "It's just for tonight."

"What's going in them?" Pete asks.

"We haven't decided."

He peers into the hollowed core. "I hear whoever wins gets to boss the other one around."

I shrug. "We'll figure it out."

"I also heard she's from Georgia." Pete raises his eyebrows meaningfully. "Does she know Anita?"

Everybody knows everybody's business around here, especially at the market. "Georgia is a big place."

"I'm just saying."

"I'm not interested in looking for Anita."

"Who's Anita?" The sound of Tillie's voice makes me jump, and flyers work loose from my arm, sliding to the ground.

Pete snickers, leaning back against a white pole like he's ready to watch a show.

"Nobody," I say, leaning down to pick up the pages, then realize both hands are occupied with coconuts.

"I'll get them," Tillie says. She has a paper bag stamped *Eff the Bozos*, the name of Mom's candle business, but she slides the handle over her wrist and chases after the loose flyers.

Anya returns. "Hey!"

"Hey?" Tillie straightens the stack and takes the rest from me.

"I'll get those," Anya says, accepting them from Tillie. "I'm the one putting them up. I didn't call you the hottie drinkslinger, though." She holds up a hand. "That was all Mendo. I'm Anya."

"I'm Tillie. And it's fine. Whatever sells drinks for Gabe."

"A keeper!" Pete booms. "Am I right or am I right?"

I hold up the coconuts. "What do you think?" I ask Tillie.

She takes one. "I like it. It's going to be perfect." She peers into the hollow. "What if people want the drinks we make? Will you sell them in the coconut?"

"I'll handle it," Pete says. "I'll bring the cart to the condos. If ya get a rush on coconuts, Bodeen and I will start whackin' them."

Tillie nods. "Sounds great!"

"I asked for ten," I tell Tillie. "That should get us started. And Pete, can you slice up a pineapple?"

"Can you keep the outer skin on it?" Tillie adds. "It's prettier that way."

Pete nods and pushes off the pole to help Bodeen.

Anya points at the bag. "Whatcha get from Mz. L.?" She winks at me, and I wonder what she saw between Tillie and my mother.

Tillie passes the coconut back to me and pulls out a candle. *Fuck Failure* is printed in big black letters on the side.

Anya leans in for a sniff. "Ooooh, peppermint?"

Tillie nods. "For focus. And eucalyptus for energy."

"Mz. L. got it going on. She's a little bit health nut and a whole lot witchy."

Tillie breathes in the scent. "She mentioned there were special ingredients to ward off negative forces."

"Mm-hmm." Anya hugs the stack of papers. "I'd burn that candle tonight. Maybe you'll get yourself a lowly assistant in that hunk of manmeat." She angles her head toward me.

I can tell the comment throws Tillie. She probably thinks Anya is flirting. "I've known Anya since we were in diapers," I say. "And I was potty trained a full six months faster."

Anya shakes her head. "And who had the accident in Mrs. Perez's third grade class?"

"Okay, time to check on our coconuts." I motion my head toward Pete's stall.

But Anya and Tillie don't budge. Anya watches Tillie slide the candle back into the bag. "Looks like Mz. L. is favoring you over her own son for the win tonight."

Tillie shakes her head. "No, it's for both of us. She wants a big, successful night."

Anya smooths down the top flyer of her stack. "It's gonna be lit. I can feel it. See you tonight!" She takes off.

We walk toward the edge of the pavilion where Bodeen is still whacking coconuts to flatten their bottoms. "I have a feeling Anya is going to favor you over me," I tell her.

"But you're her friend."

"She likes you. Mom too." And it's true. It's not usual for either of them to take to a tourist like they just did. But then, I've never brought one to the market, either.

Tillie tucks her bag closer to her body. "They were fun."

"I'm worried this challenge is going to get bigger than we think."

Tillie bumps my arm with her elbow. "We'll be fine. They think we're big rivals. But really, we're a bartending dream team."

Chapter 9

Tillie

After our visit to the farmers' market, Gabe and I part ways, agreeing to meet an hour ahead of the challenge to make sure we have time to set out everything we need. I return to the condo and stare at the contents of my suitcase, as if the perfect outfit for the evening will materialize.

Lila shows up in the doorway to my room, Rosie on her hip. "How did it go?"

I spread every top I own on the bed. "I met his mother."

Lila steps inside. "His mother?"

"Yes. She sells candles at the farmers' market where we went to get coconuts. He didn't seem too pleased when she walked up. She gave me that." I point to the *Fuck Failure* candle on the dresser.

"Oh my." She sits on the white wicker chair in the corner, settling Rosie in her lap.

The room is serene, gold sheers billowing aside the tall windows looking out on a courtyard. The smell of the ocean permeates everything like the best, most expensive perfume. Everything is gold or white: the rug, the bedspread, the satiny wallpaper. Drew really spoiled us. I've never in my life slept in a room this nice. It's calming.

And I need calm. Panic keeps bubbling up like someone put dishwashing soap in a hot tub.

"So, you met his f-bomb-loving mom," Lila says. "How did it go with him?"

I eliminate three shirts and place them back in my suitcase. They make my chest look smaller than it already is, and I don't want to deal with comments about my "mosquito bites" or "goose bumps" in front of Gabe. I can't help that when God passed out boobs, I was obviously off fixing someone a drink.

"Well?" Lila prompts.

Right. "We get under each other's skin. When I'm around him, I can't stop myself from making digs."

"It's a defense mode. You've built it up after all these years of bartending."

She's right. "Something about him makes me want to sharpen my stick for the battle of wits."

"It's how you met. The crabs. The misunderstanding. You're sensitive when someone criticizes you."

"I am not."

"Oh, like right now?"

Dang it. I start pairing the remaining shirts with shorts and skirts. Ensley took us on an epic thrifting expedition before this trip to get beach clothes. She's a maniac in a resale shop. We got a lot of great stuff for almost nothing.

"I wish I had my bar boots." I arrange my meager footwear choices on the floor at the end of the bed.

"Working wasn't supposed to be part of the vacation."

"It's not working. It's entertaining. And today I got to see more of the island on the back of a motorcycle. Tourists don't get that."

"And meet a mother who·sells f-bomb candles."

"Isn't it great? She had one called *Fuck Fear* with lemon and cypress."

"Sounds like a mother you don't mess around with." Lila leans over so that she can see my shoes. "None of those look comfortable."

"I know. I think Gabe goes barefoot in the bar. He wasn't wearing shoes when he ran at us last night."

"You better not. Your feet will kill you, and you'll stub your toe a thousand times."

She's right. I'm not exactly graceful.

Rosie babbles, waving her arms. The two of them are quite the picture with the curtains stirring behind them. Lila wears a pink shirt and white shorts that match Rosie's pink jumper. At this moment, I'm so glad Dodge took off. He might not have let her come if he were around. And she'd have obeyed him. She always did. Him leaving was the best thing to happen to her, in my mind at least.

But Asshole Dodge is another reason I can never leave her. She's vulnerable. She needs me to watch out for her now that Ensley won't be part of our day-to-day lives.

I pick up a pair of red, thick-soled flip-flops. "I think it's going to have to be these. Everything else has a heel or is too strappy or flimsy."

Lila nods. "Then go with that red shirt with yellow flowers. And the denim miniskirt. You can bend over in it?"

"Yeah. I can wear biker shorts underneath it."

"Do you think the guys here will be as awful as the ones back home?"

Rosie drops her teething ring, and Lila scoops it up and blows on it to give it back. I walk over to extract it and wash it off in the bathroom sink. After working in bars, I can't handle anything that hits the ground. "I have a feeling rowdy drunks are the same the world over."

"But Gabe will defend you."

I hand the teething ring to Rosie, who promptly chucks it to the ground again. This time I let it be. "Yes, he probably will."

But do I want that? I'm used to handling my own ugly incidents. The bars where I've worked almost never had bouncers near the bar, and if they did, they were tied up with actual fistfights, not nasty comments between drunk men and the female staff.

Rosie howls, so Lila stands. "I'll try to find a spot with Rosie to see some of it. I won't be that mom with a screaming child trying to hang out with the singles, but I'd like to at least take a peek." She scoops up the teething ring. "Time for your nap, missy."

She leaves with Rosie, and I consider the ensemble. The red, flowered shirt is cute, tied at the waist, cap sleeves. The denim skirt fits well. All in all, a good choice.

So now that I've chosen the outfit, I have to get my head wrapped around Gabe, his mother, and this crazy event I'm about to take part in.

~

Only one couple sits at the bar when I show up an hour ahead of the official start of the booze brawl.

When Gabe looks up and sees me, his face brightens from serious concentration to something lighter, happier.

A glow blossoms in my chest. We might argue like an old married couple, but he's glad to see me. He can't hide it.

He's changed into a yellow shirt with red flowers. It's a good pairing for mine, like we did it on purpose. I don't think he notices this, though. He gestures to the back and opens his counter for me to enter.

I was right. Gabe is barefoot in his bar. The smooth wood floor is well worn, but I have a feeling that my tender city feet will get awfully sore if I try to match him. I miss my bar boots.

He's brought in a small rolling cart stacked with the bottles we'll need on the top tray. The lower one is filled with hollowed coconut husks.

"I brought this from home to organize the liquors. This first row is for our two layered drinks. Then your high-end whiskey with whatever you're doing for the second drink." His palms brush the tops of the bottles in a caress that makes parts of my body tighten.

"I like it. And when things get busy, we can always wheel it to the side to be out of our way."

"Or I can have Anya or Mendo take it out of here if things get crazy afterward." He quirks a smile. "Given that you will be here all night working for me."

"You're sure you're going to win?"

He washes his hands, a chuckle escaping as he dries them on the bar towel. "I have no idea what to expect from this. We have the least impartial judges in the history of judging. Flyers all over town might draw an outrageous crowd, or potentially no one at all." He shakes his head. "I'm winging it in a way that I never wing anything."

I pull the glassware I'll need. "Same. I like my bar neat and orderly. But you never can plan for how a night goes, like a van full of jerks showing up, already drunk."

"That happens less on this remote beach. But it definitely happens." We both lean on the counter, grudgingly admiring each other for all the things that we understand about each other's work lives.

The man sitting at the bar clears his throat. "Is it possible to get another round?"

Gabe jumps away from the counter as if he's been caught stealing penny candy from the five-and-dime. "Absolutely. Sure."

I tuck away my smile that he's distracted as I continue pulling the glasses we will need for the competition drinks. Something's happening here. He wasn't expecting it. And I certainly didn't plan on it.

But I'm pretty sure the only way to handle this surprise attraction is exactly what Gabe said.

Wing it.

Chapter 10

GABE

It's not going to be possible to bring my A game to this cocktail challenge.

Tillie looks too adorable to be working, her hair twisted up in a pile of ringlets, her flowered shirt and denim skirt colorful and perfectly fitted to that lithe body.

Every time she bends down to pull a bottle from the lower shelf, it takes all my willpower to avoid staring.

Anya arrives with the flyers and starts passing them out as we approach the hour. Pete and Bodeen show up with a handcart full of coconuts ready to be hollowed out if needed.

Mendo texts to say June couldn't come judge, but Morrie and Chuck will be there. Anya will be the third.

At first, I'm not sure anyone's going to show. We have maybe ten tourists ringing the bar as four o'clock hits. I specifically set it to before the rush, not that things ever get too crazy.

The foot traffic to my hut is steady but limited to the three condo complexes on this stretch of beach. It's a long walk from the public parking, and most people give out way before they get this far.

Anya returns, having finally depleted her stack, and hangs one of those customizable birthday signs where you can choose the letters from a kit. It reads BOOZE BRAWL USA VS LA JARRA.

"You're representing your entire country now," I tell Tillie, who watches Anya crawl onto the counter to tie the banner to the posts.

"Somebody's got to do it. Might as well be me." She tucks a bar towel into her waistband.

Morrie shows up with a speaker and a microphone from his karaoke setup. I've never seen him dressed like he is today. He's a sizable man, normally in some combination of jeans, hoodie, and Converse.

But now, he's full tropics. Green shirt with parrots. Yellow swim trunks. Flip-flops. He's even wearing a straw hat with a wide brim that ends with little pieces sticking out to form a pinwheel, the kind you mostly find at the tourist market. It's pulled so low that the only parts of his face you can see are his mouth and a triangle goatee.

He plunks the black box on the bar and drops the electrical plug over the inside. "Give me some juice, and we'll get this party started."

Anya hops back down to the sand. "No party yet. Should we delay until people get here?"

I plug the speaker into a socket below the bar. "We have to wait for Chuck, anyway. He's a judge."

"Oh, right." Anya pulls a black scrunchie off her wrist and ties her long black braids together. I guess judging is serious business.

A few more tourists arrive, most of them holding the flyer. Morrie tests the speaker. "Hello, hello, hello," he says in his melodic accent. "We will start the booze brawl shortly. Get your drink orders in now if you'll get thirsty as our two professional bartenders prepare for the challenge."

Nice. The newcomers take him up on that. Piña colada. Sex on the beach. Three beers. Tillie sets to work, leaving the cocktails to me while she pulls the taps. I intend to intervene, worried she won't do it right.

But she's good, getting a good frothy head about an inch deep.

I stuff down my urge to control every detail. It's fine.

I ring up the orders, and she checks on the rest of the customers, seeing if anyone else needs a refresh. I've never had anyone work the bar with me. I vacillate between concern and relief, then finally acknowledge that the experience is nice.

We get caught up, and I realize Chuck has joined the others. Anya is handing the men clipboards and explaining something with a barrage of wild hand motions. All the seats are taken and a row of bystanders fills in behind the stools.

"You ready for this?" I ask Tillie.

She tucks her thumbs in her skirt pockets. "Absolutely. Prepare to get your butt kicked."

This riles up the tourists.

"Whoa, ho, we've got some trash talk going on!" A man in a panama hat lifts his pint glass. "Who's got more experience?"

Morrie sees the attention is on the bar and hustles over with his microphone. "It seems we have a few prebrawl questions. Tell us your name, sir." He aims the mike at the man.

"James."

"And where are you from?"

"Ohio."

"Well, James from Ohio, what's your question for our competitors?"

James glances side to side, his cheeks reddening now that he has the spotlight. "I asked who had more experience."

Morrie spins around, his belly a split second behind the rest of him. He aims the microphone at me. "We'll talk first to our La Jarra local, Gabe Landers. Gabe, how long have you mixed drinks?"

I lean in. "Since I was nineteen."

Morrie tilts the microphone back toward his face. "For those of you who aren't from this great island, the legal drinking age is eighteen. Gabe might have an edge on our American. How old are you, Gabe?"

I glance briefly at Tillie, who stands a couple of feet away, arms crossed over her red shirt. "Twenty-eight."

"You heard it right here, folks! Our local drinkslinger, Gabe, has been serving up cocktails for nine long years! Let's hear from our golden girl, Tillie!" He moves along the line of tourists to get closer to her and squeezes between two young blonde women. "Tillie, tell us about yourself."

I think she might be shy, but she surprises me as she takes the wireless mike from Morrie and walks the counter as she talks. "I'm Tillie James. I grew up in Alabama, but now I live in Atlanta, Georgia."

I spot Chuck turning to Anya in surprise, but she just nods.

Tillie pauses in front of the blonde women. "Gabe here is five years older than me, and the legal drinking age in the US is twenty-one." She hangs her head and the crowd lets out a long "Awwwww."

She snaps her head up. "However, where there is hardship, there is innovation. I got my first fake ID at age sixteen and started working as a cocktail waitress!"

A great cheer goes up. "So I have seven years of experience." She passes the mike back to Morrie.

"Both of our contenders have solid experience," Morrie says. "But what are our heroes' specialties?" He moves closer to me.

I take a page from Tillie's playbook and hold the mike myself. "On this beautiful island, I make the most colorful, perfect cocktails!"

"And we love them," a woman shouts. I turn and spot the flower-hat woman from last night.

Her pronouncement is echoed by several tourists who must have been previous customers. I don't pay much attention to the details of the vacationers who temporarily land in my space, but they seem familiar.

Tillie takes the mike. "And for those of you who like more liquor than sugar water . . ." She pauses for the crowd to react with cheers and boos. "I focus on delicious flavors that harmonize like a perfect melody." She makes a deep bow and the crowd cheers.

One of the blonde women extracts a marker from her beach bag and writes TEAM TILLIE across her friend's bikini-clad chest. Then her friend does the same for her.

This fires up the crowd, and the marker is passed around. TEAM TILLIE and TEAM GABE appear on chests and foreheads and knuckles.

Morrie takes the mike. "Look at you, lining up for your favorite bartender. Let's hear it for Team Gabe and La Jarra Island!" A huge cheer rises, and more curious beachcombers start to walk up from the water's edge.

"And now Team Tillie!" Tillie runs along the circle, holding out her hand for high fives from the crowd. Her cheer is significantly louder than mine.

Good. This is great. Lots of energy. It's going to be an epic night.

Then Morrie ups the ante. "After every round, we will pause for anyone who wants to try the drink. Is that right, Gabe?"

Oh boy. I'm not sure the two of us can handle that if the crowd gets too big. I lean over the counter to his mike. "We'll sure try, Morrie."

"Let me introduce the judges!" Morrie says.

Anya and Chuck have to wind through the bystanders to walk up.

"This is Anya, a longtime friend of Gabe's!" There are boos and cheers as the crowd realizes she might vote for me.

She takes the mike. "No worries, Team Tillie! I've got the lady's back!" Another big cheer.

Chuck doesn't want to hold the mike. He tugs his ball cap low on his forehead, leaning close to Anya to quickly say, "I'm Chuck. I like to drink."

This gets the biggest cheer of all.

Morrie takes the mike back. "This first round will be all about presentation. Gather around to watch our two bartenders make the most beautiful drinks!"

I'm not sure if we should do them simultaneously or one at a time. I turn to Tillie.

"You go!" she calls.

I nod. I pull the liquors for the mermaid sunrise.

Tillie walks the circle as I fill the glass with ice and pour in the bright-red grenadine. "Pay close attention," she says. "Layering liquors is one of the most difficult things we do. It takes a steady hand and a knowledge of how each color will behave when it encounters the others."

I place the juice in next. For a moment, it appears the yellow-orange will mix in with the red, and the crowd makes a disappointed "Awww." But then I tap the glass, and they separate again into two clean colors.

Everyone claps.

"That's how it's done," Tillie says, and I appreciate the tone she's set that we will encourage each other rather than point out any negatives.

I cut the Midori with vodka and add it at an angle, letting it slip into the glass. When it's time for the blue curaçao, I stick to my bar spoon, leaving the fancy cherry work for her.

I finish it out with the fruit garnish and the seahorse gummy, then hold it up.

Anya, Chuck, and Morrie have squeezed in together by the hinged section of the counter, where there are no stools.

"Look at that," Anya says.

The three of them make a great show of writing on their clipboards.

"I'll take one!" the flower-hat woman calls. "I had it last night, and it's delicious."

I wave my hand around the circle. "Anyone else?" Four or five others lift their hands. With a crowd this size, it's going to be challenging to keep it all straight.

I set to making more off to one side while Tillie takes my place. "I will also make a layered drink. But rather than playing to the bright side, I'm going dark." She heaves four bottles onto the counter, including the coffee liqueur. "For those of you who have black, black souls."

A long *ooooo* settles around the bar.

I glance over occasionally, watching her expertly layer the black, brown, amber, and pale liquors.

"And like any good drink, we add a bit of chocolate."

I pause to watch. I didn't know about this part. She takes the bottle of chocolate liqueur and shows it around. Then she opens a candy bar from the snack tray and breaks off a rectangle.

She uses the chocolate as a ramp to ease the liqueur into the drink. She lifts the glass, the coated chocolate bar slowly sinking into the liquor like the last gasp of a dark world.

Brilliant.

"And who wants to order this one?" she calls.

Twice as many ask for the chocolate drink as my rainbow one. As she sets her drink in front of our trio of judges and starts making more, I wonder if we could have simply used the orders to signify the win.

Morrie realizes the drinks will take a few minutes and flips on his mike. "While we wait, let's meet some members of Team Gabe and Team Tillie." He walks around the circle to interview customers while Tillie and I frantically mix cocktails.

I glance over at her. She's working swiftly, adding ice to ten glasses, then pouring liquor into each one. So smart. I've been making one drink at a time.

I take up her assembly line method. She glances over at me with a smile.

My usual urge might have been to challenge her. But I find this time, I can't do anything but smile back.

I never imagined working in my bar could be like this.

Chapter 11

TILLIE

I assume that by the time we've completed the flavor round with Gabe's rum runner and my lemon whiskey sour, the orders will slow, but they don't. Gabe and I work steadily, Anya and Pete hopping inside to wash glassware and take credit cards. Pete uses the same payment system as Gabe, so he can take over immediately.

By the time we get to the wild card round with the coconuts, Pete has already seen what lies ahead and set Bodeen to hollowing out as many coconuts as he can manage.

The crowd is tremendous, and once the dishwasher is running to ensure enough glassware to keep us going, Anya works the fringes beyond the bar to take drink orders.

I'm energized by the work, as I always get when a busy shift wears on. But, of course, it's only afternoon, and it could be a long one if this crowd makes a night of it.

I glance around to take in what we've done. The hut is circled three and four feet deep with customers, most of them with a drink in their hands. I spot Lila and Rosie on a chair a short distance away and wave.

Gabe's mom has also shown up with another woman near her age. The two of them sit on a blanket in the sand, their heads together, talking and occasionally looking our way.

The windows in the condos light up as dusk falls. Gabe flips on the colored lights. When I turn toward the ocean, the sun is setting, sparking fiery red and orange tones across the darkening water.

I love it here. I love everything about what we're doing and where. I hope Gabe knows that he's bartending in paradise. There is no inside bar that could come close to the working conditions he has. The openness cuts the noise. The breeze keeps the air fresh and moving.

Gabe bends down to locate the new bottle of blue curaçao, so I quickly squat next to him.

"Hey. Do you think Bodeen can handle a ton of coconut orders if people go nuts?"

Gabe looks behind him at the bottom row of the cart. It's piled high with coconuts ready to be filled. "It looks like we have about twenty. I say we announce only the first twenty orders will get coconuts."

I nod. "That's a good plan."

We stand up.

Morrie is ready to announce the final category. "It comes down to this—the wondrous coconut. They grow on our island. Our local farmers harvest them and prepare them for various delicious items all across La Jarra."

Gabe snatches one from the cart and hands it to Morrie to hold up.

"Tonight," Morrie continues, "our bartenders will prepare their own coconut-inspired cocktails in the husk of the fruit."

Gabe leans into the mike. "And due to the labor involved in hollowing out the coconuts, only twenty orders for these drinks will be made in the husks."

"There you have it!" Morrie says. "Be ready to get in on the final drinks of the competition!"

Gabe takes the coconut husk from him and sets it on the counter.

He pulls a cocktail shaker from the shelf and does his spin-and-toss routine. The crowd cheers.

Uh-oh. He's going for presentation on the wild card. He combines rum, crème of coconut, and orange juice with a scoop of ice. After a couple of quick shakes, he pours the contents into the coconut.

He rummages in a drawer and extracts a small grater, then a lump of nutmeg from a bag.

Nice.

He grates fresh brown flakes over the top of the drink and the lip of the coconut. Then he finishes it off with slices of mango and pineapple, also flecked with nutmeg, and places three straws inside.

He lifts it high. "I present . . . the painkiller!"

A cheer goes up, and he takes the coconut to the judges.

When he returns, he tosses his shaker behind his back to the other arm, then *plop*, sends it straight into the suds in the sink.

Another cheer.

"You think you've got me, don't you?" I say to him, curling my finger like I want him to come close.

He sidles up to me.

The crowd goes nuts. Nothing like a little romantic tension to up the ante.

I grab his shirt and pull him close. "I've got two words for you."

"Do you now?" His face is inches from mine. Our gazes lock. I was doing this all in fun, but the heat of his nearness makes me gulp a sharp shot of air.

Morrie clamors for his mike. "We're down to the last drink of the night, and the competition is heating up!"

"Those two words are something I want from you," I tell him.

Now it's his Adam's apple that bobs. "What's that?"

I lean in closer, closer, until our mouths are so near, we can feel each other's breaths.

The crowd quiets, watching, hanging with suspense.

"Two. Blenders." I push him away.

The crowd shouts with its release of tension. Gabe shakes his head and drags both blenders onto the counter, plugging in the cords.

I open both their tops.

"First, you need the lava!" I slide one blender close and drop in ice, light rum, and coconut rum. Then I bend down to the fridge to extract a tub of fresh strawberries. I lift one and run it close to Gabe's lips.

I don't expect him to bite it.

I shriek and let go, sending the crowd into a roar.

"Cheater!" I say, laughing, then quickly slice the tops off several strawberries and rinse them in the sink. I toss them into one blender.

"Now we need the flow!" I call, adding ice, coconut cream, and pineapple juice to the second blender. I pull a banana off a bunch hanging from a hook near the glassware.

I turn back to Gabe and peel one side with exaggerated slowness, my gaze fixed on him.

The spectators shriek and cheer.

When I expose the top of the banana, I act like I'm going to take a bite.

Gabe shakes his head.

I dump it into the blender instead and drop the peel in the compost. Gabe has already figured out what I'm making and covers both blenders.

With great flourish, I lift both arms and slam my hands down on the power buttons.

The blenders whir to life, one spinning a red blend, and the other a creamy, pale-yellow froth.

I shut them down, lifting the glass jars from the bases. I raise the red one higher. "Lava!" I shout. Then I lift the pale one. "Flow."

I lift the red one again, and the crowd understands. "Lava!" they shout.

Then the pale. "Flow!"

I keep it going.

"Lava!"

"Flow!"

"Lava!"

"Flow!"

Gabe removes the lids, and I pour both of the frozen colors into the coconut, not even trying to be neat. They form a red-and-yellow swirl that spills over the edge. I lift the coconut in the air.

"Lava flow!" everyone shouts.

I turn to Gabe. I know we're supposed to give the drink to the judges, but I bring it over to him.

I lean in to lick the overflow drink from my side, and he knows what to do. He licks his side.

And then something happens that I didn't plan. I don't know if it was an accident, or a miscommunication, or if we got caught in the moment.

But when both of us reach the top of the sloppy, dripping lava flow coconut, we meet above it.

In a kiss.

The crowd goes wild.

Chapter 12

GABE

What the hell are we doing?

I'm vaguely aware of the crowd cheering and the slosh of frozen lava flow on my feet. But mostly I'm feeling Tillie's lips, the press of her nose to my cheek, wisps of loose curls brushing against my forehead.

The sound is muffled, like I'm underwater. Maybe I'm drowning. Maybe this is some afterlife. My entire body rushes like the ocean wind is passing through my skin.

But then she pulls back, her mischievous eyes a fiery combination of blue and the colors of the sunset. She's amused by what we did, when I kissed her. Or she kissed me.

She looks down at the coconut and laughs that it's tilted, half of the contents on the floor. She quickly hauls it over to the judges.

People call out orders for the lava flow. Everybody wants in on it. I'm still in this weird spacy place, like I'm in a dream and hovering on the edge of waking up.

Pete touches my arm. "Bodeen is going to carve coconuts until his arm falls off. Take as many orders as you want."

I nod at him, trying to get my bearings, hoping to get the world to right itself. Tillie kneels in front of me with her bar towel, mopping up the spill and wiping my feet. This causes another whirling sensation to knock me off my equilibrium.

She's just a woman. Flesh and blood. She's not the rainbow mermaid. There is no such thing.

But this feels a lot like Mendo's story.

Her gaze lifts to my face, and her expression shifts to concern. She leaps up, her hand on my chest. "Gabe, are you okay?"

I shouldn't be standing here like a thirteen-year-old boy having his first kiss. Normally my interaction with a woman follows a pattern. A date. Maybe two. Heated encounters. A predetermined end point, chosen by me, whether she likes it or not. I'm willing to act like an ass if need be to extricate myself.

I don't stop to assess what's happening in those moments. I just do it. The only way I could describe it is that after a week or two, a woman feels like a threat, not a pleasure. So I cut her loose. I have to. It feels critical, like if I don't, I will fall into a pit I can't climb out of.

But this time I've been knocked off balance before we even get started. Like everything I ever knew to be true about how I felt about women, dating, and maintaining my predictable life might be . . . wrong. That maybe, just maybe, this one is worth staring into the abyss.

How could I ever be an asshole to this woman just to get away? She's . . . I don't know. Words fly out of my head like they're bats escaping a cave. My whole body feels foreign, like my guts were scooped out and replaced with sand.

"Gabe?" Tillie waves her hand in front of my face.

I force myself to snap out of whatever weirdness came over me and shout at her over the noise. "I have another blender around here somewhere. I'll help with the lava."

She looks relieved that I've gone back to normal. "I'll get the strawberries. You have the banana." She glances at my shorts like she's about to make a joke, then shakes herself out of whatever it was and spins back to the blenders.

These drinks work up fast, and because we're making so many, it's a simple task to fill them. Bodeen and Pete go mad whacking coconuts, and a crowd gathers around them, too.

We're all going to do well tonight.

I keep stealing glances at her with stupefied wonder. She's having a grand time, shouting at customers over the roar of the blender, pouring lava flow into coconuts, and spinning in circles to pass them to their owners with great flourish. The goldfish bowl tip jars are stuffed tight with money.

She's good at this. I think she's better than me.

I have to admire her.

But damn it, I have to take my eyes off her. I need to get my head back on straight.

So I work. And work. We both do.

When the orders seem to have settled out, Morrie flips on his mike. "We have a winner of tonight's epic booze brawl! Did you all have a good time?"

The crowd roars. Most of them have settled onto folding chairs or towels spread over the sand. Circles have formed along the beach, friends gathering to watch the sunset and drink.

The locals made the long walk from the parking lot for the competition and are enjoying the novelty of a different view. The tourists are content to hang out, feeling like they finally got an authentic La Jarra experience.

This party is definitely going to keep going. I switched everyone to plastic cups as they started moving out onto the beach with drinks. Normally the glassware stays at the bar, but the crowd is way too large.

Morrie raises his clipboard. "The judges have compiled their scores. For presentation, the winner is Gabe Landers of La Jarra with his mermaid sunrise!"

Cheers rise up, and I lift my hand in acknowledgment.

"For taste, the winner is Tillie James of Atlanta, Georgia, for her lemon whiskey sour!"

Tillie takes a bow and holds up the bottle of whiskey.

"So now we come to the tiebreaker." Morrie pauses, glancing around the crowd as he holds his mike close to his chin. "For the wild card competition, and for the win, the best cocktail in our third and final category is . . ." He lets the moment hang. The beach goes quiet.

I spot Mom sitting on a beach towel next to her friend Jessa. I wonder how long they've been there. They both have mermaid sunrises, so a while.

"Tillie James for her lava flow!"

The crowd goes crazy. Orders for the drink come from everywhere as Bodeen dumps another batch of hollowed coconuts onto the counter.

I turn to Tillie. "Congratulations!"

She stands on her tiptoes to hug me. "Thanks!"

The roar is loud as I hold on to her. I have to get comfortable with this feeling of being off-center. It will be a long night, and it's only just begun. I have to get past the idea that I'm not in control of my thoughts and emotions around her. That she's different. That something has happened here that will require a reckoning.

As our bodies press together and that full-body overwhelm comes over me a second time, I plan to say to her, "I'll do the cocktails, you man the blenders."

Or maybe even, "You've been an epic help. I'll figure out how to split the take."

But what comes out instead is, "Will you stay awhile after we shut down the bar?"

She tilts her chin up to look at me. "The strong, surly native is asking to see more of the tiny, bouncy tourist?"

It's a saucy question, but I have to push forward or I'll melt back into that astonishment and panic I felt after the kiss. "He is."

Her expression is full of mischief, but I'm not making it past her lips, anyway. If I'm headed to doom, then I might as well take the first step.

Her grin makes the ground shift beneath my feet. "The tourist says yes."

~

When midnight comes, the party is going strong, but it's closing time. We work through last call, and then I pull down the metal shutters as Tillie loads the last round of glasses into the dishwasher.

"Did you pay Pete and Bodeen?" she asks.

"Yeah. They killed themselves, but they made a haul."

She shuts the dishwasher door and punches the buttons. "Okay, good."

I close the last shutter and lock it. It's immediately stuffy, so I turn on the oscillating fan hanging in the center of the roof. Normally by the time I close, all the shutdown work is done. But tonight, we made drink rounds right to the bitter end.

Mom stopped by to kiss my head and Tillie's cheek. Tillie's sister came by to introduce herself with her baby girl.

Anya, Morrie, and Chuck are on the beach somewhere. Mendo missed the competition, but showed up a couple of hours ago to hang out and hear all the details from our friends.

I rinse out the sink while Tillie dumps a few leftover fruit preps into the compost. I'm nervous. I asked her to stay, and now I don't know what to do with her.

"Should we have a drink?" she asks. "Or are you the type of bartender who doesn't partake of his own creations?"

"I'm good for that."

She hops on the counter. "What should we make? I don't think I'll be able to look at another lava flow for a year."

I nod. "I'm not going to want to make another mermaid sunrise for a long time."

"Good thing it's not on the menu."

"Exactly."

I want to impress her, but how do you surprise someone who's at the top of her game?

Then I remember something. I open one of the back cabinets and pull out a high-end bottle of Japanese gin.

"Hey, you were holding out on me!" Tillie cries.

"These bottles aren't for customers."

"But I get some?" She tilts her head, completely carefree with her easy smile.

I feel like I'm made of rocks, bumbling around like I can't find my own feet.

But I manage to sound somewhat smooth. "Absolutely." I pull two shallow coupe glasses from the far end of the rack. They're dainty and fragile, etched with the outline of lilies. I pour gin in each without measuring, then move to the fridge for the bin of limes. I squeeze a quarter wedge in each glass, then garnish it with a spiral slice.

I hand her a coupe.

She touches the rim to mine. "To a wildly successful night in your beach bar."

"To a well-practiced partner."

We sip our drinks, and Tillie lets out a long sigh. "The classics are the best. This is an excellent gin for a gimlet."

My eyes feel glued to the long, smooth line of her throat. "Joe sometimes gets a box of something new when he travels. When we're lucky, he'll sell us some."

"I like it." She sips again, her eyes bright despite the hours of labor. She really is used to hard work. But then, I feel wide awake, too.

"How did this night compare to what you're used to?" I ask.

She glances around the closed-up hut. "The customers were nicer. The breeze and open air made a difference. The view was incredible."

"What sorts of venues have you tended?"

"Mostly hellholes. But I did work for a bar in Alabama where the head bartender was the nephew of the guy who owned it. He was terrific." She reaches up to slide all the glasses more evenly on the rows by her head.

Jealousy spikes through me. Is this someone she dated? Slept with? Loved? "So, what was so terrific about this nephew?"

"We had a great time inventing drinks, and some of his friends would come in to appreciate them. His name was Cole."

Her face is so full of admiration for him, I can't stop myself from asking, "Did you go out with him?"

She laughs, and the metal shutters echo the happy sound. "Oh no. He was in love with one of the barbacks. A male one. It was a big secret because his uncle was, well, you get it."

My belly settles even though it never should have been upset in the first place. "And he taught you to mix cocktails?"

"Totally. Cole instinctively knew what paired well. He'd take a bottle of blackberry brandy and add a Kentucky bourbon, then cut it with vanilla vodka. And it would be magic."

"I'm not sure I've strayed too far off the usuals."

"I don't get much opportunity now. Cole was an artist. I learned the nuances, how some flavors opened up others. When the bar was slow, we would experiment and practice, usually with oddball liquors so his uncle wouldn't notice them decreasing without sales to match."

"But you don't work at that bar anymore?"

"No."

"I bet he missed you when you left."

"His leaving was the reason I quit. He and his barback had an ugly breakup. The jerk outed him. His uncle kicked him out of the bar, his house, everything. I never saw him again."

"Damn."

"Yeah. I was the only decent bartender there, so I left the uncle in a big lurch, right in the middle of a Saturday night rush. Of course, for my impetuousness, I had a hard time getting another job. Lots of the bar owners know each other. But I always have acted impulsively."

Did she? Was she being impulsive when she kissed me?

"Where did you go next?"

"Really crappy bar. Nothing but shots and beer. Not much mixing. I moved to experimenting at home."

"So you love it enough to do it in your spare time."

Her face tilts, and my breath catches at the happy serenity in her expression. "I do."

"Well, you kicked my butt tonight."

She laughs again. "I did indeed."

We sip our gimlets until they're gone. She takes my coupe and hops down to wash the glasses in the sink. "Was there any special reason you wanted me to stay after the brawl?"

I have to gather my courage to ask the next question. "How long are you here?"

She shakes the glasses and sets them on a towel next to the sink. "Eleven more days."

Almost two weeks. "That's a hefty vacation."

"My brother-in-law, Drew, got a deal on the condo if he took it longer. Lila and I decided we wouldn't get somewhere like this again, so we took all our time off at once."

Tillie dries her hands and turns to lean against the counter. "I know that's not long. If you're rethinking whatever made you want me to stay tonight, I get your hesitation. I'm hesitating, too. But it will be fun, right? I don't like to overthink something like this."

I'm not overthinking anything. If someone were to run up with a stop sign, I'd pitch it into the surf.

"How about breakfast tomorrow?" I glance at the clock over the highball glasses. "Or, I guess, later today."

"Sure," she says. "Where should I meet you? I have a car, although driving on the wrong side of the road is pretty unnerving."

"Maybe Americans drive on the wrong side."

"Probably. It's hard to get used to!"

"I'll come for you, then. Eleven?"

She laughs. "That's practically afternoon for the baby. But sure. We'll call it an early lunch. Is the bar open tomorrow?"

"Yes, but not until two on Sundays. And the hut is closed Monday and Tuesday."

"So it'll be your weekend!"

"Exactly."

Her smile tells me this will be all right. I only need to adopt her attitude. My usual attitude. That can't be hard.

Whatever happened earlier was some weird trick of the light, a mirage in a desert. I'm rational. She's realistic.

We're not embarking on some long-term love affair. I'm not sure I even have that in me. As long as I keep my head on straight, this will work just fine.

She heads for the back counter and opens the hinged section to duck below the shutters. "See you in the morning, Gabriel Adam Landers, loser of the booze brawl, maker of rainbows."

Her words pitch me sideways again. Maybe I'm destined to feel off-kilter with her. "See you tomorrow."

She bends low to blow me a kiss, and I almost reach out to catch it, a strange, sentimental urge.

That would be too much. We barely know each other, and I'm way out of my depth here as it is. I simply wave until Tillie's legs have disappeared, and the sand outside the door is empty.

But then I reach into the air and snap the invisible kiss into my palm. Got it.

Chapter 13

TILLIE

I try to stay focused during my turtle expedition with Lila and Rosie. The morning is sublime, warm and breezy. The sun hazes through light cloud cover, making the water turquoise.

The turtle center focuses on experiences for children. Kids can get in the water in small concrete pools to play.

I sit on the ledge as Lila holds Rosie in the water. Rosie glances up at her mom, her face shadowed by her flowered hat, as if to ask if it's okay to be there.

Her only words are "mama" and "bye-bye," so she calls the turtles "ma-bye." Her hand connects with the water right as a turtle glides by, and it grazes the green-brown shell.

I capture her look of shock with my phone. Lila laughs. "Turtle, Rosie. Turtle. Turtle."

"Ma-bye," Rosie says, kicking her legs and lunging after the turtle.

Lila holds her by the waist and zooms her through the water after it. "Turtle. Turtle."

"Ma-bye!" Rosie shouts, her hands slapping the water.

Lila lifts Rosie to her face. "Turtle."

Rosie stares at her a moment, then says, "Tuhtuh."

Lila looks over at me. "Did you hear that?"

"I did!"

Another turtle lazes in the corner, and Lila moves toward it.

"They like it when you rub their necks," says the man in a red uniform. "You can pick them up."

Rosie seems to understand and reaches down, grasping the edges of the shell. She picks it up for only a moment, the turtle waving its flippers, then slides it back into the water.

"Awwww," Lila says, shifting Rosie to one knee so she can reach out to pet the turtle herself. "It's so beautiful!"

My eyes prick with emotion. It's been wonderful to see my sister grow as a mother, confident and happy. Despite the rough start with our difficult upbringing and her deadbeat ex, we're good. We're really good.

Our turn in the pool ends, and we walk over to the rails where the giant turtles are being fed. Lila and Rosie leave a drippy trail. I shoulder the bags as we lean over the metal bars.

Turtles so large that they wouldn't fit in Rosie's plastic wading pool climb over each other's backs to snap up bits of feed tossed into the water.

"Turtle," Lila says. "Big turtle."

"Tuhtuh," Rosie repeats.

Lila looks at me. "She's saying it!"

I nod, training my phone on them. I'm sad Ensley is missing this, but I'll send her the video. She's on her honeymoon, and the vacation has been well earned.

A large iguana with rings on its tail saunters by as if it's an ordinary creature normally among humans. I tap Lila's shoulder and point.

"Oh!" Lila says. Our eyes meet, and I see the emotion on her face, too.

"We're a long way from Poorsville, Alabama," I say.

She nods.

Our childhood was a struggle in every way. Dad checked out after Mom died, leaving us four kids to fend for ourselves. I was a baby, so I missed the worst of those days, blissfully unaware of the hardship.

But later, I was the one lowered into the donation bins in parking lots, grabbing as many clothes as I could get and still fit through the slot as Garrett and Ensley pulled me out.

If we were lucky, there would be kid outfits in there, or something we could sleep in at least. Otherwise, back down I would go, or if we determined everything in there was from some old lady's closet, we'd sneak to another one and try again.

Later, many of the boxes put spiked wheels inside the openings to prevent people like us from taking the donations before they got where they needed to go. I hated that. Hated stealing more. But there was no other way to get what we needed.

Dad never asked where we got things. We almost never saw him. When we did have food for dinner, during the years some ladies' group or teacher realized our plight and helped with casseroles or take-home bags from the cafeteria, he still didn't come to the table.

He became a shadow of a person, only leaving his room at random hours to do odd jobs that must have paid rent. We did always have a home, even if there wasn't anything much in it. Ensley sometimes excused his absence by saying he was in there with Mother's memory.

His absence was no great loss to me. I'd never known him any other way. But it was hard on Ensley and Garrett, who often knocked on his bedroom door only to be ignored.

He's never met his only grandchild, and he didn't even respond to the news that his oldest daughter was getting married.

I've never known a happy father other than in the old photo albums that abruptly end with my mother's death. His only smile with me in the picture is from the day I was brought home from the hospital.

There are precious few childhood pictures of me. Ensley carefully saved the proof images sent home from school on order forms we never could send back in. That's the only documentation of what I looked like as a kid.

I run my fingers across Rosie's cheek. We will never let her have a life like that. Never, ever. I'll work in the worst run-down, backwater bar before I let that happen. It's a promise I made long ago: Rosie comes first. Then my sisters. And with Ensley moving on, more of the responsibility is mine to shoulder.

"What's got you so thoughtful?" Lila asks, settling Rosie on her hip as we walk down a trail lined with palm trees. "That bartender?"

There's an edge to her voice. She doesn't approve.

"I'm having brunch with him after this."

Lila stops. "Why? This is just a vacation. You'll never see him again."

"And that makes him a perfect fling. Have you seen those biceps?"

Lila takes off in a speed-walk, her jaw set. She's really mad.

I rush to catch up with her. "Hey. What's getting you?"

She shrugs. "You seem so happy."

I want to fire back, *And I'm not supposed to be?* But I don't. I get it. She doesn't want me to ruin our sisterly escape by running off with a man.

I don't argue. Fighting isn't really what we do. Instead, we keep walking, letting the tension dissipate in the beauty of our surroundings.

But then she stops and points to the trees. Up among the leaves are parrots, bright green and yellow. Rosie sees them and claps her hands. And just like that, the hard moment is over.

The birds look down at us, cocking their heads, making us laugh. Rosie's infectious giggle must annoy them, as they extend their colorful wings and tweet down at us in high-pitched chirps.

I don't snap their picture. Some things you always remember, even when there is no evidence the moment happened.

This is one of those. My sister, my niece, and me in the most beautiful place we've ever been. And she's right. I am happy.

∼

I realize I don't have Gabe's phone number when we run late. I frantically lunge out of the car and dash down the sidewalk that cuts through the condo complex to the beach.

But he's there, leaning against his closed-up hut, the wind ruffling his sandy hair, a half smile on his lips.

"I'm so sorry. The turtles went longer than I thought. And I can't drive fast, not on the wrong side of the road—"

"Now don't go apologizing." His eyes crinkle with amusement. "This is island time. It's all good."

I tug my white T-shirt self-consciously. It's damp over my wet bathing suit, revealing the yellow-flowered bikini top. My butt is wet as well.

"I didn't get to change," I say. "Should I go do that?"

Gabe is wearing long khaki shorts and a yellow shirt that fits tightly across his chest and biceps. "You can change if you like, but where we're headed, most of the people are coming in off the beach."

"Okay." I touch my cheeks. I don't have a lick of makeup on, either. But he's already seen me.

We head to the hedge where he hid his motorcycle yesterday. Soon, we're in helmets and flying down the highway, this time going in the opposite direction.

I could seriously ride through the tropics, hanging on to Gabe's back, for the rest of my natural life. The tangy air, the wind on my knees, and his muscled back against my chest are an intoxicating mix.

I close my eyes and revel in the rumble of the bike and his lean into a turn. We're all one working part—Gabe, me, and the motorcycle.

The smells change from sea air to something mossy and damp. I look out, and we're surrounded by trees and ground cover. The few buildings have wood bridges leading to them, as if the earth is too soft to walk over.

Another one of the ring-tailed creatures I saw this morning dashes from one cluster of leaves to another. I'm in another world entirely.

There is nothing familiar about this ride, this man, this vision. Every one of my senses is taking in something completely new.

We break through the surround of trees and the ocean returns. Gabe slows down and signals for a left to a rambling restaurant on tall stilts.

Stone stairs lead down to the beach on one side, and just like Gabe said, people are wandering up from the shore to the restaurant.

We park near the front. I've mostly dried out after the windy ride. Gabe gives me a crooked smile as we cross the sandy asphalt. The wind is high. A bright red-orange bird like nothing I've ever seen before struts across the sand and pauses next to the building's steps.

"What is that?" I ask.

Gabe pauses to look. "A scarlet ibis."

"But it's orange!"

Gabe chuckles. "Yeah, I'm not sure if it's the light or the type of shellfish they eat here, but they definitely skew orange."

The bird tilts its head at me, opening and closing its long, curved beak. Its tiny circular eye seems to mock me.

Two young boys from a family walking up from the beach see the ibis and run toward it, shrieking. The bird takes a few cautious steps backward, then wings into the sky, soaring over the parking lot and heading toward the ocean.

"So sorry," the mother says, trying to rein in her boys.

I'm disappointed not to get a closer look, but we smile at them and head into the restaurant.

"Gabe!" A man holding an armful of menus brightens at spotting us. "You brought a woman? This must be the Georgia hottie drinkslinger!"

He realizes what he's said a moment too late and pulls his straw hat off to hold in front of his chest. "I am so sorry. I mean no disrespect to the lady."

"It's fine," I say. "I think I'm going to have to get used to it."

"This is José," Gabe says. "He's worked here since I was a kid."

"I'll never leave here," José says. "My ghost will seat diners for centuries. Come, let me find you a good table. By the beach, yes?"

Gabe nods, and we follow José through tables covered in plastic tablecloths until we reach the back deck overlooking the ocean.

"'Tis beautiful, no?" José asks as he sets two menus opposite each other on a small table near the rail. "I hear Gabe lost the competition."

"He did," I say. "And now he's buying me breakfast."

"Good, good." José leans in. "Order the lobster taco and stick it to him."

"Hey!" Gabe says. "I thought we old-timers had each other's backs!"

José smacks Gabe on the shoulder. "Old-timer. That's a good one. I used to snatch you up by your overalls when you tried to run off the deck to the water." He shakes his head and leaves us, laughing as he goes.

I spread the menu out on the table. "So, do you know everyone on the island, or are you taking me places where you know people?"

"A little of both."

I scan the drink list out of habit. My head rushes when I see the prices. I lean in closer to Gabe. "If this is what drinks run here, you're seriously undervaluing yours!"

He nods. "Probably so. This place is more high-end than average."

Oh. I shift to the food prices. I feel my face flush at the lobster taco. I've never in my life paid that much for a taco.

"It must be really good," I say, quickly scanning the rest to look for anything reasonable. One egg and toast is more my speed.

"It is. I'd take José up on the lobster taco. It makes you feel a little faint when you eat it."

"From how much you paid for it?"

He laughs. "From how insanely good it is."

"I could drink three mermaid sunrises for the price of that taco."

His eyebrows draw together. "I don't mind."

And now I've upset him somehow. Maybe he's getting the idea that I think he's cheap.

I go for honesty. "I'm not used to eating at fancy places. I grew up in . . . hard circumstances." I let out a half laugh. "I know I'm staying someplace fancy, but I didn't pay for it. My sister's husband did. So maybe I gave off the wrong vibe. Everything I'm wearing was five dollars or less at a thrift store." I'm about to keep going when he reaches out and squeezes my hand.

"Hey. Does this place make you uncomfortable?"

"No, I . . ."

"You worked incredibly hard last night."

"And you gave me all the tips! I only deserved half!"

He holds my gaze, and I will myself to shut up. Why can't I be like the girls at the bar back home, forcing guys on fancy dates and bragging about how much they spent?

I mean, I know why. Nobody who grew up like I did can spend stupid amounts of money on things that should cost less. But I would like a smidge of their girl power right now. Their ability to splurge.

"I'd like to treat you, Tillie." The way my name comes out of his lips makes me shiver. "It's your vacation, and I took a day of it away from you. Let me show you a place you wouldn't go to on your own."

He's right. "Okay," I say. "But I can't order a lobster taco."

"That's fine. I will and you'll promise to take a bite."

"Deal."

The server arrives and Gabe orders a carafe of mimosas and his lobster taco. I get the egg and toast.

He grins. "It's going to be different today working without you."

I sip my water. "It's going to suck and you know it. I can't believe you do the whole thing by yourself. What if you run out of ice? Or need change? Or twenty people show up at once?"

He shrugs. "I handle it. And I plan ahead. The only real challenge is if I need a day off. I lose the day's sales."

"But probably it's not quite enough work to justify a second server."

"Bingo. Last night was unusual."

"Maybe we could do it again."

The mimosas arrive, and he pours us each a glass from the carafe. "A booze brawl rematch?"

"Sure. Or some other competition. And you should think about events. If you did something once a month, you could really goose your income."

He sips his drink. "Just one problem with that idea."

I grip my cold glass. "What's that?"

He meets my eye, and even though I know what's coming, I can't stop the way my whole body feels like it's swooping when he says it.

"I won't have you."

Chapter 14

GABE

In the end, Tillie can't stop at one bite and eats my entire lobster taco, which is fine by me. I'm good with egg and toast, and I'm amused she feels so strongly about what to spend money on.

José returns to clear our plates and remarks that it's a good day to see the stingrays.

"I heard about those!" Tillie says.

"My son runs a boat out to Stingray Bay," José says. "The stingrays know the sound of the engine means they will get food. You haven't truly experienced La Jarra until you have pet the silky belly of one of those beasts!"

"I'll try to get there," Tillie says. "I saw the turtles this morning."

"Another good expedition." He nudges me. "Of course, Gabe here has a best friend, Mendo. He runs a boat out to Stingray Bay, too."

"Mendo does tours?" Tillie's eyes light up. "I think he owes me after getting the whole town to call me a hottie drinkslinger."

"I would agree with you," José says. "Give him a call."

"You want to go?" I ask Tillie.

"Of course I do!"

I nod. Mendo will think it's great. I send him a text that Tillie wants a tour in exchange for his hottie drinkslinger nickname that seems to be sticking.

He says sure, he has space for two on Monday.

"I have to open the bar in an hour," I tell Tillie. "But Mendo says we can go tomorrow afternoon. The tour leaves at one. We'll want to meet at the hut at twelve thirty to ride to the dock."

She squeals. "Yes!"

"Is it okay if you leave your sister behind? It's not a trip for a little one."

"Oh no. They nap in the afternoon. It's perfect."

We wander back through the restaurant, and when our wrists bump, we end up holding hands. A zip of adrenaline darts through me, and I don't fight it. At this point, I suspect my mother is burning candles day and night to bring about a romance in her son. She worries, I know, that I don't connect with anyone beyond the easy friendship I have with Mendo and the gang. She's told me.

"Aren't you exhausted after the late nights and early excursions with your sister?" I ask her.

She shrugs. "I keep weird hours. Always have."

We load onto the motorcycle. She stands on the pegs, resting her chin on my shoulder before I start the engine. "I love riding across the island with you. I feel like I see so much. I can smell everything. The wind has a taste!"

"What does it taste like?"

"Like the dregs of a margarita, when it's watered down with the salt from the rim and tidbits of lime."

"Huh." I'd never thought of the air having a flavor.

As we fly down the highway back to the condo complex, I try to taste the wind.

Watery lime and salt. She's right.

I drop her off and ride on to park in my usual spot in the lot down the beach. The crowd is picking up, rented chairs and umbrellas dotting the sand.

Quite a few people have spread their blankets near my hut. They perk up when I walk by and unlock the low door.

"The barman is here!" one shouts. "Whoop, whoop!"

A cheer rises.

Interesting. That's never happened before.

By the time I lift the shutters, almost every stool is occupied.

"Lava flow!" a man calls.

"Make that two," says another.

"Can you make the chocolate layered one, or do we need the girl?" A lady in a big straw hat eyes me.

"I can get it done."

"Good."

It takes nearly an hour to get everyone settled and orders filled. I lean on the counter, drying my hands on a towel, looking out over the sprawling collection of pale-yellow condos with white trim. In one of them, Tillie is sleeping.

The thought of lying next to her sends a jolt through me.

I'd like that.

I realize I still don't have her phone number and shake my head. We'll remedy that tomorrow, when we meet for the boat tour.

For now, it's probably a good thing I can't foolishly spill my unexpected feelings in a text. I'm used to thinking in the short term, but something about her inspires more.

But that's impossible. She's a tourist. I need to hold something back. The remainder of her two weeks in La Jarra is a lot of time to spend feeling this off-center.

But I'm already guessing it won't be near enough.

~

When Tillie walks up to my hut the next day in a red polka-dot halter bikini under a white mesh cover-up, I know I'm a goner. My whole body sees that outfit, not just my eyes.

She doesn't seem to notice me gawking. "I heard you had a crowd last night."

I spin my keys around my finger to harness my jitters and lead her to my motorcycle. "Where did you hear that?"

"An elderly couple on the deck that adjoins ours. Lila and I made dinner and ate it out there, and they were saying they could barely get a drink order in edgewise."

It was true. I had a harder time keeping up than I usually do. "It's residual from the booze brawl." I pass her the extra helmet. "It will wear off over the next few days as all the tourists who came to it go home."

She pulls the helmet down. "You should text me if it gets crazy. I'm happy to work it with you to help you catch up."

I swing my leg over the seat. "It's your vacation. No working."

"But I like it. At least with you." She fits in behind me.

Does she? "I don't have your number."

"Right. I realized that when I was late yesterday. Give me your phone."

I tug it from my pocket and unlock it. "Here."

She takes it and types in her number, then calls herself from my phone so she'll have mine. "There." She passes it back. "We can take photos for the contacts on the boat."

A photo of her in that bikini. I'll never want to look at anything else.

I crank the motor, and we take off for the marina.

As we cruise along the highway to the bay, I try to see the island as Tillie does. I'm aware tourists view La Jarra as a paradise, and it is. But when the long beaches and turquoise waters become an everyday scene, the beauty of it wears off. You go through the rainy season, when the roads flood, or get the threat of a hurricane.

I know that behind me, Tillie is inhaling deeply and tasting the air. We have to cut through a neighborhood to get to the docks, and I sense her interest in the everyday life of regular residents as she turns her head back and forth, the butt of the helmet rubbing across my spine.

La Jarra, like most islands, has its rich and its poor, its professionals and its laborers. This neighborhood is upper class, the houses painted in pastels with tidy yards filled with plants and palm trees. Mom lives in one like these on the opposite side of the island, long paid for by her career as a conservationist specializing in native wildlife. I had the best of everything growing up. I don't take a moment of it for granted.

Then we turn down the road to the dock, and the white boats line up in a row.

She squeezes my waist, and I swear I hear an excited shriek almost lost in the wind.

I pull up behind Mendo's Jeep and park against his bumper.

Tillie hops off the bike and jerks her helmet from her head. "There are so many boats!" She rises up on her toes to see more.

I spot Mendo on the dock, checking in his passengers. His brother, Zeke, waves from the rooftop over the deck. He's coiling a red line.

Tillie waves back. "He has to be related to Mendo. They have the same posture."

"It's his brother."

"They work together? Like Bodeen and Pete?"

"Lots of families have small businesses here."

We wait until the regular passengers have all loaded to approach the boat. Mendo extends a hand to Tillie. When she gives it to him, he kisses the back of it. "I'm here to steal you away from this lug," he says. "If it can be done, I'm gonna do it."

"You'll give him a run for his money," Tillie says.

Mendo releases her and turns to me. "I heard the bar was crazy again yesterday. You should skip your days off until it dies down. Unless there's something better than money." He flashes his eyes at Tillie.

I'm not even touching that. "I appreciate you fitting us in." I clap him on the back.

"It's restitution for the crime of my word choice." He puts his arms around both of us, taking up the middle. "Even though I'm pretty sure it was my flyers that got you all the biz."

"You're right," Tillie says. "Gabe owes you. I'd make him pay."

Mendo releases me and whirls Tillie away. "I'll take the hottie."

Tillie ducks under his arm and slides up next to me, wrapping her arm around my waist. "Gabe's done got me hooked, Mendo. You snooze, you lose."

I feel pulled in five directions at once. One, Tillie's closeness. We've only held hands before, and now she's connected to me without the rumble of the motorcycle and the necessity of her hanging on.

And the familiarity of all this talk. It's like we've been dating for years, and this is the same ol' shtick she and Mendo always play out.

For a moment I think, *This is what my dating life could have been like all this time.*

But that isn't true. I shed the women before because I had to. I was compelled to shake them loose. With Tillie, I won't have to. She has an expiration date.

"Had to take my shot," Mendo says.

We follow him down the dock, and he extends a hand to lead Tillie onto the boat.

"I've got this," I tell him.

Mendo jerks his hand back. "I see how it is." He grins. "You two are already a thing."

He's thrilled I'm seeing her. It's as plain as his foolishly happy expression.

The boat is cleaner than I remember, everything bright white. Zeke has climbed down and waits in the cabin for when we take off. Behind him is a door that leads to an open deck with seats on both sides.

We join a group of six tourists. I recognize two of them from the night of the wedding, the honeymooners who asked for Mendo's card.

"It's the bartender and the goddess!" the woman exclaims. "This will be so fun!"

Mixing business and pleasure. I'm really breaking my rules now. I give them a nod.

Mendo starts his spiel about the stingrays and to wait until he's brought them around to interact.

A tall man in yellow swim trunks raises his hand. "Isn't a stingray how Steve Irwin died?"

"It is," Mendo says. "But stingrays are very docile creatures. They are not known to go on the attack unless you're a tiger shark."

The man seems placated and settles back onto his bench.

Mendo claps his hands. "Let's head out to Stingray Bay! The bay is only three feet deep, so it's an ideal place to interact with these majestic creatures."

Tillie turns to me, her eyes bright. "I'm both excited and terrified."

I'm not worried about the stingrays, but I still understand exactly how she feels.

Chapter 15

Tillie

The ocean air over the water tastes and smells different from the version on land. I hold Gabe's hand as the wind barrels over my face, freeing tendrils of hair from my messy topknot.

"Would it be weird if I bit the air?" I ask Gabe.

His chuckle, so close to my body, reverberates in my chest. "Everyone here is a tourist. You'll never see them again."

I peer around him to check whether Zeke and Mendo are watching. I can see only Zeke's back as he steers the boat. Mendo is up there with him, but he's not visible at all.

I'm clear.

I open my mouth and bite down. More of the tangy flavor fills my mouth. It's wild. Normally when I breathe in, it's blank air. But not here.

I catch the honeymoon woman watching me, and her eyebrows shoot up. Dang it. Caught.

Gabe leans in. "What's the verdict?"

"Tastes like chicken."

He laughs again. "Do you mean seafood?"

I turn so that I can't see the staring woman, not even in my peripheral vision. "Maybe. It's definitely meatier out here. The land air is fruitier. Still very salty."

"Never in my twenty-eight years have I tried to bite the air on a boat." His amused gaze holds mine, and I'm caught off guard by how handsome he is.

His sandy hair has curled up on the ends from the wind and humidity. There are fine white lines around his eyes, creases that haven't tanned like the rest of his face.

He wears a tight blue shirt that I'm praying he's going to pull off when we get in the water. I want to see the thing that I've kept feeling when riding behind him on the bike.

He seems amused that I'm staring at him, and the white lines around his eyes disappear into the crinkles.

I lean a little closer so that I can say, "The honeymoon lady saw me biting the air. I can't even look in that direction now."

He pauses a beat, then casually turns his head in her direction. His lips press to my ear. "She's still staring. Should we give her a show?"

My heart hammers. "What do you have in mind?"

Two fingers press against the bottom of my chin, making me tilt my head up to him. Then his mouth is on mine.

Yes.

At first, he tastes salty, like the air blasting against our faces.

But as we relax into the kiss and his arm moves behind my back to draw me closer, I settle into the taste of him. Gabe. Warm and simple, maybe the tiniest bit like spearmint gum.

I imagine him popping a piece in his mouth before he came to meet me, knowing he would kiss me. The thought that he planned ahead makes me smile against his lips, which makes him smile back.

Soon, we're grinning like idiots against each other, and the kiss isn't spicy or moving in any hot direction, but fun and full of laughter. Like a vacation. Like joy.

We break apart, and I glance at the honeymoon lady. She's stopped watching me, peering out over the waves like a good tourist.

"I think your ruse was successful," I whisper to Gabe.

"Oh, it was no ruse." And then he leans in again, and this time there is no laughter, but white heat.

I feel this kiss from my lips to my knees, everything in between liquid and hot.

It's a promise for things to come. Encounters I can only imagine. The cocktail *sex on the beach* immediately springs to mind, and I know I will never think of that drink the same way again. I want it. Naked skin. Sand. The ocean washing over our legs like a travel commercial.

I think I can have it. I think Gabe will want it, too.

His hand on my back presses against the mesh cover-up. His fingers slide through the strings to touch my skin.

I scoot in closer to him, reveling in the hardness of his chest.

His fingers spread against my back, pushing me into him. His mouth slants over mine, lips parted, our tongues slipping alongside each other.

A paradise romance. I'm *in*. This will be more than a vacation. It will be an unforgettable memory. I'm short on those. And I'm confident I'll be able to walk away when it's time. No one has ever made me feel any differently.

Our kissing might have gone on and on, but the engine suddenly drops in intensity, then cuts off entirely.

"We're here," Mendo calls out.

Even though my eyes are closed, I can feel Gabe's gaze on me.

"For those of you not already engaged in a *pressing* matter, please move forward and prepare for a demonstration on how to approach these amazing creatures. The water is quite shallow, but do be mindful of your step as you disembark."

Gabe and I break apart, snickering at each other a moment more before turning to the back end of the boat. I plan to say something snarky to Mendo as a retort to his comment, but then I see the stingrays.

I twist away from Gabe. "Look at them!"

Gabe wraps his arms around my waist and pulls me against his chest. He rests his chin on my head. "I have to admit, they never get old."

I peer up at him. "Do you come out here often?"

"I haven't been here since a school field trip."

I slide forward on the bench seat to get closer to the rear of the boat. Mendo has lowered a ladder.

The semicircle of the bay has no beach. The water laps directly against a crumbling shore that leads into a forest. The water is shallow and blue-green, and the wide, thin-tailed stingrays glide forward and back, waiting for Mendo to feed them.

I squeeze Gabe's arm where it rests across my belly. "I could never have imagined something like this."

Mendo splashes down into the ocean. They're right. The water is only waist deep. Zeke comes forward to help the passengers down the ladder.

We let the others go first, given that they're the ones who paid for this expedition. When they are all down, Zeke turns to us. "You two good?"

Gabe nods. "We're good."

Zeke opens a metal box affixed to the inside of the boat and extracts a camera in a waterproof housing. Photography upsells. Smart.

He drops to the water and starts taking pictures, leading each tourist to a stingray. They pat their bellies and run their hands along their backs.

"It's amazing how tame they are," I say.

"You ready?" he asks.

I nod. I stand and reach for the bottom of my cover-up, but Gabe moves behind me and breathes in my ear, "Allow me."

I shiver as he bends down to grasp the bottom hem of the cover-up and lift it over my head. Even though the loose white mesh hid very little of the swimsuit underneath, it feels a lot like he is undressing me. My heart speeds up, and the low, heavy thrum in key places of my body starts to pound.

"Are you wearing that shirt in the water?" I ask.

"Wasn't planning on it." His voice is low and gruff, and I can tell taking the cover-up off me affected him, too.

"Then allow *me*."

I take my time removing the shirt. His chest is deeply tanned, although possibly a shade lighter than his arms and legs.

His belly is a smooth, flat plane with well-defined abs. I really want to touch them. They're so close.

The ground beneath me sways, though I'm not sure how much of it is the boat anchored in the bay, and how much is what I'm feeling looking at Gabe. I wonder how long this excursion will last. I want to be somewhere with him. Alone.

But we're really far from that. We approach the ladder at the stern of the boat. I turn and take the rungs down carefully. Gabe's eyes are all over me as I lower into the sun-warmed water in front of him.

Then he's beside me, his arm on my bare waist. If he's touching me, I'm touching him. I rest my hand on that flat plane I was just admiring. A rush of heat blasts through me, and I'm glad I'm in the water, surrounded by people. I am sorely tempted to do wild things with this man.

Zeke turns to us with his camera. "Mendo, get them some squid."

Mendo tosses a pink bit of something at Gabe.

"What's that?" I ask.

"To feed the stingray. Give me your hand."

He lays the strip of pink meat in my palm and closes my fist, leaving part of it sticking out of the top.

An enormous stingray glides forward to us. He's almost as wide as I am tall.

"I had no idea they were so big!" I exclaim.

Mendo runs his hands along the stingray's back. "These are monsters. They tend to be much smaller when they are not fed so well."

Gabe takes my arm and guides it beneath the creature. "Put your hand underneath him until you find his mouth. He'll help you by shifting. Then he'll—"

I gasp. "He sucked it right out of my hand!"

Mendo laughs. "That's what she said."

I slide my palm along the stingray's dark-gray surface. It's soft. So soft.

"Now pucker your lips for a kiss," Mendo says. "Gabe, don't get jealous. You got plenty of action today already."

I lean forward with my lips puckered.

The stingray glides upward, and for a moment, his cool, gentle mouth is pressed against mine. Then he slides back.

"Thank you," I tell him. Another tourist walks forward with squid, so we're abandoned.

We wander around the bay. Other boats also pull up, dropping more tourists to vie for the stingrays' attention.

The sun bears down, and Gabe pokes my shoulder. "I'm guessing you put on your crappy Georgia sunscreen?"

I nod. "Why?"

"You're turning pink. Come on. Let's get back on the boat, and I'll coat you properly."

So he'll be putting his hands on me.

I can definitely go for that.

Chapter 16

GABE

I coat Tillie's shoulders with real sunscreen, the kind that's probably rare in the States but necessary in the island sun.

She lets out a sigh as I move down her back, shifting aside the long strands of hair that have fallen out of her loose bun.

I take longer than I need to, letting the sounds of the tourists in the water fade out of consciousness. Mendo and Zeke go through their shtick, taking pictures and video and making sure the customers know they can buy them in a digital package.

I don't need to listen. I only want to focus my attention on the feel of Tillie's body in my hands.

The bikini covers so little of her. I fight the urge to kiss the dimple between her shoulder blades. Tiny silver earrings dangle below her ears, sparkling as she moves.

She's worn a different bathing suit on other days, because the ghost of a tan line tracks from her midback, over her shoulder, and down into the red bikini. I give myself a moment to admire the shadow of the cleavage leading into the top.

But we're stuck on a damn boat.

"That was fun," Tillie says. "Thanks for watching out for my ghostly complexion."

I press my thumbs into her spine, enjoying how she groans with the pressure. The red string on the back of the bikini top tempts me sorely. It takes self-control not to untie it.

I want her alone. I want to see her. Taste her.

"How long will we be out here?" she asks.

"Not much longer. Do you want to go back in the water?"

"Not necessarily. I had my stingray moment." She glances at the clusters of people in the bay. "There's a lot more now."

"Mmmm." I lift her thigh to swing it across the bench so that she faces me. The heat of her sun-kissed skin settles against mine. I push her hair off her forehead.

She reaches up self-consciously. "I'm sure I look a fright."

I wrap my hands around her back. "I don't think you see yourself the way others do."

Her blue eyes hold my gaze. "I'm a skinny bartender from Georgia whose only real skill is drinking customers under the table."

"You are a gorgeous, savvy businesswoman. But really, you built a tolerance?"

"Sure. I saw *Indiana Jones*. I wanted to be Marion. She was fierce. Being able to hold your liquor, but pretending you don't, is a critical skill when you're tiny enough that drunk jerks think they can throw you over their shoulders."

I run my thumb over her cheek. "Well, I see a woman who is fierce. And beautiful. And doesn't know her own worth."

She swallows, her gaze dropping. "I better figure it out before too long, or I'm going to be bartending in my seventies."

I can't help but laugh. "Because twenty-three is so close to seventy."

"The way it's been going, it is. I feel like I was born old."

I draw her close, resting her wet head on my shoulder. "Not right now. For the rest of your two weeks here, we have all the time in the world."

Except I have to work a lot of it. I wonder if I should take a vacation. Close up the hut for a while. Wednesdays are slow. I could take a third day off. Maybe only open on Thursday close to dinnertime.

That's the perk of working for yourself, right? You make the rules. My contract with the condo complex never stipulated hours. They don't pay that much attention to me as long as I keep the hut neat and pay my lease on time.

I have to do it. The urge to make the most of our time together is overwhelming. I won't think about the crash at the end. Only about what happens today.

"What's that head of yours thinking?" Tillie asks.

"Whether I can take off Wednesday, too. And open later on Thursday."

She lifts her head. "Because of me."

My throat almost catches, but I clear it. "Yeah. Because of you."

"Huh. The big entrepreneur is going to take some time off."

I glance out at the tourists. Zeke and Mendo are rounding them up.

I slide my thumb across her bikini top, enjoying how she sucks in a breath and her nipple tightens into a pucker beneath the wet fabric. "I'm going to enjoy every inch of you for every moment you're here. You in?"

Her eyes lift to me, half-lidded as she slides her hand up my thigh. "I'm in."

"Do you have a beach fantasy?"

"Sex on it."

"There's sand, you know."

"I'll learn the hard way."

I lean closer to her ear. "Tomorrow morning then? There's a secluded beach we can reach by kayak."

She shivers. "Yes."

Mendo climbs the ladder, shaking his head at us as he turns to help the tourists into the boat.

Tillie turns around in my arms, leaning her back against my chest.

I get a magnificent view of her slender, pink-tinted legs as we wait for everyone to return to their seats. They chatter happily about the stingrays.

The boat fires up again, and then the wind races over our bodies.

I hold Tillie tight, my hand flat against her bare belly. My entire body hums with anticipation of getting to know her better. Not just the savvy, entertaining, sharp-witted bartender who worked with me for a night and beat me at my own game.

But the woman in my arms, falling into my kiss. Tomorrow, we're going to have sex on a beach. Over and over again. I already know my thirst for her will be difficult to quench.

The bracing gusts of air with random sprays of ocean water add to the sense that I'm moving in an uncharted direction, taking a new tack, ready to try something new.

And I'm definitely throwing caution to the wind.

Chapter 17

TILLIE

The next morning, Gabe drives us out to the marina, a backpack strapped to his motorcycle.

"I thought you said we were taking a kayak," I say as we secure our helmets.

"First, we boat out to the private island a couple of miles off the coast of La Jarra. Then we kayak."

The boat ride is longer than to Stingray Bay, and Gabe and I spend it wrapped together, the wind blowing our hair together.

I chose a turquoise bikini for this excursion because it makes me look tanner than the others. I lean against Gabe's chest and compare our outstretched legs.

"How is it that you're a bronzed god and I'm a plaster peasant?"

He laughs. "You're perfect."

"You'll probably have to slather me in your super sunscreen when we get there."

He leans close to my ear. "Happy to."

We arrive at the new dock. Only a couple of tourists wander the area. Gabe rents the kayak. "Do you want a set of paddles, or should I treat you to the ride?"

"Hook me up! I want to paddle!"

Soon we're gliding away from the pier, aiming for a small island with nothing but sand and trees. Nobody else is headed that direction.

We run the kayak into the shore, and Gabe jumps out to drag it farther onto the beach. My heart hammers. We're really doing this. By my request.

There isn't a soul around. Even so, Gabe tosses the backpack over his shoulder and we walk down the beach until the kayak is far behind us.

I head to the water's edge. It's shallow as far as I can see. Shells dot the sand, and I wander the shoreline, searching for intact ones.

I've amassed a collection when Gabe asks, "Thirsty?"

I turn back. He has a blanket spread. Two, actually. A thick one over a thin one. "Totally."

"Water or booze?"

"Both."

He grins. "In what order?"

I catch his gaze. "Simultaneous."

"All right, then."

He's shucked his shirt, and the heat in my cheeks isn't from the sun. I watch his arm muscles shift and move as he opens a small cooler and passes me an insulated bottle. "Water."

I kneel on the corner of the blanket, mindful of my sandy feet, and pull off my cover-up before taking the bottle. I line the shells along the edge of the blue tassels as I drink.

Gabe drops ice into a clear plastic glass. He adds orange juice, cranberry, vodka, then peach schnapps.

I grin. "Sex on the beach."

"Mm-hmm." He passes it to me.

I take a sip. It's sweet and cold and heavenly. "Delicious. People should drink this for breakfast."

He lies on the blanket on his side, watching me. "I agree."

I take another sip and glance around. "We could be the only two people left in the world, and we wouldn't know it."

"Best place to ride out the zombie apocalypse." He reaches for the water bottle and takes a long drink.

I'm obsessed with how his throat moves. And his chest. His abs. Everything. "So if there was a zombie apocalypse, who would you bring to your sanctuary? Who matters?"

He lies back on the blanket. "Mom. Mendo, probably. Probably Anya and Morrie. Those two need to get together already. Everybody sees it but them."

"Really? They've never dated?"

"No. Anya was born here. Morrie came when his parents arrived as seasonal workers when he was six and got long-term permits."

"What if they tried it on the sly and decided not to move forward?"

"I'd know. I know them like you know your sisters."

"Oh. Huh. Well, anyone else?"

I know he won't say me. Of course not. I'm a tourist. I'm temporary.

When he doesn't answer, I lie beside him and close my eyes to the sun, the cool drink resting on my belly. It doesn't matter. I should enjoy this moment. The sand. The ocean sounds. The mellow breeze. He's good company, even if we have nowhere to go as a couple.

He reaches for my hand. This is good. I'm about to remind him of the sunscreen when I feel a drop of something cold on my belly. I shade my eyes to look.

Gabe is squeezing a lemon over me.

"What are you doing?"

"I've heard bars in Cabo do body shots."

"Bars everywhere do body shots."

"Mine doesn't."

He sprinkles sea salt on the dribbles of lemon.

"Did you plan for this?"

"Maybe."

My body revs up. "What liquor did you bring?"

"Tequila."

"I hope it's the good stuff or you will regret this in the morning."

"It's the good stuff." He opens a small bottle and pours the chilled liquid into my belly button.

I have to hold myself still from the tickle or I'll spill it.

"So, you're going to lick me?"

He catches a trickle of liquor that threatens to spill down my hip. "Yep."

"Without my consent?"

"Hmm. Tillie James, may I please lick the mess I've made on your skin?"

I laugh, but this sends another dribble of alcohol out of my belly button. "What were you going to do if I had an outie instead of an innie?"

"Mmmm, good thing you're right for it."

He hesitates over my body, his hair blowing in every direction, sand sprinkled over his shoulders. He's beautiful. I'm desperate for him to lick me.

His eyes meet mine. "You haven't said yes."

"Yes," I breathe. "Yes, yes, yes."

I'm guessing this is why I'm not covered in sunscreen yet.

His hair tickles my ribs, but I don't laugh because his tongue has found the hollow over my belly button. It slides down my sun-warmed skin, sending my pulse to skittering.

Then it dips into my belly button, his lips pressing against me.

He swallows but doesn't lift his head. "Some got away," he says, then runs his tongue across my hip bone.

The turquoise bikini is tiny. I don't need much to cover me. He licks along the edge, so low on my pelvis that my vision swims.

Then he's back on the other side, sucking against my waist.

"You got it all yet?" I ask.

He lifts his gaze to mine, and our eyes meet in the haze of the sun. "You have a tan line," he says. His finger slips just inside the bikini. "Right here."

"Are tan lines a party foul?" I ask. I can feel my heartbeat between my legs.

"What I'm saying is we could even things out." His finger flirts with the string, tugging on the end.

"Okay." I watch him pull out the bow, then slip his thumb beneath it to untie the knot.

Then he works the other side. "I think I've found a spot I missed earlier."

"There's still salt?"

He eases the bikini down. "Mm-hmm." He presses his tongue on the pale triangle of skin I shaved clean this morning before our outing.

"Down there?"

"Mm-hmm."

"You better get that."

He spreads my knees, settling between my legs. The ocean waves rush against the sand in a roar. Birds caw in the distance.

His tongue gently dips along the folds, making my body quiver. He goes in deeper, and my hands grasp fists of sand on either side of the blanket as everything falls away but him, his hands holding my thighs apart, his mouth working me.

I cry out, sucking in the salty margarita air, ready to bite down on life, ingest it all, memorize every sensation.

He cups my bottom and lifts me higher, delving deeper, sucking, flicking his tongue against the bud he's exposed.

The sun sears my eyelids, and the world is a haze of bright light, sand, and pleasure. He reaches one hand up to untie the bikini top, exposing the rest of me to the dazzling sky.

His fingers work my breasts, his mouth tasting all of me. The vibrations gather in my belly, tightening, throbbing, growing in strength.

"Gabe . . ." I feel lost in the heat and the fervor. He's learned my body, what it needs. He moves with me, my pelvis rocking into him. The pressure increases, and my body draws in. My breath is fast and raspy.

I need Gabe to take me over the edge. I need everything.

And then it goes, all the tension releasing at once. My body pulses against him as he holds still, drawing out the orgasm, keeping me firmly against his mouth.

My cries disturb the birds and they squawk their displeasure, rushing off in a flap of wings.

I laugh, coming down but feeling high, like the perfect moment when you have just the right buzz. Not drunk, not sober, but in the ideal in-between.

A shadow crosses my face, cooling my skin. I open my eyes to see Gabe hovering over me, grinning like crazy. "Let's skinny-dip. That's on your bucket list, right? Or have you done it before?"

I shake my head. "Never." I don't say I've never had a chance. Those kinds of wild outings weren't something my friends ever did.

He leaps to his feet and unties his swim trunks. I'm already naked, and sit, waiting to see the rest of him.

The trunks fall into the sand, and I suck in a breath. His skin is lighter, but not pale. And his erection is . . . a lot.

"You must skinny-dip a lot."

He looks down. "Not really. I'm never very pale."

"But your hair is so light."

"The sun."

His mother's hair is raven black and her skin a shade darker, but I don't think about this any longer because he holds out a hand to me.

I take it and then we're off, running to the water.

The breeze on every part of my body is wild and intoxicating. I want to do more things. I'm ready to get crazy. "Can we do it in the water?"

"Sure," he says, his eyes taking me in as we splash through the shallows. "There's the matter of protection. Not sure condoms and salt water are a fit?"

Oh, right. "I'm on the pill, so babies aren't a thing." I tilt my head at him. "It's been a while for me. I think I would know if I had anything."

Gabe nods. "Same."

"Then let's do it." That behind us, I run, lifting my feet high so I can rush out into deeper water.

He shouts, "Hey!" and races after me.

He catches up right as we hit waist-deep waters. He crashes into me, and we both fall into the surf.

When we come up for air, he's got me, his arms around my waist, my body buoyed by the water.

I kiss him, clutching his shoulders. I can feel his every muscle. I glide up and down his belly, trapping him between us as I move.

His breath gets ragged and fast. "Tillie James, I'm going to fulfill my promise now."

"Yes," I say, reaching up to slick my hair out of my face.

He lifts me with both hands, then slides me down over him. He fills me, and we're together, all the way. I settle against his body, holding on to his shoulders, warm and wet.

Every stroke is glorious and wild, like every beach movie fantasy I could imagine.

I lean back on the water, exposing my breasts to the sun, letting my hair fan out. The waves rock us as he moves me forward and back, gliding in and out like we are one with the ocean, sky, and wind.

I lose myself in that moment, the water holding me up, his body sending flashes of pleasure through me. This is perfection. This is the ultimate. It can't get any better than this.

Then Gabe reaches between us, his thumb circling my nub. I gasp, realizing I need to hold on to him.

I reach for him, and he lifts me against his chest. I wrap my arms around his neck as our bodies crash together, making the water around us splash.

It's so intense. So much. When my body tightens down on him, the pulses flashing between us, he lets go, too. I feel the rush of warmth of him flowing in me like the water that surrounds us.

We're all one thing, one nature, one world.

I drop my head to his shoulder and he holds me tightly.

If I paid the price of twenty-three years of hardship—hungry, poor, and barely clothed—to earn this moment, it was worth it.

Totally worth it.

Chapter 18

GABE

It's my fault that Tillie is completely incapacitated the next day.

We forgot the sunscreen.

We were naked for hours.

We had sex so many times in the sun.

She texts me the next morning asking what standard tourist sunburn protocol might look like.

I tell her I can bring it, but she says no, she's hiding her condition from her sister and could I please come get her before she's busted?

So I do, going for the car instead of the motorcycle so that she won't have the friction of riding close to me to aggravate the burn.

When I arrive, she's hustling down the sidewalk toward the parking lot. I quickly halt the Mercedes handed down from my mother and run around to hold open the door.

She eases slowly onto the seat, her face scrunched. "Oh, man. This is bad."

I help her with the seat belt to lessen any twisting she might have to do to get it latched. She wears a light cardigan and a T-shirt with a high neck, so I can't see the damage.

"Still worth it," she adds, finally sitting back against the seat.

I hurry around to the driver's side and crank the air. Her cheeks are flushed, but I have a feeling that's not what hurts.

"I have aloe and cooling creams, and I'm happy to fan you gently." I ease out of the lot, trying to avoid any jostling turns.

"I'm glad you got me away before I got a big lecture from Lila. She's been pestering me about sunscreen every day, and I've blown it big-time."

"I'm sorry. I should have pestered you, too." I glance over at her as she stretches her arms forward, grimacing.

"You were busy doing other things." She flashes a quick smile. "I'm not showing any signs of sickness. It just hurts."

"Any blistering?"

"Not yet."

It's a short drive to my apartment. I'm about to apologize in advance for the rather humble living arrangement when she says, "I like this car. I always wanted to ride in a Mercedes."

"It's probably almost as old as you."

"Is not. But I like that you've kept it so nice."

"It was my mom's, back when she had a regular job. She bikes everywhere now."

"She hasn't always sold candles?"

I signal to turn into my complex. "No. She used to be the director of a conservation group on the island. They did studies on indigenous plants and animals and how to protect them. She's a PhD."

"Ah. The crab incident makes sense."

"Yes and no. Most people here know the value of the crabs. They aren't just part of the animal life. They feed and sustain a lot of local families who catch and sell them."

"I can't even imagine eating that nightmarish black-and-red thing that invaded the wedding."

I chuckle. "They're not exactly cute. People are used to seeing crabs in the context of dinner plates or Disney movies. The real thing can be unsettling."

There's a spot close to my door for once, and I slide into it. "Let me help you out."

"I'm not an old lady."

Despite her protest, Tillie lets me help her out of the car. I spin a dozen excuses for my place, its plain carpets, white walls, and sparse furnishings.

But when I open the door, she takes in everything with wide eyes. "I love it. It's so big and tidy. There's no clutter anywhere." She turns to me, an accusation ready. "Does your mom come over here to clean?"

I shake my head. "She'd be more likely to chase me with a broom until I cleaned it all up."

Tillie skirts the coffee table to sit on the edge of the beige sofa. "She taught you to be neat."

"I guess so." The truth is closer to me never feeling particularly attached to the place, so I didn't feel the need to decorate. I sit on the chair near her. "Can I help you with the burn? Does it hurt to wear clothes?"

She tilts her head. "Gabe Landers, are you trying to get me naked?"

"Yes. Yes, I am."

"It won't do you much good."

"I've guessed that."

She shrugs the cardigan off her shoulders. Her arms don't look too bad. "Is it your back?"

She shakes her head. "Mostly the front. It would have been *your* back."

I picture her in the water, lying with her face to the sun. "You want to show me?"

She stands, but before she takes off anything else, I lead her through the living room to the hall and into my bedroom.

"Okay, there's more mess here," she says, running her hand along the edge of the dresser that's filled with shells, keys, business cards, and random items dumped from pockets. "Good to know you aren't perfect." She kicks off her shoes. "You're not allowed to gasp or freak out, okay?"

I nod. I'm about to flip the light on when I decide, maybe not. There's plenty of indirect sun from the shutters.

She grasps the bottom of her T-shirt. I've already figured out she's not wearing a bra beneath it, which makes sense. That would be tight and painful.

When her shirt hits the bed, I see it. She's quite red across the chest in a deep, even tone.

"In a couple of days, your lack of tan lines is going to be fucking hot," I tell her.

She laughs. "Probably." She looks down. "I do tan, but I don't get much opportunity. I keep vampire hours."

"How's the rest of you?"

"Belly is about the same. Warning—there are no panties here."

I hold up my hands. "I'm prepared."

She slides the skirt down. The color of her skin is bold and unbroken.

My dick goes into overdrive.

"I know. It's sexy. I guess this is why women get naked in tanning beds."

I nod. "It's torture just looking at you."

"I know, right? It should only hurt for a day, though."

I mean me not being able to devour her, but I don't say it. "Let me get the aloe."

She shifts carefully to the bed, working hard to avoid bending her midsection any more than she has to.

I stand in my bathroom, staring at my reflection for a good minute. I will not do anything to that woman. I will apply aloe like a proper gentleman, and I will leave her alone.

As if it knows better, my dick twitches.

I'm doomed.

I open the cabinet and pull both the aloe and the cream I always keep on hand even though it's really rare for me to burn.

When I return to the room, Tillie is stretched out naked on my bed, the lines of light from the blinds' wood slats crossing her body.

Damn. That's a sight. I want to photograph it so I can see it anytime I like.

But no. I commit it to memory instead and sit next to her with the two containers.

"We'll try a bit of both and see which one works better."

She nods.

I squeeze aloe gel on my finger and paint a line on one side of her belly.

"That's nice," she says, closing her eyes.

I spread it gently, my rock-hard need for her threatening to overtake me.

"Here's the other one," I say, clearing my throat when the words turn into a croak. I'm not in control here. Not at all.

I squeeze the cream and cover a similar amount of territory on the other side of her belly.

"Mmmm. That one nips the pain, but the aloe is better with cooling."

I reach down to adjust my shorts.

She opens her eyes and catches me. "This is a lot, isn't it?"

"I won't ravish you in this condition."

She sighs. "It's just as hot for me lying here as it is for you looking at me."

Is it? "Will it help if I'm naked, too?"

She grins. "Things will get risky."

"Nope. I won't do a thing."

"Even if I beg?"

Yeah, no. I couldn't resist that. "Okay, I'll stay dressed."

"Please don't. I like to look at you." Her gaze stays on me.

This is one hard-core game of temptation we're playing. But I sit up and pull my T-shirt over my head.

She reaches out to touch my chest and abs, stoking the fire I'm feeling.

I unbutton my shorts and pull them down. My boxers are the fitted kind and, in my current state, don't even contain me.

"Nice," she says. "Those need to go."

Bloody hell.

I tug them off.

She reaches for me, sliding down my length. "It probably won't take much, will it?"

"Not in the current situation."

"Scoot closer," she says.

I obey, and her fingers slip easily up and down me. I feel like I'm drowning in my need of her.

"Can you spread your legs a little?" I ask.

She does, and I reach for her, teasing those pink folds.

The room darkens as a cloud passes over the sun. We keep working each other, learning more about what makes each other tick.

When her breath speeds up, her hand slows, but it doesn't matter. The closer she gets, the more I feel like I might burst myself.

When her hips lift, and her muscles clench around my fingers, she grips me hard. She cries out, and my control evaporates at the sound of her orgasm. I flow out onto her hand, spilling over her fingers.

We both start laughing at the same time.

"We're crazy," Tillie says. "Look at us. Sticky in every way."

I snatch up a Kleenex box. "I know."

"Maybe we can relax now."

"For a while."

She drapes one arm over her forehead as she smacks my thigh with another. "That's going to have to do us until I'm better."

"Agreed."

I pick up the aloe bottle. "Let me get the rest of you cooled off."

Chapter 19

TILLIE

We sleep the morning away until Gabe's phone beeps an alarm.

I glance over at his phone. It reads "Time to open bar."

Right. It's Wednesday.

He stirs next to me. "How's the sunburn?"

I sit up. "I feel okay. It's sensitive, but it doesn't actively hurt."

He clears his alarm with a sigh.

"You going to open the bar?"

"I'd rather spend the time with you." He spreads his hand across my belly again.

"I'm not sure I'm *that* okay. Why don't we work it together tonight? Then tomorrow morning I'll probably be in good shape for all the things."

"All the things?"

I nod. "All."

"Mmmm." His thumb slides across my chest.

"What do you think?" I ask.

"I think you shouldn't work on your vacation."

"It's not work when it's with you."

His gaze rests on my face. "You're serious."

"Yeah. It's a good time. Then we could have a late dinner. I assume there is somewhere on the island open at midnight."

He nods. "There is. Okay. Let's do it." He leans over and presses a kiss to my belly, then drops another one farther down. "And tomorrow, let's really do *it*."

I push his head away. "Absolutely. Now get off me, you brute."

Getting off the bed is easier than when I got on. The aloe helped. We both work to spread another layer on me. His hands on my body make me heat up again, this time from the inside out. It's more than the physical attraction, though. He's taking care of me. Like a partner. Like someone who cares.

As he sweeps my hair aside to cool my shoulders, I realize this is already more than an island fling. Something deeper has already engaged.

Leaving is going to be impossible.

~

The bar is rapt as Mendo tells his story one more time. "And then Gabe here rowed her out to the secret caves." He leans close to the man near him. "I have a secret boat tour that goes to them." He sits up again. "But when he helps her out of the boat, he slips, and accidentally pulls her over the side."

I glance over at Gabe. He's shaking his head while he fills a pint glass, as if he wants no part of the story.

"Did she die?" a woman asks, her hand at her mouth.

"Did he kill her?" The wife of the man near Mendo grips her drink with both hands.

Mendo waves his hands. "Oh no. He heard a splash, then a strange whoosh of a giant fin. And he never saw her again. Later, he realized there were rainbow scales on the edge of the boat, same as the ones he sometimes found in his bathroom."

I lean against the counter, in awe of how Mendo has the whole bar enthralled. He's missed his calling.

"And now he makes his secret rainbow drink, the mermaid sunrise, in her honor." He spots me and his eyes go alight. "But this story doesn't end there. Only a few days ago, this beautiful creature you see inside the bar arrived, with the same dark ringlets and cornflower eyes. She goes by another name, but the way the two lovers connected so swiftly . . ." He shrugs. "Who is to say who she really is?"

It's my turn to shake my head as I dry my hands on a towel.

"I love that story," a woman says. "Can I get a mermaid sunrise?"

I push away from the counter. Gabe is still drawing beers. "I'll make it," I tell him. Then I turn to the lady. "If you spot any unusual scales on the glass, keep it between us."

She laughs, and I start pulling bottles. "We'll want to pick up more blue curaçao tomorrow," I tell Gabe.

He nods, ringing up the previous order.

It's nice and easy, working this space with him. I mentally tally the orders and glance at the tip jar. It easily supports one. Probably it could do two.

Then I chide myself for the thought. I can't stay here. Of course not. For one, that wasn't the arrangement. For two, I have to be there for Lila and Rosie, especially now that Ensley's married. And for three, I barely know the guy. He might not be as great as he seems once the shine wears off.

The sun has long gone down, and the beach is dark.

But from somewhere beyond the light of the condos, a chant begins. "Lava flow! Lava flow!"

I peer into the distance. Several flashlights bob.

"That's Anya and Morrie," Mendo says. "I called them down."

Oooh. I'm curious to watch them to see if what Gabe said is true. Should they be together?

"You guys going to make this a regular spot?" Gabe asks.

Mendo shrugs. "They forgot how much they like this beach."

The two friends arrive and collapse on stools next to Mendo.

"That's a haul, and I'm out of shape," Anya says, her braids swinging as she shoves Morrie. "Next time you drop me off."

"Girl, I'm not walking that stretch by myself." He turns his ball cap around so the bill faces the back. "Someone might take advantage of my innocence."

Anya tweaks his ear. "Aww, poor Morrie. Hasn't gotten any action lately."

Now that's a strange thing to say to someone you may or may not be interested in. I think Gabe's wrong. These two act like siblings.

Anya flattens a fifteen-Jarra banknote on the bar. "Get us both a lava flow, pretty please."

"We don't have the coconuts," I tell her.

"That's fine by me," she says. "I don't like to drink out of hairy balls."

Mendo slaps the counter. "That's not what I heard!"

Anya shoves him so hard he falls off the stool into the sand.

I glance over at Gabe, who's grinning by the register. He pulls the blenders out since I'm layering the mermaid sunrise.

"Oooh, is that another drink not on the menu?" The woman who was concerned about Mendo's story picks up the laminated card.

"They have a ton," Anya says. "This is the best bar on the island."

"It's two frozen flavors swirled together," Gabe says. "Strawberry and banana."

"Sounds divine," the woman says. "I'll have one, too."

"Me too," says another woman.

Gabe opens the blenders. "Anyone else? It's easy to blend a bunch at once."

We end up with five orders. I finish up the mermaid sunrise and start making the banana half of the lava flow.

"It's coming up on closing time," Mendo says. "Should we hang out?"

I glance at Gabe, who hesitates.

"Awwww, the lovers have a date." Mendo flutters his eyelashes.

"Where ya goin'?" Anya asks.

Gabe and I pour the two halves of the lava flow together. His jaw is tight. "Don't know," he finally says.

"Aren't many spots after midnight," Anya says. "Tino's is about the only one worth doing."

"Nah, a bunch of bars stay open late if it ain't a Saturday," Morrie says.

We fill the five drinks and stick straws in them.

"We can all go to Tino's," Anya says. "We won't cramp your style. It'll be fun."

I follow Gabe to the far side of the hut to deliver the other drinks. I lean in. "No action till morning," I remind him.

He sighs. "All right, Anya. We can all go to Tino's."

"Yesssss," Anya squeals. She leans over to grab one of the red-and-yellow drinks. "This one mine?"

I nod and push it closer, then slide another in front of Morrie.

"This was the bestest drink the other night." Anya takes a swig and pretends to swoon onto Morrie's hefty shoulder.

He acts like he's going to steal her drink, so she pops her head up. "No way, mister!"

Now I think Gabe could be right. They're being flirty.

It's fun having them around, and I don't mind extra people coming along after the shift. After sleeping through lunch, I feel awake and ready for a late night. It's what I'm used to. Lila and Rosie went to bed ages ago.

And I want to know Gabe's friends. I don't have a circle quite like this and haven't since I left Alabama. I don't regret moving to Atlanta to help Lila with the baby. She had it real hard when Dodge left her, pregnant and puking and barely able to work.

But it's nice to feel part of a social group again.

As midnight approaches, the tourists dribble out, and Mendo, Anya, and Morrie go ahead of us to Tino's to get a table. Apparently, it gets crazy there.

The two of us companionably put away the preps, wash glasses, and close out the receipts.

"How's the sunburn?" Gabe asks.

"I only notice it when I lift my arms. Mostly, I'm fine."

He pulls me to him. "So maybe we don't have to wait until morning."

"Except now we're meeting your friends."

He groans. "I knew I would regret that."

I rest my head on his shoulder. "It's been a good night. Thanks for letting me work it with you."

"I should be thanking you. You're the one using up your vacation."

I pull away. "You keep saying that, but I wasn't doing much. I can't afford to do many activities. Although because of the booze brawl bonus, I can probably buy a few more."

"Mendo can take you on any of the local excursions."

"That's sweet, but I should do it like a regular tourist. I don't want to take away his paid slots."

He drags me close again. "I don't think you know how excited everyone is to have you around."

"Because I'm a Georgia hottie drinkslinger?"

"Because you're great."

Am I? I think I'm typical. Average looks. Below average sex appeal. Definitely below average earning potential.

"Whatever you're saying to yourself in your head, be nice," Gabe says, his gaze piercing mine. "At least be as good to yourself as you would be to your sisters."

Oh, he's got me. "All right."

The waves crash against the shore beyond the hut. The night is dazzled with stars and a salty breeze.

I want to sink into the perfection of these days with Gabe.

When we get to Tino's, it's more than just Mendo, Anya, and Morrie there. A couple dozen people take over three booths and four adjacent tables, all mashed together in a way that has the server annoyed.

"How am I supposed to get anyone their drinks?" He's tall and lean and clearly from somewhere else. Being chill is the island way. He's the opposite of chill.

"We'll pass them down," Anya says. "Don't worry."

He lowers a huge tray of plastic cups. "Orange juice. Water. Water. Water. Four beers. Sweet tea. Two swankies."

I drop into a chair next to Anya. "Swankies?"

"Tourist incoming!" someone in a booth calls out.

Anya flips the person off. "Reggie, shut up. It's Gabe's girl."

All the attention turns to me. "Hey," I say with a wave.

It's an eclectic group, some dressed down in pajama bottoms and crop tops, others in jeans, still more in athletic wear. One man wears a three-piece suit, the jacket draped over the back of his chair.

"She doesn't even know what a swanky is," the voice says, but I don't scan the group fast enough to see who's speaking.

Morrie stands. "No bullshit or I'll sit on you."

"Promise?" This time I spot him, a guy with a sideways ball cap and a Steelers jersey.

"I could crush you like a bug," Morrie says.

I'm thinking that nobody needs to crush anyone when Morrie turns to me. "But I'm happy to."

Uh-oh. I said it out loud. "Thanks," I add, like I meant to say the rest. I have to keep my mouth shut.

I lean close to Anya. "So, what's a swanky?"

"Simple drink." She raises fingers as she lists the ingredients. "Brown sugar. Lime juice. Water."

"It's coconut water," someone argues.

"No, you wanker, it's plain water," Anya says.

123

"My aunt uses coconut water." This person, a youngish woman in a pajama-and-crop-top combo, thrusts her chin.

"Then your aunt is an idiot." The Steeler jersey man tosses a balled-up napkin at her.

She picks it up and tosses it back. "I like it with coconut water. You ought to try it."

"I don't drink swankies." He holds up his beer. "Alcohol for me."

The server turns to us. "Can I get you anything?"

"I'd like to try a swanky," I say.

"Just water," Gabe says. When the server leaves, he says, "Sorry about the craziness. We've all known each other for years. We're tight."

"I can tell."

The napkin lands in a ball in front of his chest.

"Don't go apologizing for our behavior, you lug nut," Steeler Jersey says. "You're one of the worst when you're not trying to impress your tourist."

I shake my head. "We gave up having sex for this?"

A roar rises from the group.

"Who is this chick?" Another girl in pj's leans forward to get a better look. "She's cool."

"I'm a bartender," I tell her. "I'm used to a rowdy bunch."

Another "Oooooh" rounds the tables.

"How'd you meet her, Gabe?" Steeler Jersey asks.

The second Pajama Girl agrees. "Yeah, Gabe. Cough it up."

"She'll probably tell it better," Gabe says.

"Well," Mendo says with a dramatic swoosh of his hand to get their attention. "It all started with a case of crabs."

More napkins launch through the air, and sugar packets, too.

The waiter brings our drinks and stares everybody down. "I'm not your mother, and I'm not picking up your mess."

"Awww, don't be like that," Mendo says. "We'll be nice."

The waiter whirls away.

"I hope nobody wanted food," Mendo says. "I think he just quit us."

"Don't get Tino on our case," Anya says. "He'll kick our sorry asses out, and then where will we drink our swankies?" She pushes mine closer. "Take a drink, then tell us the story."

Everyone's eyes are on me as I lift the straw to my lips. It can't be too crazy with so few ingredients. It's the color of iced tea with a hint of green. I take a sip.

"Oh!" I say. "It's brown-sugar limeade!"

"You should have it with coconut water," the girl insists.

I turn to Gabe. "Do you sell this with vodka? Or maybe tequila?" I sip again. "No, it's sweet. So rum, maybe."

He shakes his head. "Haven't thought to."

"You should. Tourists love to feel like they're drinking something they can't get anywhere else." I take another swig. Rum. No, tequila. I can't decide.

Gabe leans over to sip mine. "We can try it with different liquors."

"And coconut water." The girl won't let it go.

"So, the story," Anya says. "I didn't even hear the whole thing."

"Well, I was there—" Mendo starts, but the group shushes him.

I look out over the vast group. This is a lot for barely knowing Gabe, but this is an accelerated relationship.

So I launch into it.

Chapter 20

GABE

I can't take my eyes off Tillie as she tells the crab story.

She leans forward so she can see more of the listeners, her red cheeks appearing glowingly tan in the diner's feeble lighting. "So, I'm beside my sister as she's putting the ring on her husband, and suddenly I see the biggest, ugliest, blackest crab that ever crawled from hell."

"Land crabs!" someone yells.

"That's it!" she says. "Only it wasn't alone. It brought a legion of its minions, bent on attacking those of us innocently watching the happy wedding."

Now that's an exaggeration. Most of them were scared to death and trying to escape.

Anya's friend Kelly, in pink PJ bottoms, holds both hands in fists by her mouth. "I hate when they come in groups."

Tillie swirls her straw in her swanky. "Same. I had no idea this could even happen. Of course, chaos erupted. Guests jumped on chairs. I considered climbing the trellis."

"You did?" I had no idea she was that scared.

"Totally. My sister made us all go barefoot, and one of those *things* was going to snap off my toes!"

I can't let her keep saying that. It isn't true. "They don't attack people like that—"

Kelly jumps in. "Don't interrupt the story with facts!"

Tillie loses it for a moment with laughter, then goes on. "And then, in dashes our unlikely hero, snatching up the crabs and flinging them into the ocean."

"Carefully setting them in the ocean," I correct.

"Stop with the facts!" Kelly insists again.

I give in and sit back in my chair. They can tell the story however they want.

"And the wedding is saved." Tillie wraps her arm around mine. "So, of course, I walked over to thank him."

"And the rest is history!" Mendo says. "Until she beat his ass at a booze brawl in his own bar."

"We were there!" Mitchell says, plucking at his Steelers jersey. He's all about the Steelers even though he has to ship the merch from the States. "I got one of those lava drinks."

"Best drink ever," Anya adds.

"How long are you here for?" Kelly asks Tillie.

"Two weeks. Well, I guess I'm down to seven days now." She glances up at me, and I squeeze her arm. We have avoided saying the day count out loud.

"That's gonna feel short, man," Mendo says. "Or maybe you can have a quickie wedding and live happily ever after."

Soria shakes her head. She works at the airport. "Yeah, no. We can't get her a visa that fast. She'd have to go back. But if you get married, maybe you could get an emergency request through. Gabe could go to the States to wait out the visa."

"Oh no," Tillie says. "We're happy with our two weeks." But her smile falters.

"Don't worry about us," I tell them, but a hush falls over the group.

I know what they're thinking: I finally date a girl, and it has to end. I break my no-tourist rule, and for what? Heartbreak.

"Isn't she from Georgia?" Kelly ventures, but Anya sends her a murderous look.

Right, let's not go there.

"What's this everyone keeps bringing up about Georgia? Have you been there?" Tillie asks.

"For sure," Kelly says.

"No," Anya counters.

Tillie looks at me questioningly. It's not a time for this conversation. I try to flash a smile. "It's old, old news."

Mendo saves me by standing up. "Where's that server? I need some grub!"

The conversation moves on. But I can feel the curiosity in Tillie, the way her hand grips me more tightly, how her gaze lingers.

Yeah, I'll be talking to her about Anita sooner or later. I thought we could go the whole two weeks without the subject coming up.

But I was wrong.

~

After a long, languorous morning where we took our time and were careful of Tillie's lingering sunburn, I ride my motorcycle to the bar. Tillie's headed to a starfish boat tour with her sister and niece. They already had reservations with Mendo's rival, although I told her she should still do one with Mendo and Zeke to compare the experiences.

The bar feels different without her. A few tourists from the night before tell the others about the off-menu drinks. I mix a swanky and try it with various liquors until I find the one I think works best.

Maybe I can get a chalkboard and cycle through some of these new drinks, adding the favorites to the menu. I'm starting to see Tillie's point. While I focus on beach cocktails, I don't aim for La Jarra–specific recipes.

She texts me late afternoon to see if I would like company. I would.

She arrives with tacos, and we wait for a quiet moment with only a couple of tourists on the stools to eat them together.

She spots the bottles I've set out. "Are those for the swanky?"

"They are. I've been taste testing."

"Without me! I want to try."

"Sure." We grin at each other, and that easy feeling comes over me. We fit so well together. The dark thought of the end intrudes, but I push it off. This is good. Focus on right now. It's what I've always been good at.

I pour an inch of swanky in several shot glasses and add a splash of the liquors I've been considering.

She sips each one, her gaze on the ocean. "Which one did you go with? No, don't tell me. I choose . . . this." She picks up the tequila. "It makes the drink something between a margarita and a paloma."

"You're right. I was going with the rum."

"I like the rum, but the tequila keeps it refreshing rather than heavy."

"Consider it done. What should we call it?"

"It doesn't exist?"

"I did some rudimentary googling, and a few people add rum, but—"

"No rum! It needs to be tequila!"

"Ours will have tequila."

"Good. So let's name it. I can add it to cocktail sites. I used to do that a lot." She walks the circumference of the hut, holding the clear shot glass with the pale-green liquid. "It looks like ocean water."

"Not the ocean here. It's too dull. Too green."

Her eyes get big. "What if we added blue curaçao to make it match the water?"

We experiment with a full-size version, getting the ratios down. More tourists walk up, and while they order more typical drinks, they take an interest in our work.

"I'll try one of those," says a woman in a yellow sundress.

"Sure," Tillie says. She mixes a fresh one and holds it up. "Does it look like the water here?"

"It sure does," the woman says, and accepts the glass. "Is it something local?"

"We're perfecting it right here," I say.

"I love it." She holds the drink up to examine the color before taking a sip.

Tillie and I lean on the counter, staring at the line of shot glasses as if they could produce a title.

"It should include 'swanky,' I think," Tillie says. "That way people can get a regular swanky or an alcoholic swanky. And *not* with rum!"

"Agreed."

We concentrate, the breeze ruffling our hair. We stand there so long that I almost forget we're in the hut, that I'm working. With Tillie there, her ringlets dancing, her white T-shirt hugging her body, I feel perfectly at peace.

With Tillie, I only want to be right here. Right now. Future be damned.

I wait for the fear to creep in. For the need to escape. For the abyss. It doesn't come.

"What was the name of that place we went to swim?" Tillie asks.

"With the stingrays?"

Her eyebrows lift. "No, you know, when I got burned."

Oh. "Burr Island."

"Hmm. The Swanky Burr. Oh no. Not that."

I laugh, but I like the direction this is going. A drink to commemorate our time together.

She smacks the counter so hard that the tourists all look up. "I have it."

"By all means," the hat lady says. "Tell us!"

"Swanky panky," Tillie says, her eyes alight. "Like sex on the beach, only La Jarra style."

I lift her by the waist. "I love it."

She smiles down at me, and I lower her slowly, our bodies in full contact. When she's low enough, I kiss her, and everyone claps.

"Swanky panky on the house!" I call, spinning in a circle with her in my arms. "You all were right here with a birth of a new cocktail!"

She holds on to me, her face nestled in my neck.

The tourists whoop at the prospect of a free drink.

A week from now, making a swanky panky might feel painful.

But the memory of everything that went into it—our time on Burr Island, Tillie's first swanky with my friends last night, and this moment when we coined the name—those feelings will always be good.

Chapter 21

TILLIE

My sister Ensley texts me the next morning to ask if I want to go on an excursion with her and Drew before they fly home. They're doing a bioluminescence tour, and they can get me a spot on a clear kayak. Lila knows she can't do it with Rosie, so those two are having an early dinner with the newlyweds.

Gabe is working, and even though I want to be in the bar with him, it's a long shift. I can meet up with him afterward.

It's been only a week since the wedding, but Ensley seems changed. When I walk up to the kayak launch, she stands with Drew, looking out over the ocean. They both wear bicycle shorts and T-shirts, ready to paddle.

I hesitate, trying to figure out exactly what's different. Her dark, curly hair is piled inside a ball cap. She's not dressed in anything new or unusual.

It's the way she holds herself. She feels safe. Secure.

She's relaxed.

Out of the four siblings, she seems to have shouldered the most of our rough childhood.

When Mom died, Ensley was five and had to figure out how to keep us fed and clothed. If it hadn't been for a church school and day care giving us free tuition during those early years, I guess either social services would have removed us or we would have starved.

But even with that help, there was still dinner and weekends. Sometimes I imagine kindergarten Ensley trying to be a mother to infant me and toddler Lila. I don't know how she did it.

Garrett was the oldest, but he found friends to hang out with almost all the time, at least by Ensley's account. I was too little to know. Ensley doesn't resent him for escaping, at least not anymore. But it put a lot on her. I sometimes feel anger at him for it, though.

But not as mad as I am at Dad.

She and Garrett feel beholden to our father. I assume it's because they have good memories of him. But for me, my rage burns hot. He ignored us, day in and day out, for decades. And he still does. Grieving or not, whatever is going on with him wasn't right. He abandoned us and never got help for himself or his kids.

But when I was small, having this shadow figure I never saw felt normal. It's all I knew.

To Ensley, it was a double loss. Mom died. Dad locked himself away. She bore the hardship, the anxiety, and the fear.

But not today.

She's good. The best I've ever seen her.

As I cross the sand near the row of flat yellow kayaks, she turns and sees me, her smile enormous. "There she is!"

Drew is happy, too, more smiley than I've ever known him to be. He used to be a grump deluxe.

"You two should take more vacations," I tell them, wrapping my arms around Ensley. "You look great."

"It's been nice," Ensley says.

"Probably having you work at the clinic wasn't the smartest move," Drew says. "Now it's doubly hard to get away."

Ensley nods. "But we're here. I'm super excited about this tour."

The kayaks are lined up in the sand. As the sun goes down, the man leading the tour activates glow sticks on the kayaks so we can start the journey to the bioluminescent bay.

I'm paired with another young woman on a two-seat kayak.

"I hope my arms can hold up to this," she says. She's younger than me, barely twenty, I'd guess, with freckles across her face and two long braids.

"Me too."

"I'm Kayla."

"Tillie."

We shove our kayak near the water and climb in. Two men drag us the rest of the way into the ocean and push us off.

We shouldn't have worried about the paddling. The lead kayak takes its time around the peninsula, and the leader pauses often to talk about ocean life and give us a moment to rest.

It's full dark by the time we reach the bay.

Kayla asks, "Do we know when we'll . . ." She trails off because the water under our kayak is suddenly a swirl of blue light. "Did you see that?"

Drew and Ensley move close to us, aligning their kayak with ours.

"This is wild," Ensley says.

Each motion of our paddle leaves a trail of blue.

"Such beautiful creatures," Drew says. "It's simple plankton, and our movement ignites their bioluminescence."

"Does it hurt them?" Kayla asks.

"No," Drew says. "It's part of their physiology, like our blood turning red with oxygen."

"Drew's a veterinarian," I tell her.

More kayaks enter the bay. A few larger boats glide along the edges.

I lean over and run my hand through the ocean. It lights up, but I don't sense anything different about the water. The creatures are too small to feel against my fingertips.

I wish Gabe were here.

"Who's Gabe?" Ensley asks.

Oooh. I said it out loud.

This is a huge mistake. They don't know what's happened the last week. They've been cut off.

"No one." The moment I say it, I know the denial won't fly with my sister.

"He doesn't sound like no one."

I think fast. I'll have to downplay him or Ensley will freak. "A bartender at the hut near the condo."

Ensley exchanges a look with Drew. "Have you been hanging out there?"

"Some."

"Enough to wish he was here?" Her voice is slightly shrill, and Drew lays his hand on her arm.

"We bonded over cocktails." My throat feels thick.

Her voice sounds exactly like it used to when I did something wrong as a kid. "Tillie, have you been seeing this guy?"

Her older-sister radar is too good.

"Maybe a little."

Ensley leans so hard toward my kayak that her own threatens to tilt. "Are you *seeing* seeing him?"

Kayla gets wide-eyed.

I decide silence is my best recourse, running my hands through the water to avoid having to look at her.

"Tillie!" Ensley prompts.

Now I'm annoyed. "Ensley!" I fire back.

"Come on, Ensley," Drew says, his voice a gentle undertone. "Let's paddle."

Saved by the brother-in-law.

"I'm going to text you!" Ensley says, but her voice gets lost as Drew moves them farther down the bay.

"Sister, I'm guessing?" Kayla asks.

"Big sister. I'm the youngest."

She trails her hand through a line of blue. "I have two older sisters. Always in my business. They say baby sisters are pests, but I think the older ones are just as bad, but with *power*."

"Right?"

We're quiet, watching the water light up all around us as other tourists activate the plankton.

"Are you really seeing a local on your vacation?" Kayla asks.

"Yeah. We know it can't be serious. I'm only here two weeks."

Kayla grins. "Two weeks is longer than some of my relationships have lasted."

"Same."

We laugh. It's nice to talk to someone completely unrelated to what's happening, who has no opinion about any of the players and can judge the situation for what it is.

"Well, have a good time," she says. "Live it up."

"I am."

"Are you the sort to get your heart broken?"

"No." But the word feels like a lie, heavy on my tongue. Something's already happened. Gabe and I started out as rivals, arguing, jabbing each other with wordplay. But somewhere along the way, it shifted. When? The kiss at the booze brawl? The first brunch?

No. It was Burr Island. That feeling of being the only two people left in the world. All our hang-ups evaporated without the pressure of work or family or any mention of who we used to be. We became better. Shiny and new for each other.

No wonder Ensley freaked. She can see it, same as I was able to see the change in her when I walked up on her and Drew waiting by the kayaks.

We three sisters have always been so close. Something this momentous can't happen without the others knowing. And of course, Ensley acknowledging that she spotted my new feelings means that it is, indeed, a big deal. She had to say something.

Kayla dries her hand on her shorts. "I think it might be hard to compare a brief love affair in paradise to normal dating. It's bound to feel perfect."

"It definitely isn't the same." Even as I say the words, I know I'm guilty of thinking Gabe is the best, most important relationship I've had.

But Kayla's right. It's only been a week.

It's like cruise hookups or convention flings. Outside of reality.

Beaches. Cocktails. Sex and sunburns.

Nothing about what is happening between me and Gabe bears any resemblance to regular life. What we're feeling might not be permanent. While we're in it, there's no way to know if it's anything more than a vacation romance made magical by this perfect place.

Kayla and I keep paddling, the blue glow trailing our movements like a shower of stars.

Despite all these doubts brought on by Ensley's overreaction, I wish Gabe were with me, his strong arms propelling us through the water, telling me all the juicy details only a local could give.

And then, an important realization hits me.

The idyllic love affair on a gorgeous island is outside of *my* ordinary existence.

But for Gabe, it's another day of work in the place where he lives.

The only thing special about what's happening now . . . is *me*.

Chapter 22

GABE

Tillie walks up to the bar a couple of hours before closing.

"How was the tour?" I ask.

She opens the hinged counter and sets her bag on the floor. "Magical. Missed you being there."

I wrap my arms around her. "I get it. It's nice to share something beautiful."

"It was so amazing." She pulls back to fix her gaze on me. "Tell me you've been there recently. Something like that is too wonderful to leave to tourists all the time."

"It's been a while. I'll admit that." And she's right. There's plenty of time to go when the tours aren't running.

She releases me and assesses the crowd. "Looks like you're caught up."

I grab her shoulders and turn her to face the right side of the bar. High on the post is a small black chalkboard Mom made for me, the edges covered in driftwood to match the bar. It reads, "Thursday special. La Jarra's own cocktail: Swanky Panky."

"I love it!" She walks closer. "It's perfect."

"I only need five daily specials since I'm off two days and most tourists leave within a week."

She turns around. "Except me."

My throat tightens. "Except you."

She pulls out her phone. "You should have two weeks of specials planned. We can brainstorm."

She's right. I pull glasses from the sink to load into the dishwasher. Everyone has fresh drinks. It's a good time to talk business.

She leans against the counter, studying her screen. "Will you want the mermaid sunrise on double rotation since it's such a hit?"

"Sure."

Tillie reaches for the stack of laminated cocktail menus and tugs one out. She studies the drinks. "I've never owned a bar and probably never will. But I'm noticing you're missing a luxury tier. There's nothing outrageous. Something a customer would buy to show off."

I wasn't expecting her critique. "This is a tourist space. Vacationers want to be cheap drunks."

She shakes her head. "I don't think so." She points toward the condos. "Do you know how much one of those costs to rent? I'm only there because my brother-in-law got a place big enough for a bunch of us. The people stumbling upon your beach hut have money."

A man in a fedora calls out, "I wouldn't mind a high-end scotch."

"See?"

"Point taken. What should I do?"

She faces me, elbow on the counter. "You want to give them something to make them raise their eyebrows. Something to say, 'Holy crap, look at the price of this drink!' An option or two like that makes the midlist items look reasonable and will come off as a dare to anyone who can blow thirty bucks on a single drink."

"You're saying I should add a drink that costs thirty bucks?"

She stands taller. "I am." She gestures toward the fedora man. "You already have the right customers. I say we choose several new drinks for your secret menu. Have a few friends mention it on some review sites." She stabs my chest with a finger. "Then you're making higher daily receipts."

"But what am I saving it for?"

"You don't know?" She watches me curiously. "Did you plan to work this beach hut to old age? It's not a bad gig, for sure. But is it your dream?"

And now we come to the real crux of everything. My whole life rushes at me in an unsettling swoop. Aimless. Untethered. "I take each day as it comes. You're doing better than me at planning already."

She laughs. "Right. I can barely pay rent. Don't listen to me. I like to spin ideas. Doesn't make them good."

Everything she's said so far has been sound advice. She should be more confident about her skills.

She starts pulling bottles off the shelf. She squats low, rummaging through the liquor. When she looks up at me with fire in her eyes at the possibilities, I can't even speak.

I'm sunk. It's happening. Right now, in my bar. I can finally see what's next. Us, making cocktails. Working together. Living together.

Being together, always.

Never in my life have I seen my future like this.

Why her? Why now?

But I know. It's how we fit. Our being together isn't hard. It isn't *work*. No treachery. No posturing. Just sand, sun, cocktails, and sex.

We match.

And the realization that she's the one, the woman who has pushed me out of my dead zone, who's got me looking forward to a future, comes at a price.

Because there is no way to make this work.

I've figured it out, only to have to let her go when she returns home. The universe really has it out for me.

She has no idea my thoughts are so heavy as she lets out a happy squeal at her discoveries among the bottles. "Can I get a highball glass with ice?"

I'm happy to escape my own thoughts. "Coming right up."

She examines her choices on the bar. "Where did you learn the trade?"

I force myself to focus on her question and set everything else aside. "One of the resort bars. We had highly specific recipe cards to memorize, and we never strayed."

"That's no fun." Tillie measures coffee liqueur into the glass. She works concisely, with minimal extraneous movement. I see how she can manage a busy bar on her own. She knows exactly how quickly to fill a shot glass for a perfect pour. I'm surprised she needs to measure.

She must read my thoughts, because she says, "I've never worked with this liqueur. I want to measure so that I can adjust the next one if I get it wrong."

She locates a bottle of bitters and adds only a drop. "Bar spoon?" she asks, and I smile as I open the drawer.

"Not for amateurs today?"

"I can't use a cherry in this drink. It's too serious."

"A serious drink." I pass her the spoon. "With your surgical precision, this feels like the bar version of *Grey's Anatomy*."

Her face lights up. "I love that show. Which characters would we be?"

"Dr. McDreamy, of course."

"Hmm. I can't picture myself with hair as short as his, but I do rock the curls." She grins up at me, and my chest catches.

"I guess I'll fall upon the sword, then. But you'll have to be my Meredith Grey."

She laughs. "Tragedy aside, I don't think she'll work for me. I don't have a bar legacy to uphold. Although the bad family dynamics might fit the bill."

I'm about to ask about the bad family when the fedora man signals for the bill, and the other couple, realizing they'll be the only ones left, also decide to close out.

Then the stools are empty.

"Should I shut down early?" I ask Tillie.

She checks her phone. "Hmm. Half an hour." She looks out over the beach. It's empty, only the moonlight-tipped waves crawling up the sand. "I don't think anyone else will come. The breeze is nice."

True. Might as well keep the sides up.

She goes quiet, carefully maneuvering a bottle of a pale lavender liqueur over the glass. She didn't cut it with water, so it's a tricky topper.

I wonder if I should let her comment about family dynamics go, but she was with her sister tonight. Maybe she wants to talk. "Did everything go okay during the tour?"

"I guess." She hesitates. "Oh, right. I brought up my bad bloodline."

I sense we've strayed into deeply personal territory, but I press on. "Let me guess. If you're Meredith Grey, then maybe it's a mother who expected you to be as good as her or better?"

"My mother died when I was only a few months old." Tillie focuses on the flow of the liqueur as it layers on the drink, so her unexpectedly dark answer makes my heart thunder to my feet.

I fumble with what to say in return. I end up with, "My birth mother abandoned me two days after I was born."

We both watch the liqueur spiral perfectly onto the surface. We stay quiet until she sets the bottle down. "So that wasn't your biological mother with the candle?"

"She adopted me."

"And your bio dad?"

"I have no idea who he is. And Mom never married. The father of the species is something I know precious little about."

She steps back from the drink. "Your mom seems great."

"She's terrific."

"My dad . . . he . . ." She fumbles the bar spoon, and it hits the floor. I scoop it up. "We don't have to talk about this."

"Sure. Right. Two weeks is too short to focus on tragic backstories." I drop the spoon in the sink. "Should we drink instead?"

She nods. "It's a heavy drink. Seems appropriate."

"It's almost a shame to disturb the layers."

We both admire the varying muted tones of the drink. It looks classic and expensive, the complete opposite of my rainbow drink.

I carefully lift it to the light. "Hopefully it's all right. The bitters are almost as old as you."

She smiles. The hard moment has passed. "Will they just get more bitter?" She takes the glass and sips, letting each layer take its turn. When she sets it down, it's only minimally mixed, the layers holding together with fluffy edges.

"Your bitters are fine." She passes the glass to me.

I bring the rim to my lips, and then my mind is erased by the avalanche of flavors. "This is good. Really good. It's not what I would've expected from those heavy liquors."

She smacks the counter. "I know, right? It's the vanilla vodka." She takes another sip. "You should add this one to the secret menu."

"But it's yours."

"I like the idea of leaving you something of mine."

"We have the swanky panky."

"That one is *ours*."

I stare at the floor. Her toenails are still blue, matching the dress she wore the day we met.

Right. The bridesmaid dress.

For the wedding.

For her vacation.

Because she's a tourist.

And our time is short.

Everything keeps coming back to that.

She walks to the sink to rinse out the glass. She hums as she works, and something in me starts to give. She's perfect, better at my job than I am. She loves it more.

But when I'm with her, I love it more, too. She elevates what we do into something that matters to me.

Like *she* matters to me.

And I'll have to do something about this, or in a few days, I lose it all.

Chapter 23

TILLIE

When I wake up with Gabe, I feel hungover. It's not the liquor. I didn't even feel any effects from the one drink.

It was the talk.

He's adopted. His mother gave him up. He never knew his father. This feels so important. A set of matching holes in our childhoods.

I cuddle up against his bare back. He's still sleeping.

I'm torn about how to handle the rest of the vacation. I've spent way less time with Lila than I planned.

But these days with Gabe are so precious.

Something inside me feels like it's tearing, a thin veil wrapped around my old life. I've been treading water for years. And not ocean water, either. Sour, dank dishwater from a bar.

There's no way to fix this. I can't stay here. I already gathered from some of Gabe's and his friends' comments that La Jarra is a difficult place to move for foreigners. This was solidified by my sister's midnight texts after the kayak trip. She sent a ton of links to articles about the permit process required to immigrate. She's doing her older-sister thing, trying to make me see reason.

But all that information is for people trying to live here permanently. Lila was in on the texts, and she added her counterpoint, an article about the island requiring more service workers. Work visas for tourism jobs aren't nearly so hard to get as residency. The resorts always need waiters and housekeeping help.

Gabe stirs and turns around to draw me to his chest. "You look serious for so early in the morning."

"I'm good." I tuck my head into that tempting space between his shoulder and his neck. It's my favorite place, and I'll only have four more mornings to get it.

He sits up, taking me with him. "It's Saturday. We have the whole morning before I open the bar. Let's do something to remember."

"What's that?"

"A cave."

"Oh, I saw those excursions. We didn't book one because Lila was worried about having to carry Rosie."

"Not the tourist ones. There are those you can only access by small boat."

"I'm intrigued."

"Grab a bikini. Something easy to take off."

My blood starts pumping. "Now I'm really intrigued."

He kisses my head. "Good. I'll call in some sandwiches for a picnic. You think you can row today after doing it last night?" He squeezes my arms.

Before I can assure him I can, he says, "Never mind. I'll row. You sit back and be my motivation."

"Done."

We pack beach towels and water bottles and plenty of sunscreen. When I pop out of the bathroom in my yellow bikini, I turn to the side and pluck at the string on my hip. "Easy access."

Gabe lets out a growl as if he's going to come for me. I shriek and dash out of his grasp. "You promised cave sex!"

It takes a lot to keep packing and head out. He kisses me by the front door, and I wrap my legs around his waist.

But eventually, we're flying down the highway on his bike. We turn into a neighborhood of small houses set close together. We cut down a dirt road and I can smell the water again, not as salty and clear, but earthy and damp.

We park among leafy trees and shrubby bushes. Birds flit from branch to branch. A scratchy sound in the undergrowth makes me squeal.

"Are those crabs?" I ask.

Gabe pulls off his helmet. "Not likely. Even during breeding and egg laying, they move mainly after dark. Unless you're out here with flashlights at midnight, you only see them at dusk."

"Then what's out here?"

"Lizards, mostly."

I uncurl my toes in my tennis shoes.

Gabe stows our helmets and unlatches the basket with our food and beach towels. "We're taking one of Mendo's canoes. The cave isn't far from here."

We tramp through the leaves until we reach a muddy bank. There's no sand here, but a silver canoe lies waiting, tied to a metal post with a red nylon rope.

Gabe drops the basket into the center. I step into the end.

He kicks off his shoes and pushes us out into the water. As soon as we're afloat, he hops inside and picks up a paddle.

I reach for the other one.

"Nope," Gabe says. "You're going to reveal that bikini and let me look at you."

My cheeks warm over. I've gotten used to letting him see me, especially after Burr Island. I've let my tiny-boob hang-ups go.

"I'm waiting." His muscles ripple as he paddles us away from the shore and out into the bay.

I take off my shoes and unzip the front of the cover-up.

His eyes never leave me as I shrug it off my shoulders. I glance around. This is a super private area, no beaches, just leafy trees lining the shore.

"I might have forgotten to sunscreen something important," I say.

His eyebrows lift, but he says nothing as I flip open the basket and extract the bottle of lotion.

After one more check to make sure our path along the shoreline is private, I untie the string behind my neck and let the front of the bikini fall.

I'm rewarded with a long groan from Gabe.

I squeeze lotion on my hands and spread it across my chest, which is evenly tanned now. His swim shorts tent appropriately as I work the lotion into my skin.

"You're killing me," he says.

"I'm just being safe this time."

He lets out a long gust of air. "We're almost to the cave, so you can leave that top off."

"Sure." I untie the last string and fling the bikini top at him. It lands squarely on his lap, as if it's about to be hung out to dry.

"I guess we're eating last," he says.

"Depends on what's for lunch." I lean back, elbows braced on the edges of the canoe. I feel high again, like I did on the island, body bared to the sky. Who knew I was a nudist?

Yeah. Might as well do it right. I untie the sides of the bikini bottom.

"Bloody hell," Gabe mutters.

I slip it off right as he steers us around an outcropping of rock.

Then we're in shadow, the cave engulfing us.

It's not dark. Plenty of sun comes in from above, holes in the ceiling shining light through in perfect beams.

I realize he can't come for me in the boat. It will capsize.

"It's not deep here," Gabe says. "You can step out. Just be careful of the algae. It's slippery."

I picture this mysterious Anita here and wonder if she's the source of the legend. "Hey, is this the infamous mermaid cave? Where your lover left you forever?"

He laughs. "That's a made-up story. The only time I've been here is drinking with friends."

I'm glad.

Gabe paddles us to one of the cave walls, where the trunk of a long-dead tree sticks out over the water. He wraps the red nylon rope around it and ties a sailor's knot.

I take in the cave. It's cooler in here, out of the sun. The water laps the boat and shifts in a lazy wave, revealing the green line of algae on the walls.

Gabe throws his legs over the edge and hops out, holding on to the boat to avoid slipping. He's right. The water doesn't pass his waist.

"And now for my naked mermaid." He reaches for me.

"Don't slip and knock me unconscious," I say. "There's only so many mermaids you can lose before there's an inquiry."

He chuckles, easily snatching me from the boat and cradling my body against his chest. "I'm never going to lose you."

My eyes smart at that. He will, and soon. I'm very careful to keep my thoughts out of my mouth. I don't want to wreck this perfect moment with reality.

This is fantasy, and I'm going to live every delicious moment.

He sets my feet in the water and doesn't let go until I'm safely standing.

He wastes no time, his mouth on mine, hands running down my body.

A beam of light pierces the ceiling to fall on us in this private sanctuary. The smells of the ocean, green growth, and salty air fill my senses.

I untie his swim trunks and push them down. He steps out of them and flings them into the canoe.

He's hard and pressed between us. I feel on fire after stripping for him on the boat. I'm high again, every inch of my body hypersensitive and ready to be overcome.

Gabe grasps my waist to lift me against his chest. Water rolls down my knees and calves as he shifts my body over him.

Then I slide down, and he's inside me. I wrap my arms around his neck, drawing in a long, filling breath as my body opens for him.

His muscles tighten and flex as he lifts me and brings me back down in long, even strokes. I'm already keyed up from the canoe ride, the nakedness, and our seclusion in paradise.

I lock my ankles around him and work with him, sliding in and out of the light as we move.

He groans, his hands grasping my butt, driving me down on him.

Water splashes where my feet hit it, making the light sparkle on its surface. My body starts to tighten around Gabe, and my breath speeds up, drawing in the pure, natural air.

Then I clench hard, a long, low shriek coming out of me. Gabe moves faster, puffs of air blowing my hair off my face.

Then I feel the rush of him inside me, warm and good. I hold on tightly, letting my body sink into this moment, him pulsing inside me, me convulsing around him. I feel exhilarated, like I've taken a shot of pure adrenaline.

I realize my eyes are shut tight and I force them open. The sky is above, visible in the gap of the rock. Another day with Gabe. Another act of pure passion. Another stolen moment.

A new feeling creeps in, not just heat or sex. Something deeper, something scarier, something that floods through me in a tidal wave.

I clutch him, burying my face against his neck. I'm not feeling this. No. I can't. It's been nine days. It's not possible. I'm confused.

I cannot be falling in love.

No.

It's only the magic of the moment. The sex. The beauty around us.

I'm Tillie James, damn it. I kick jerks out of my bar for fun. Men are awful, by and large. Look at Lila. I won't fall for the miracle, even if it looks like Ensley got it.

I get control of my thoughts again, holding on to Gabe's shoulders.

He walks us to the cave wall. "There's a rock shelf here," he whispers against my ear. He turns his back to it, shifts my legs, and sits down.

The water settles around us, even and still. In the distance, I hear birds and the occasional splash of some creature diving into the sea.

Gabe wraps his arms around my back. I don't know if he has guessed where my thoughts have gone, the battle inside me. But he says, "Just be here. Just be now."

He's right. I'm where I need to be. Cocooned with him. Safe with him.

This is the place where we can forget anything else exists. Even time.

Chapter 24

GABE

I work the bar alone that night. Tillie is off with her family. It's the last night before Ensley and Drew head back to Georgia, so they're having dinner.

I could have closed the bar and gone along. Tillie asked if I wanted to.

But it's a Saturday, a night a bar should be open, and Tillie told me that Ensley has been playing serious big sister and warning her about getting her heart broken with an island fling. I'm not sure I'm charming enough to win her over.

Mendo shows up with two plastic cups of conch stew. His mother knows I love her version.

"You catch the conch?" I ask, pulling off the rubber band that holds the plastic wrap over it.

"Nah, she had Violetta do it."

"Hard to believe she's old enough to find conch." Mendo's baby sister is ten years younger than him. I search around a drawer and locate a couple of plastic spoons.

"Growing like a weed."

I dig into the stew. It's filled with peppers and perfectly cooked bits of pastry. "So good."

Mendo grins. "I know, right?"

We eat for a moment, savoring the classic La Jarra dish. Mom isn't much of a cook, and her conservation career was sometimes intense. I grew up on takeout and box meals. It was fine. Besides, I met Mendo when I was six, so I didn't have to wait long for all the best local food.

"She still helping out at Carrianne's?"

"Yeah, she's doing all the do-ahead dishes." Mendo holds up the cup. "That's why we have this stew. She served us some before taking the batch to the restaurant."

He stares out at the ocean. He's younger than me and feels stuck on La Jarra. He'd like to travel, maybe work somewhere else for a while, but he has boat payments, and his family is firm about him staying on the island. He feels obligated to provide a job for his brother.

Three youngish men wander up and plunk onto stools to order a round of beer. They were here yesterday. I set down the stew and wash my hands. "Same brew?" I ask.

"You remember!" one says.

"I do." I'm about to pull the pint glasses down when one points to the new chalkboard. "What's a La Jarra boilermaker?"

"La Jarra Stout and Macallan." It was Tillie's brainchild. Pair a beer with premium whisky to do a high-end beer drink.

The men confer.

"Is Macallan the best?" one asks.

"Right up there."

They order three.

Look at that.

By the time I've served them, Mendo has taken off for a night tour he booked. I lean on the bar, wondering if I'll see Tillie tonight, when I spot her walking down the path from the condos.

And she's with the whole crew.

I recognize her light-haired sister, Lila, holding Rosie. I didn't get a good look at the bride and groom from the crab wedding, but I see the resemblance in the woman. She has the same dark hair as Tillie, only hers is shorter. The man with them must be Drew, her new husband.

Here we go.

Tillie slides onto a stool. "Hey, Gabe."

Lila sits beside her, and Ensley next to Lila. Drew remains standing behind the women even though there's another stool.

I decide the baby is the best tactic and lean over the counter to touch her tiny hand. "Welcome, Rosie." Only when she grins at me do I straighten and greet the others. "Hey, everybody. Can I get anyone a drink?"

"No," Ensley says on top of Tillie's "Definitely."

I hesitate, not sure who to obey.

Tillie waves off Ensley's refusal. "Get Ensley a blue Hawaiian, extra rum, less vodka, heavy on the pineapple juice. It's her favorite."

I pull a hurricane glass, then pause. "You mean a blue Hawaii, then?"

I realize my mistake when Ensley snaps, "I think Tillie knows her drinks."

My forehead beads with sweat. A blue Hawaiian has coconut crème, and a blue Hawaii doesn't. I can't mix the wrong thing and make this sister angrier than she already is.

Is this a test? And if so, what's the right answer?

But Tillie sees my distress. "He makes La Jarra versions of some drinks." She gets up and circles the hut to come in through the back. "Make a mermaid sunrise. I bet it's her new favorite. I'll do the blue Hawaii as a backup."

She says it correctly this time, and I get it. Ensley has misunderstood the drink somewhere along the way, and Tillie won't correct her.

I pull bottles, feeling the eyes of the entire group on me. The men with the La Jarra boilermakers talk among themselves, oblivious to the drama unfolding on the other side of the hut.

I layer the mermaid drink, occasionally glancing at Tillie.

"That's so pretty," Lila exclaims. "Look, Rosie! It's a rainbow."

Despite me having layers and Tillie having a simple mix, I finish first. I push the drink before Ensley.

"I'll wait for the blue Hawaiian," she says. She's going hard core.

Tillie stirs the drink but doesn't give it to her sister. "Not until you try the mermaid."

"Fine." Ensley takes a sip. Her eyes widen, but then she catches herself. "It's all right."

Tillie can barely hold back her laugh. "It's *fine*. Best drink on the island, and the most beautiful." She passes the second drink to her sister. "But it's *fine*."

Drew places his hands on Ensley's shoulders. "Did you win the cocktail challenge, Tillie?"

"I did. But this mermaid beat my layered drink. And mine had *chocolate*."

Two women in red hats are sitting down as she says it. "A drink with chocolate?" one asks. "I'll have that."

"Coming right up," Tillie says. She pulls more bottles.

"Do you really have to work right now?" Ensley asks. But she keeps drinking from the mermaid.

"I like it," Tillie says. "Better than arguing with you."

I'm guessing dinner didn't go well, so I stay quiet as Tillie starts making her dark-layered drink.

Ensley stares me down. "So, what are your intentions, Gabe?"

"Ensley!" Tillie says. "Nobody needs intentions! And why aren't you asking *me*? Maybe I'm the one forcing myself on this poor, unsuspecting man!"

That quiets everyone. The two red-hat women exchange a glance.

"We're dating," Tillie tells them, sinking a square of chocolate into the glass. "My big sister doesn't like it."

"I'm her big sister," one of the hat-women says, pointing to the other. "So I understand."

The other one leans forward. "And so do I."

"That's on the house," Tillie tells her, and sets the glass in front of the older of the two sisters.

Ensley shoves a loose piece of hair out of her eye. "And this big sister thinks it's unwise to get hot and heavy with someone on vacation. Someone she'll never see again."

"You mean this hot hunk of muscle here?" the older hat-sister asks. "I say go for it."

Ensley shoves the straw back in her mouth, scowling.

I'm not sure what to say or do. I don't want to get between the women.

"The men are struck dumb," says the younger hat-sister with a laugh.

"Probably for the best," says the older one.

I try to come up with something to smooth things over. "I respect your concern," I say to Ensley, who has already made it halfway through her mermaid. "Tillie and I discussed from the beginning our expectations for the end."

But even as I say it, I wonder, *Did we?*

The older hat-sister pushes the drink to the younger one to try. "Who asked whom out first?"

Tillie glances at me. "Um, technically, he asked me first. But I kissed him first."

"Oooh." The sisters exchange a glance.

"You're going to get your heart broken," Ensley says with a hiccup. She claps her hand over her mouth. She still hasn't touched the blue Hawaii.

"Hearts aren't involved," Tillie says, and my own sinks a little. Of course hers isn't. She's going home soon.

"I'm leaving in the morning," Ensley says. "I don't want to leave poor Lila to deal with both a crying baby and a crying baby sister on the plane."

"She won't," Tillie assures her. "It's not like that."

I busy myself with wiping the bar, holding my expression intensely neutral. Even so, I wonder, *How did I get here?* From brief encounters, shedding women like wet socks, to standing here, my stomach a well of lava over Tillie's assertion that we mean nothing to each other.

Ensley shakes her head, realizes her mermaid is empty, and pulls the blue Hawaii closer. She takes one sip and grimaces. "What did you do to this?"

Tillie takes it away. "The mermaid is sweeter. You'll need a palate cleanser to make this one taste right."

Ensley turns to Drew. "I need a palate cleanser."

He takes her hand to lift her from her stool. "Probably we need to take a boat back to our island." He frowns. "Can you handle a boat?"

Ensley stumbles to her feet. "Of course I can handle a boat."

Behind her, both sisters make slashing motions with their hands. Lila pretends to throw up to get her point across.

"Put her in the extra room," Tillie says. "Garrett's room. She can sleep it off."

Drew nods. "I'll pack up our things and bring them here. It's an easier trip to the airport from your condo than from the private island."

"I'll go with you." Lila moves Rosie to her hip. "Tillie, will you come by tomorrow to see them off? They don't fly out until noon."

Tillie nods. "Sure."

Drew leads Ensley toward the condos, followed by Lila.

Tillie dumps the blue Hawaii down the sink. "That went well."

I busy myself folding bar towels. "She liked the mermaid."

"Can we get one of those?" The sisters have finished their chocolate drink.

"Sure." I'm more than happy to focus on a complicated drink.

Tillie puts away the extra bottles. "Sorry to put you on the spot about the blue Hawaii. She got it in her head that it's a Hawaiian, and I've never corrected her."

"It's all right."

"Most people in the States make it the blue Hawaii way no matter how you order it."

"All island bartenders make a distinction."

"I bet." She twists a long length of curls around her finger, lost in thought.

The men order more boilermakers, and Tillie snaps out of it to prepare those, happy to see her drink idea working.

More tourists come. I glance down at the red heels that match Tillie's long dress. "You're not in working gear. Why don't you sit down?"

"I like it back here." She kicks off her shoes. "I can't think of anywhere I'd rather be."

This is almost the complete opposite of what she said to her sister. Maybe she really is able to set a deadline for herself and cut off her feelings.

If she can do it, I certainly can.

But when we get a break in the orders, the way she settles into me, her head on my shoulder, tells me that maybe, just maybe, neither of us knows a damn thing about how we're going to feel when her vacation is over.

Chapter 25

TILLIE

My sister resumes the argument first thing the next morning, this time with a hangover.

"Tillie, promise me you won't fall apart on Lila when you leave." She shoves shoes in her bag as if they have personally offended her.

"I promise. It's going to be fine." But I don't sound very convincing. Even though I have three more full days here, it already seems like the end. And this terrible sinking feeling in my gut refuses to go away.

"Tillie, I've known you since you were born. I've lived with you. You have never looked at a guy the way you look at this bartender. You've put yourself in an impossible situation. This is going to be your first heartbreak. It's written all over your face." She moves her smaller suitcase to the floor and starts working on the bigger one.

Drew sits on a chair in the corner by his neatly packed bag. His hands are folded together in a picture of quiet patience. It's what he needs to manage his firebrand wife.

Ensley looks over at him. "What do you think? What are we going to do with her?"

Drew notoriously speaks only when he has all his thoughts together. This time is no exception. "I think your anger is far too late. Tillie obviously already has feelings for Gabe. It's up to them to manage how they part and what form of communication, if any, they will have from here on out."

Communication. I hadn't thought of that. Will we keep texting? Do phone calls? Try to hold it together?

This is no ordinary long-distance relationship. Gabe lives in another country.

And I'm poor. I can't afford tickets here. And he shouldn't buy tickets to come see me for a hookup that is ultimately doomed. I can't abandon Lila. He can't simply give up his bar.

Ensley shoves the last of her toiletries in the bag and pushes down on the top to force it to close. "Have you thought about what it's going to feel like when you get home? When he's been ripped away from you? You refused to date anybody before. Now it will be so much worse."

"You don't know that." I lean over the top of the bag to help her press it down to zip. "Maybe this will be the change for me. Maybe I'll understand what it's all about. Maybe I'll take a chance on someone next time."

Ensley finally manages to close the zipper. "Are you sure you're not going to sit around and pine for him? I feel like this is the worst time possible for me to be moving away from the two of you. You've always been so stable and reliable. And now this."

I step away from her. "Is that what this is about? You're putting your guilt for leaving us on me because I decided to have a fling?"

"No." But even if she says it, she stares at the floor.

"Ensley, you deserve this happiness. Nobody is upset that you're married and moving in with Drew. We're happy for you. If you remember, Lila didn't have our help before we moved to Georgia."

"And look what happened to her! She got pregnant, and the asshole left her."

Lila peers in the door. "You know I can hear you."

Ensley stares at the floor again. "Dodge was a jerk. That's not your fault. But we have to look out for each other. And I don't like the fact that I'm leaving right as Tillie's made this huge change in her personality."

Lila crosses her arms over her sunny yellow shirt. "If I can raise a baby on my own, I can manage a brokenhearted sister."

I want to stomp my foot, but I have to stop myself from doing it. It'll prove their point. "Who says I'm going to have a broken heart? It's not like I'm in love with Gabe. I've just been banging him."

All three of them look at me. "Oh, sweet summer child," Ensley says. "I know the look you've got. You've totally fallen for this guy. The whole package. The beach. The island. The bar. It feels like fate, doesn't it? Like a dream made just for you."

This time I do stomp my foot. "Do you think I don't know what I've gotten myself into? I do. So go back to Georgia and live your happy life. I'll figure mine out."

I clomp away, out of their room and into mine. I don't really want to say goodbye this way. Because Ensley's right. When we go back to Georgia, nothing will be like it was before. Ensley will have moved out. The home duties will be split between only two people.

And there won't be endless blue skies and turquoise water and perfect beach sand. There will be no swanky panky and light bartending and meeting new people every week because a constant flood of customers comes through to spend their idyllic days drinking cocktails by the water.

I plunk down on the floor of my room at the base of my bed. How am I going to leave this place? Leave him?

I have no choice. None.

Ensley comes in the room and sits on the floor beside me. She wraps her arms around my shoulders. "I might not live with you, but I'm still here. Please call me when you get back into town. We'll spend some time together. Okay? We'll get you through this."

I will not cry. It's not time for that. I have three more glorious days to spend with Gabe.

Ensley pulls me close for one of her long sisterly hugs. "You are worth every beautiful moment you've had this week. And you will be worth every one that's to come."

"Is this one of your stupid positivity mantras?"

She laughs. "Just truth bombs, sister. Just truth."

Drew waits at the door with the bags. "It's a tiny airport, but we have to get through security."

We stand up. "I'll drive them," Lila says. "You should go find Gabe. We probably scared him."

I let them go, but when the house is empty, I don't go to Gabe. It's a couple of hours until the bar opens, and I need to pull myself together. This is going to end. I am going to have to go home. And Gabe will stay here.

The only smart thing to do is to close myself off. Finishing this romantic interlude is like putting the perfect head on a beer. You can't keep the tap on all the way to the brim. Shut it off early and let the beautiful foam rise exactly the right amount.

Otherwise, it spills over the top, making a mess, getting your hand and the glass sticky, and leaving you with the feeling that you wasted something.

So I'll wean myself off him so that the end isn't so abrupt.

The tap shuts off now.

Chapter 26

GABE

Sunday is long with Tillie tied up with her family in the morning, and then me working the bar the rest of the day. When evening arrives and she hasn't stopped by, I text her, but she's off shopping with her sister.

She's right, I've taken her away more than I should have. I shouldn't lure her to the bar during her vacation.

But the timing feels off. Her sister's upset. Now her distance. I finally text her the tough question. Are we already done?

She doesn't respond for hours, but when the words come, they're not easy. Maybe we should wean ourselves off early.

I shove my phone in my pocket. She's right. It was going to end anyway. There's no sense causing a family disruption just to say goodbye.

I'm off Monday, but Mom claims the early part of the day for brunch. I pick up two jerk chicken plates at our favorite roadside shack and head to the lighthouse on the rocky side of the island where tourists never go.

The lighthouse is old and shabby and not particularly picturesque. It was decommissioned decades ago in favor of the new electronic beacon system to ensure cruise ships and other boaters arrive at the safer side of La Jarra.

We park in the crumbling space near the front door, which is completely boarded up to discourage trespassers. On the back side of the lighthouse, overlooking the cliffs, is an old stone picnic table that has weathered centuries of wind and sun.

Mom ties her wild black hair back so it won't get in her food. There's something approaching a chill up here, and she wraps a sunny yellow scarf around her shoulders as we sit down and take our foil-covered platters out of the bag.

Mom peels back just enough foil to stick her fork in the rice. "You seem really down, Gabe. Has your friend gone home?"

I shake my head. "Wednesday morning."

"And you were willing to meet me? Shocking."

"She's with her sister and niece." I don't even know what they're doing this morning. I don't know how to follow up on her last text, or if I should.

Mom examines the chicken on her fork. "It's tricky, dating tourists. They come and they go."

Her tone is kind. My mother doesn't have a mean bone in her body. But the words cut.

I make a show of unwrapping my plate, but I don't feel like eating it. Is this awful feeling worth the high?

But I remember the cave, Burr Island, and countless encounters in my room.

Definitely, yes.

Mom sets down her fork. "I've never seen you poke at Micah's jerk chicken. Letting go of this girl must be a real gut punch."

I force myself to take a bite rather than respond to that. She's not telling me anything I don't already know.

She passes me a napkin. "I think it would be good for you to go to Georgia."

I swallow the bite. It tastes like chalk. "She may not even want me to."

"Have you asked her?"

"No."

"You don't think her coming here is a sign?"

"She's not one of your candle sayings."

Mom presses her lips together, her gaze drifting to the tumultuous sea. The waves crash against the cliffs. Getting too close to La Jarra on this side would mean certain destruction of a boat of any size.

I realize she's poking at her chicken, not eating, either. I've upset her.

"I'm sorry," I say. "I mean it's not that simple."

Her dark eyes hold my gaze. "Those sayings are truths, Gabe. *Fuck cancer* isn't just an expression. It's a mantra of strength and determination. *Fuck the haters* reminds us to love ourselves no matter what."

"I know."

"Do you? You know Anita is out there. You know she's unfinished business."

At that woman's name, I flinch. Of all the people I hate bringing her up, Mom is the worst.

She closes her foil. "I've known where she is for years. Facebook makes it easy to keep track of someone."

She's told me this before. We don't discuss it often, but sometimes Mom gets determined to make me face my past. She's sure I won't heal until I do.

"I'm not sure I want that."

"I know. And I get why. But it's part of you. Part of your history. What if you learn something that frees you from these demons?"

"Who says I have demons?" My voice has a higher pitch than I like.

"Every woman who has tried to love you. Don't think I don't know about your string of broken hearts."

"What has that got to do with Anita?"

"Everything, Gabe. One thing an adoptive mother always struggles with is when and how to tell the baby left in her care about the adoption. We lay it softly in a cocoon of how much we wanted you. That we chose you. That your arrival was a miracle."

"You saying it wasn't?"

Her metal bracelets jingle as she reaches across to grasp my wrist. "Of course I'm not saying that. You have been the joy of my life. But the unsaid other half of this story is that someone did leave you behind. They also made a choice. And probably that choice was the right one. Likely it was painful and selfless. It was about your safety, your future. But I could always see in your eyes that you saw yourself as abandoned. As unworthy. And I never knew exactly how to help you with that."

"You did all the therapy. You tried."

"I did. They all felt you were very well adjusted."

"But I'm not?"

She tilts her head, her gaze holding steadily on mine. "I think you are perfect. But here we are. And you're all torn up for the first time, and I can't help but wonder if the decisions you're making are for the right reasons."

"The decision to see Anita or the one to let Tillie go? It's not like I can keep her here."

"Both. I think it starts with Anita."

"What if I learn she's been way better off without me being a weight around her neck?"

"That could happen." Mom's fingers squeeze my arm as she holds on to me. "But then you'll know. Sometimes it really is the devil you don't know that gets you."

"And what about Tillie?"

"Georgia means more time to figure things out with her. Two weeks is not enough. Take more."

I'm not sure she's right. But the roiling unease in my gut tells me plenty is already wrong. It's always been wrong.

I stare at my chicken. I love the island. The food. The people. But I've never felt like I really belonged. Not deep down. Is it Anita's fault? Or did I always hold myself away from where I landed and the people who came into my life?

When I look at Mom, she's rummaging through her enormous canvas bag. She keeps everything in there from Avon Skin So Soft to firecrackers. She always says you never know when you might need soothing, or when you ought to cause a disturbance. Or both.

But this time, she extracts a candle. "I'm not saying I'm brilliant. But I'm probably brilliant." She passes it to me.

I turn the label. It reads: *Fuck the darkness (especially when you're sitting right next to a light).*

~

I'm just out of the shower after a workout, which I've sorely missed out on lately, when I get a text from Tillie: Need you naked.

My entire body flashes with relief. She'll see me after all.

I send a shot of myself, the towel still wrapped around my hips.

Tillie: I double dog dare you to send one without the towel.

Of course I do.

Tillie: Hold that pose. I'm coming.

And she does. A few minutes later, she crashes through my apartment door and tackles me right on the sofa.

The hard texts seem far away, like they happened to other people.

When we're quiet again, lying side by side on the narrow cushion, the need to know what happened overwhelms me. "I didn't think you were coming back."

She presses her head to my shoulder. "I couldn't stay away."

"What changed your mind?"

She sits up on her elbow to pierce me with those blue eyes. "It was Rosie."

"The baby?"

"Yes. She was crying and upset and toddling around in despair. We couldn't figure out what was wrong. She wasn't hungry or thirsty and didn't need a change."

"What was it?"

"Her stuffed turtle. She wanted it. And as soon as she had it in her arms, she was back to her happy, goofy-grin self."

I'm not sure I get the connection. "Isn't that normal for kids?"

"Sure. She got the thing she needed and it turned everything around. I was moping around and upset, not doing much better than a toddler, and I decided—this is dumb. I'm going to go get the thing I want."

"Even though it's going to be taken away again?"

"All the more reason to hold it close for now."

I pull her back down to my shoulder. Maybe it really is that simple. Maybe we are making all this harder than it has to be.

We decide not to get dressed the rest of the day, ordering no-contact delivery pizza and eating it in bed while watching black-and-white movies.

Every time anyone kisses, we kiss, too, and end up missing half of the films.

She stays with me all night, and we get up to swim in the morning. It's early and no one is at the quiet beach, so we get more *swanky panky* in.

We don't talk about how it's the last day she'll be here. That in the morning she'll pack her suitcase.

We don't mention the future or plan anything beyond the next five minutes.

We hold on to our stuffed turtles as long as possible.

But night still comes.

Her sister texts, asking if she'll wait until morning to return. There's a lot to do to get the condo closed up. You promised to help.

Tillie looks up from her phone, sorrow on her face. Tomorrow has intruded.

I follow her to the condos on my motorcycle. When we get there, Lila sits on the floor with Rosie, who is activating a starfish squeaker toy by bouncing on it with her butt. In her arms is a stuffed turtle.

"Hey, you two." Lila helps Rosie stand, and the baby toddles over to Tillie, who picks her up.

I watch the two of them interact. Tillie bonks Rosie's nose, sending the baby to giggling. Then Tillie starts giggling. Then Rosie laughs harder, and Tillie laughs harder.

"They're always like this," Lila says. "Two peas in a pod."

"Auntie Tillie needs some water," Tillie tells Rosie. "Can you come with me to get some water?" They head to the kitchen. "Do you need a drink, Gabe? Lila?"

"I'm good," I call.

"Nothing here," Lila says.

And we're alone.

Lila picks up colorful bead-stuffed lizards and adds them to a mesh bag. I recognize the set from a tourist stand near the cruise port.

"I apologize if I took up too much of Tillie's time," I say.

Lila continues gathering toys.

Okay, so she feels put out.

"I didn't intend to take her away from you and Rosie."

Lila holds up a hand. "It's fine. I'm glad Tillie got to do some grown-up excursions. With the baby, we were pretty limited, and Tillie doesn't like doing things by herself. So don't worry about that."

"Is there something I *should* worry about?"

The toys go more forcefully into the bag. "Tillie isn't much of a dating person. I think this goodbye is going to be hard on her."

"Same here. I don't usually do this."

Lila ties off the bag with a jerk. "Maybe that's true, maybe it's not. But I'm asking you to go easy on her as this trip ends. We need Tillie. She's how Rosie and I get by."

"I will do my best."

Her gaze pierces me. "If she cries, the baby will cry. Did you see them? They have a connection. I need her. We're a family. So please make your goodbye before we have to get on a long flight home and all this is more difficult than it had to be."

I understand her point.

Tillie returns with a glass of water. Rosie looks down at the floor and lets out a howl.

Tillie squeezes her. "Oh no! Where did all your toys go?"

"It's time for bed," Lila says, reaching out for the baby. "I'll see you in the morning. Flight's at one. We have to turn the car in before that."

Tillie passes Rosie to her. "That's not early. We'll get it done."

Lila smooths Rosie's hair, her expression hard. "I'll empty the fridge in the morning. And take out the trash. The sheets need to go in the wash as we leave. It's hard to manage all the chores if I'm alone with Rosie."

"I can do it."

"Really? You're not going to drink half the night or get sunburned or try to sneak in another cave visit?"

Tillie takes a step back. "Lila! I understand what we need to do."

"Okay." Lila flashes one more look at both of us. "Nice meeting you, Gabe."

"Nice meeting you, too."

We head to Tillie's room and she tosses her suitcase on the bed. "I'm not sure what's gotten into my sister. I don't have much to do. Just a few dresses to pull down." She walks to the closet and drags them from their hangers.

She seems on the verge of tears. I don't know what to do. Lila said to take it easy on her, but how?

"Are your bathing suits hanging up?"

She nods.

"I'll get them." I step into her bathroom. All the bikinis I got to know so well are lined up on a small rack by the bathtub. The red polka dot. The yellow. The blue.

They're dry. I bring them to Tillie, who is trying to fold the same dress she was working on when I left.

I drop the swimsuits on the bed and wrap my arms around her. "I refuse to regret this time we had."

"Me too." She lets go of the red dress and it falls in a heap.

"I'm never going to forget it."

"Me neither."

We stand that way for a long time.

There are a lot of things I could say. That she's been the best thing to ever happen to me. That I'm glad I broke all my rules for her.

That I'm better than I was before I knew her.

I could tell her more about Anita, give my birth mother a name. Even tell her that Mom thinks Tillie has broken my curse, that I can get attached to someone now. That my feelings for her are new to me, proof I can move forward, that I can plan for a future like she does.

But those admissions won't make things easier, not like Lila insisted.

And they're pointless if this is the end.

It feels like the end.

Her tears drip on my arm, and the only thing that makes sense to do is just hold on.

The future has arrived. Our time is done.

Chapter 27

Tillie

I don't sleep much in the condo. I'm flooded with a thousand regrets about not spending the last night with Gabe.

I'm grumpier than I should be with Lila the next morning as we pack our things. I know I chose to stay and help rather than be with him. But big-sister guilt trips are hard to shake.

To her credit, Lila knows not to poke the beast. She gives me easy tasks. Empty the fridge. Gather the laundry.

When it's time to take the garbage bags to the dumpster, I volunteer. But after I drop them off, I can't help myself. I take the path to the beach for one last look at the closed-up bar. Gabe won't be here for hours to open it. But I wanted to see it one more time.

I take a shot with my phone, something about the shuttered hut against the gray sky a match for my melancholy.

I need to think happy thoughts about our time together, not sad ones. But it's impossible.

I'm reminded of an embroidered pillow we had growing up. Mom must've bought it at some point. By the time I was old enough to read the words stitched on the front, it was ratty and stained. But I remember what it said.

Don't be sad that it ended. Be happy that it happened.

Ensley hated that pillow. She felt it was some terrible message from the universe that we should see the silver lining about Mom dying. I remember her punching it on bad days, her girl fists flying. But it was indestructible. The seams never gave way.

It disappeared sometime during high school, and I never asked anyone about it. I wouldn't be surprised if Ensley finally tossed it. By then she was out of school and working and helping out. Things weren't nearly so dire, and tossing something we could still use would have felt less wasteful.

I want that pillow. Or maybe one of Gabe's mother's candles that says *fuck sadness*. It would smell like cotton candy and happiness. I bet she has one.

I toy with the idea of taking a stick and digging the pillow words into the sand, but several tourists wander by, and I can't bring myself to carve such a lengthy expression in front of an audience.

Even so, I like the idea of leaving a message behind. I walk to the back side of the hut and smooth the sand right where Gabe will step when he unlocks the swinging section of the counter. I'm in the shadow of the bar and nobody's looking back here.

But what to say?

Ensley has no end of positivity mantras, but I can't text her about it. She'll insist on knowing what it's for, and that won't end well.

I choose a stick and draw a big heart. Cheesy, but timeless.

Then I scratch out, *We'll always have La Jarra.*

Not exactly original, but it's a classic. And true. Nothing that happens in our futures can take away the two weeks we had here.

I back away from the message carefully to avoid wrecking the pristine sand. Then I run, knowing Lila will be wondering where I am.

We have a plane to catch.

An hour later, we're sitting in a line of chairs at the rental car place, waiting to turn in our vehicle, when both of our phones buzz simultaneously.

Lila can't get to her phone with Rosie sleeping in her arms. "What is it?" she asks.

I turn mine over. "Our flight has been delayed by two hours."

"Two hours!"

She looks down at Rosie. "What are we going to do for two hours? The airport is so tiny."

"Be glad we haven't turned the car in. We can always drive around the island."

Lila nods. "It's true. Rosie likes napping in her car seat."

We go back to our car. There's no returning to our condo. We already dropped the keys off at the rental office. But I'm happy to drive around, maybe reminisce a little. It beats sitting in uncomfortable chairs with a restless toddler.

Lila reinstalls the car seat she pulled out only a few minutes ago. "Maybe we can get something to eat?" She carefully shuts the door to avoid waking Rosie. "I'm starving."

My mind is on Gabe, of course. He'll be at the hut, unlocking the shutters and starting the prep work.

I could see him.

The need to look at him one more time overwhelms me.

"Lila?"

She already knows what I'm thinking. "It's fine. I'll drop you off at the condos. Rosie and I can drive around. I can eat in the car."

I jump into the passenger seat, and we race back across the island to our complex.

Only after she's driven away do I feel nervous. Gabe and I said our goodbyes last night. I shouldn't push this. I should let it end where it did.

But the pull of him is strong.

I walk to the end of the path through the buildings until I see the ocean.

And then he's there, lifting shutters to his bar.

My feet start running, barreling down the path toward him.

Gabe spots me, and the look of pure happiness on his face tells me I've done the right thing. He doesn't even bother to go around the back, but leaps right over the counter into the sand.

Then I'm in his arms, my face against his chest.

He kisses the top of my head. "What happened?"

"Our flight has been delayed. And I had to see you again. I needed to hold on to you one more time."

He tangles his fingers in my hair. "I know. Me too."

My mouth keeps talking, way out in front of my brain. But I have to say what I need to say.

"I know it's only been two weeks. But I feel so much with you. So, so much. It's hard for me to walk away. I know it's paradise. I know it's vacation. I know it's hard to figure out what's real." I pull back and look up at him. "But it's not that for you. This is your home. Your ordinary work. Please tell me what you're feeling."

Now I've done it. I've broken our unspoken pact. The one where we're just having fun. Where we part with easy feelings. I watch his face, looking for any trace of emotion, any sense of what he's going through.

He runs his hand over his forehead, then through his hair. His gaze fixes on the ocean. He can't look at me.

I've wrecked the ending. Botched the whole thing.

"I'm sorry," I say, backing up. "I should have let it be. I'll head out."

But when I turn, he grabs my arm. "Tillie."

I look back at him, and I see it. The pain in his eyes. The uncertainty. "I don't—I don't know how to quit this. How to quit you."

He pulls me to him and leads us over to the stools. He lifts me by the waist to sit on one, standing so close that my knees rest on either side of him.

He closes his eyes a moment, and I can almost see him trying to pull words from the sky. At last he says, "I feel it, too, Tillie. I feel everything. And you're right, this isn't vacation for me. Except it was. My job stopped being work. When you're here, when you're inside the bar with me, nothing is work. It's the best life I can imagine."

I gasp, almost a sob. My emotions are like a storm on the ocean, threatening to break over the sand. I can't contain them. I choke out, "So what do we do?"

He drops his head to rest on top of mine. "I know you don't want to leave your sister. I could come to Georgia."

"And leave paradise?"

"It's not paradise without you."

My heart surges. I swear it no longer fits inside my ribs. "But you would be leaving your mom."

"For now. Maybe not forever. And there's . . . something I should do there. Everyone's been telling me the fact that you arrived, and that you're from Georgia, means I should go."

I pull away. "Is this about Anita?"

He nods. "You know about her?"

"Her name came up a few times with your friends." My heart is thundering so loud it drowns out the crash of the waves.

"My mom kept tabs on where she is."

Despite the fact that he's coming, and I should be singing, my chest feels heavy. "Did you love her?"

He sucks in a breath. "No. I never really knew her."

But does he know me any better? "But you're going to Georgia to find her again? Where do I fit in this?"

"There's this thing experts explain about people like me." The rasp in his voice tells me this is hard for him to say. "They call it the primal wound. And I never thought much of that mumbo jumbo. Just because she left me doesn't mean that I had something wrong with me."

"Gabe, of course you don't!"

He shakes his head. "But I never got attached to anyone. I barely even attached to my mother. And certainly no one else. And then you came and I was so attached to you. I knew it meant something. But you're not even from here. And moving here isn't easy."

"We'll figure that part out."

He seems completely distressed. His brows are knitted together, his face tight. "Everyone wants me to find her, and I'm afraid if I don't, I'll mess up this thing with you."

Damn. Well. Okay. "If it is important to you, it's important to me," I tell him. "We can find her. Is she in Atlanta?"

"Mom says she is. I've never looked."

I picture a beautiful tourist. Gosh, maybe it's even the origin of Mendo's mermaid story. I imagine someone gorgeous and well put together with big boobs and a smart brain. Basically, everything I'm not. And she wrecked him. And now he has to find her.

But he just said he didn't love her. That he didn't know her.

"What if she still loves you?"

"I don't think she ever did."

I'm not sure I understand. "Maybe you should start from the beginning."

He lets out a rush of air. "She's Anita Clemens. She was pregnant when she got to the island. She was young. Nineteen, I think. She worked a six-month visa, and by then it was apparent to everyone that she was far along."

Oh God. Some pregnant woman did a number on Gabe? To this level of distress? My anger rises. "What did she do?"

"She slept with so many people. Like everyone she came in contact with. Later, when it was clear she was pregnant, people speculated she was trying to trap someone and find a way to live here."

I want to ask if he was one of the people she slept with. Maybe she was his first, and that's what got him so worked up? But I just listen.

"My mom met her. She was doing volunteer work at the hospital. She thinks she might be the last person who saw her. All I know is that

Anita Clemens gave birth to me, and then the day we were supposed to check out of the hospital, she left me there."

My brain stutters. Gave *birth* to him?

Oh my God. Gabe isn't talking about some girl he knew. He's talking about his *birth mother*. I press my hands to his cheeks. "Gabe."

"I mean, it's not like she had me, refused to even look at me, and ran. She actually knew me for a couple of days. She nursed me. She *tried*. I don't know. Maybe I was cranky. Maybe I wasn't cute enough—"

"Gabe. Stop. You were a baby. An infant. She was obviously a mess. This is on her. All of it." My head is swirling with all the new information. I knew he was adopted, but not the how or the why.

Gabe holds up a hand. "I know all that. I know it all intellectually. I can rationalize it all day long. People can say it to me like you are doing now. A million therapists taught me to cope. But something about being left behind has stuck with me. That's where my actions stop making sense. Like I'm behaving irrationally. Mostly, I don't give anyone the chance to let me down."

"I know what you mean, Gabe. My dad—he was right there. Just on the other side of a bedroom door. And his hungry, scraggly children couldn't get him to come out and help them. I've ignored it, too, how awful he was. I told myself that it didn't matter because I never really knew him, just like you never really knew Anita. But maybe both of us carry this terrible load."

"Your dad was right there?"

"My whole life. He's still there, sixty years old, and has to be frozen inside. I can't imagine what goes through his head. So I know what you mean. Maybe we're supposed to figure this out together."

"You think so?"

I take both of his hands. "Let's find her, Gabe. Let's go to Georgia to track her down and get some answers. Maybe it will connect these pieces. Maybe she'll be a horrible person, someone you can easily write off. Or maybe she'll have a reason. Something you couldn't even imagine. And that will change your perspective on why you think you're broken. Which you're not. I think you're perfect."

"Will you see your dad?"

"We've tried. Over and over. And maybe it won't work for you, either. But trying helps. It really does. It passes a load from you to them."

He hangs on to me like we're lashed together on a boat in a storm. The sun beams down on us. Tourists begin to fill the beach chairs. A couple of them sit on the stools, peering into the hut as if wondering where the bartender might be.

But we hold on. Life can't intrude. Not yet.

Then my phone buzzes. I pull away from Gabe. It's Lila. Got food. Be there in under an hour.

"I don't have a lot of time," I tell Gabe. "I can't change my flight. I don't think I can afford the change fees." I laugh a little. "I'm really poor. I apologize for that."

He nods. "I've been waiting for a future I've never been able to visualize." He runs his thumb across my lips. "But maybe I see it now."

We walk to the back of the hut, carefully hopping over the heart I left him.

"I took a picture," Gabe says. "I was going to frame it for the bar."

I squeeze his hand. "That's perfect."

He looks around. "My lease isn't up for another year."

I open the dishwasher and start unloading the glasses. "Don't think that far ahead. Just get these people drinks, and I'll help you set up. I'll stay right here until Lila comes."

"You're going to work your last hour in paradise?"

I laugh. "I wouldn't want to be anywhere else but here."

We serve the first round of customers, peering at flights to the US in between orders.

Gabe chooses one to Georgia in two days. "I'll see if anyone wants to run the hut. Otherwise, I'll shutter it."

"Who do you trust?"

"Morrie might do it. He's forever trying to get DJ gigs, so this will at least be steady work."

"Can he mix drinks?"

Gabe huffs a laugh. "No."

Lila texts me. She's waiting in the parking lot.

I nuzzle his cheek, drinking in the smell and texture of him. These are the parts I won't get once I'm gone. Only his voice, and maybe a video chat. "I have to go. I will see you at the airport in Georgia in two days. Okay?"

"Yes. And you can show me your town."

"We can find your mother."

He nods again, his eyes closed as if the thought of it is painful.

"I'm going to be with you," I say. "I don't know much about moms, but if she's no good, I'm ready to throw down."

He laughs. "I'm glad you're on my team."

I kiss him again, our lips careful and lingering, but not too crazy in front of the customers. Then I open the back counter, hop over my message to him in the sand, and race to the front of the condo complex.

My heart is light. Gabe is coming to Georgia.

We're going to figure everything out.

There's no telling how this will work in the end, but I don't have to give him up.

Not now. Not yet.

Chapter 28

Gabe

Everyone shows up at the airport. Mendo, Anya, Morrie, Mom. They're all going to pitch in at the bar while I'm gone, even if they have to cut the options down to beer and basics. It's not a long-term solution, but for the week I'm in the States, it will have to do.

"Good luck, brother," Mendo says, clapping my back. "Bring me back some killer kicks."

Anya's next. "I want some real jeans. I'll send you links. Bell-bottoms. By the time I could order them, I'd have to wait another thirty years for them to be in style."

Morrie bumps my fist. "I'll try not to run your bar into the ground."

"I'll watch over them," Mom says. "This old lady can still wink at the cute tourists of a certain age."

Anya bumps her hip. "Gabe-Mama, we're going to rock that hut. The tourists won't know what hit them. Bring some candles."

Mom's face lights up. "I'll make one that says *Fuck bad tippers*."

Anya snaps her fingers in the air. "Now that's what I'm talking about!" She and Morrie twirl in circles, Anya having a good time, and Morrie uncomfortably looking around to see who might be watching.

"Let's go, A," he says.

"Party pooper." She draws me in for a shoulder squeeze. "Hug Tillie for us."

Then my friends are gone, and it's only Mom.

"You have Anita's information?" she asks.

I nod. "I haven't figured out how to approach her."

She straightens my collar. "It will come to you."

I kiss her cheek. "You know you'll always be my only mom."

She pulls me in for a hug. "Of course, silly goose. I'm the one who changed all those terrible diapers!"

"You have to bring that up now."

"I will bring it up until the day I die. My tombstone will say, 'Here lies Taralyn Landers. She changed all the diapers.'"

"I'll let you know when I land."

"Don't forget to switch to the US SIM card."

"I will."

"And let me know where you're staying."

I didn't book anything yet. Tillie assured me the low-end hotel near her house with Lila never has more than five cars and would certainly take me. "I will."

Mom kisses my cheek and steps back. "Don't miss your flight. You know how slow they can be to get everyone through."

I wave and head to security. Anya's oldest brother is working it, and he thrusts his chin at me. He waves me over to the priority line.

Nice. Now to get to Miami, then a connection to Atlanta.

And Tillie will be on the other side.

~

It's been only two days, but when I spot a bright bit of yellow shirt topped with dark ringlets, I swear I'm a dying man in a desert, finally spotting water.

She jumps up and down, and amused bystanders watch as she runs up to me, almost knocking me down as she wraps her arms and legs around me.

I let go of my suitcases and hold on to her. The sea of arrivals parts and flows around us.

She smells of shampoo and sunshine, but a different sort than I'm used to. There's no salty air, no sea. Just Tillie.

She finally sets her feet down.

"I didn't know you could climb me like a tree," I say.

"I'm going to climb more than that later." She takes the handle of my smaller bag and rolls it toward the doors.

I follow her with my larger one.

It's bright outside, but a duller sort of shine than the island, as if there's something coming between us and the sun. We cross the flow of cars waiting to pick up passengers, then the line of buses, and into a garage.

Tillie's car is a battered green Ford that has seen better days. She kicks the trunk twice before it pops open. But the back has been cleared out and vacuumed. You can still see the stripes from the suction.

A palm tree air freshener hangs from the rearview mirror. Tillie notices me looking at it and says, "It's supposed to smell like an island breeze, but I'm thinking maybe they meant Isle of Dogs."

I lean forward to get a good whiff. "Yeah, it's not exactly tropical."

She pulls it down. "That's as good as it gets here for salty breezes." She backs out of the slot and heads to the exit. I pay the fee for her, and then we're sailing down a highway.

"You've never been here, I'm guessing," she says.

"Nope. Didn't really plan to visit the city of my bio mom."

She reaches across the center console to squeeze my arm. "I'm glad you changed your mind. Are you nervous?"

"I'm a lot of things."

We decided over texts that the first day, we'd go over the plan. We know Anita lives somewhere in the heart of Atlanta, and we also know she tends to spend Saturday mornings at a specific coffee shop.

We have four options. One, message her first. We can do that through several social media outlets where she has accounts.

Two, call her. There's an option to ring her phone on Facebook through Mom's secret account. The two of them have been connections for years without Mom ever letting Anita know who she was. I have the log-in. The account for Mom, who goes by "Janet" on it, claims she lives in Atlanta, so Anita won't suspect it's a La Jarra spy.

Anita might not respond to a message or a call, though.

The third option is to hang out all morning at the coffee shop and see if she comes. A fourth one is a public library book club she attends. It meets Sunday afternoon.

When I decided to fly to Atlanta, Mom quickly read this month's book and gave me some talking points if I wanted to show up and check Anita out without giving away who I am.

Tillie seems to recognize I'm lost in thought and lets me ruminate in silence as we drive out to the suburb where she lives with Lila and Rosie. Only when we turn into a neighborhood does she finally say, "This will be all right, one way or another. Whether she becomes someone you meet once or a part of your life, you'll have done it. You'll have some answers."

"Right."

"Plus, you get to bang me on the side!"

I smile at that.

We pull into a cracked driveway. The house is small, and the green paint is peeling. But it looks serviceable enough.

Tillie kills the engine, which chugs a few times before actually stopping. "Home sweet home. Ensley keeps trying to subsidize a better place for us, but we don't want her money. We don't need much."

"A roof over your head is plenty good enough."

We step out. "I guess we don't need your bags," Tillie says. "You ready?"

"Sure." I follow her across the scraggly dirt yard. There's so little color here. But it's her home.

Tillie unlocks the door and pushes it open. "We're here!"

I'm not sure how Lila will be after our last conversation back on the island. Tillie has assured me she's fine with me coming, but I'm braced for whatever happens.

The baby looks up and babbles at us as we step inside. The living room has a flowered sofa and a scarred coffee table. Rosie and Lila are on the floor on a spread-out blanket, rolling a big green ball back and forth.

"It's Tillie!" Lila says. "And Gabe." She says my name much less enthusiastically.

"Tuhtuh!" Rosie babbles.

The women laugh.

Tillie turns to me. "We taught Rosie 'turtle' in La Jarra, and now she calls me that."

"Turtle. I like it." I kneel next to Rosie. "We should all call her Aunt Turtle."

Tillie nudges my ankle with her flip-flop. "Don't even think about it."

I sit on the sofa, and Tillie falls in place beside me.

"What did you all decide to do?" Lila asks.

Tillie glances at me. "We haven't."

Maybe this is my opportunity to reach out to Lila. "Did you have thoughts?" I ask her. "Tillie feels an ambush is best."

Lila watches me for a moment, as if trying to decide if she wants to get involved. She rolls the ball to Rosie. "I guess I kind of agree. You could spend days waiting for a message that never comes."

She's right. "So, coffee shop?"

Tillie nods, squeezing my hand. "I'll be there."

"Did you get tonight off?" Lila asks. "Badger was being a dick about it."

Tillie tugs on her shorts. "Nope. But I might no-show."

I didn't know about this. "You have to work?"

"Badger put me on the schedule even though I asked for tonight off."

"I don't mind being a barfly and watching you work."

"You sure? He can't fire me. He's short-staffed already."

"I'm sure. It'll be fun watching you in your own space."

"Just don't punch anybody who comes on to me. It's going to be all of them, and I can handle it."

I chuckle. "I'll leave them to you."

We order Chinese takeout, and the evening moves on until it's time for Tillie to work her shift.

I don't know what tomorrow will bring, but I know tonight is going to be awesome.

Chapter 29

TILLIE

"Why's a fine filly like yourself working in a dump like this?"

The man, at least twice my age, leans against the counter. He reeks of cheap whiskey and cigars.

I glance down at the end of the bar, where Gabe has taken up residence. He looks amused, so I decide to have my usual fun.

"I'm waiting for some gorgeous hunk of love to come and rescue me and make me his." I say this without a bit of irony as I pour two shots of tequila for one of the servers.

The man laughs, sending both a stream of smoke and a stronger stench of booze across the bar. "Then this is your lucky day. I might be in the mood for a lady for the night."

I quickly mix a rum and Coke before I respond to that. "Well, that's a disappointment. I was thinking of getting hitched in Vegas. I guess you're not up for that."

The man takes a step back. "Whoa, slow down, little lady."

I set the drinks on the rubber mat so the server can grab them. Then I stare the man full in the face. "Aww, come on. Let's get married. Then I'll be all yours!"

"I think I hear my friend calling me." He takes off across the room.

Gabe laughs so hard that he snorts his glass of water, and this makes me giggle. "I amuse you?"

"I love the way you handle these guys. Nobody's ever taken you up on Vegas?"

I wipe down the bar to look busy. "Every once in a while, somebody does. I tell them to find a flight because I want to go tonight. Generally, the price tag of the same-day ticket to Vegas is more than enough for them to rethink their hastiness."

"You don't actually turn them down. You let them excuse themselves."

I tuck the rag into my apron. "I mean, some of them I have to handle roughly. But most of them can be toyed with and there's no big scene. I don't like scenes. My boss definitely doesn't like scenes. He always blames me if some guy gets mad when I refuse to give him a blow job in a bathroom stall."

Gabe's jaw tightens, and I know that look. He's angry on my behalf. His fingers tighten on his glass until they're white, but otherwise, he keeps it together. "And you like it here?"

A guy down the bar holds up his empty beer glass, and I give him a nod. "I didn't say that. But it's a job. The boss blaming me doesn't come up that often because I know how to handle people here. Deep down, he appreciates that. Plus, I'm fast. And I'm good."

I pull the beer and slide it down the bar to the man. Three seats from Gabe is Old Slim, who looks to be at least eighty years old but, in reality, is probably closer to fifty-five. He's a regular. I've never had an ounce of trouble from him.

Slim rubs his thinning mop of gray curls. "You sure are talking to this guy a lot, Tillie. Are you sweet on him?"

I move near Gabe. "I might be."

He nods. "About time you got yourself a feller."

"Now, Slim, a girl doesn't need a feller to be happy."

Slim grips the beer he's nursing. There's only an inch left, and it's bound to be warm. "That's what two of my ex-wives said."

Gabe and I exchange a glance.

"Draw one up for him on me," Gabe says.

"Thank you, kindly," Slim says.

I refresh Slim's beer. It's a typical crowd for a Friday night. Seventy percent men. A handful of couples. Very few single women. It's not a safe place for them.

I really should find another bar. I'm sure there are plenty that would take someone as experienced as I am. Maybe a hotel, something classy where the tips are better and the pace a little slower.

I make my way back down to Gabe.

"You look lost in thought," he says. "Tell me all about it."

"I was thinking maybe I should apply around. Find another place. I could probably do better than this."

"Hell yeah, you could," Slim says.

I frown. I should keep quiet. I don't need Slim accidentally blabbing to my boss that I'm looking elsewhere.

Gabe must think the same thing, because he changes the subject. "How far is the coffee shop?"

"It's downtown. So a ways, but nothing crazy."

"What time do you think we should get there?"

"As early as we can bear it. We don't want to miss her."

Gabe flips his phone over in his hand. He's nervous now that we're talking about Anita. "Mom says she posts her croissant picture around nine in the morning when she goes."

"Does she post something every week?"

"No." Gabe stares at the back of the bar, and I know he's not really looking at anything. Just thinking. "But she's done it enough that it's a good shot."

"And you're prepared to go to the book club if not?"

He nods. "I am."

The doors open with a roar. A group of at least ten young men in steel-toed boots, several wearing orange safety vests, burst in like a thunderstorm.

"Where's your barback?" Gabe asks.

I shrug. "He was supposed to be here an hour ago. It's not unusual."

"You're about to get behind."

Three of the cocktail waitresses walk up at once, all shouting orders.

The group of men heads toward the bar.

Here we go.

Gabe jumps from his stool. "Exactly how mad will your boss be if I help you?"

"I guess we can find out." I grin at him. It might be important to have a job reference for my next gig, but honestly, I can't count on a good one even if Badger's happy with me on the day he gets the call. So, what the hell.

Gabe circles the bar, and one raised eyebrow at the ladies arriving with their trays sends them giggling.

"Hold your flirting," I tell them. "He's spoken for."

"Oh, shucks," Arlene says. "Can we at least look at him?"

"Looks are free," Gabe says. "So, tell me what I need to make."

I elbow him. "I'll handle the ladies. You take on the dudes."

He nods. "An even better plan." He scoots down the bar.

And it works. There might not be a tropical breeze. No sand or ocean view. But the two of us are magic together behind the bar. Gabe starts flipping the bottles, making everyone laugh when he tosses one to me and I shriek, certain I will drop it.

"Don't be a clown in my bar!" I shout at him.

This gets everyone laughing.

We realize that his silliness and my seriousness play against type, and we give everyone a good time.

Soon our antics have drawn a good chunk of the people to the bar, and the tip jars are stuffed.

Deborah, a waitress who's worked here for twenty years and is the unofficial mom to us all, says, "I've seen this movie. Which one of you is Tom Cruise?"

"She's the good-looking one," Gabe says.

"And he's the idiot!" I shout back.

There's another roar of laughter. We upsell quite a few customers, an additional layer of protection in case Badger gets wind of Gabe working back here. He's nowhere to be seen, though, and unless the cocktail waitresses blab, he won't even know.

I can't worry about it. I decide to adopt the same attitude I had on the island. Live for right now. Have a good time. Do a good job. Enjoy every minute.

By midnight, the crowd has thinned, and Gabe is safely back on his stool. Most of the people who were entertained by our antics have gone home.

Even Old Slim has called it a night. Badger finally shows up to check out the register and review the receipts. He raises his eyebrows at the stack of printouts pierced onto the metal pin.

"We get a bunch of chicks in here or something? Why are there all these cocktails on here?"

I shrug. "Yeah. There were a lot of women today. You shoulda been here. Found your next ex-wife."

Badger snorts. "Must've been quite a rush. You floated two kegs."

I nod. "And me without a barback. You ought to give me a raise."

Badger snorts again. "It ain't like you got much need for money. It probably don't cost a dollar a day to feed a mite like yourself."

"It might surprise you. I once won a pie-eating contest." It's a lie, but I like poking him.

He shoves fistfuls of bills into his lock bag and shuts the register. "I guess you better close since there's nobody else here."

"All right."

He glances down the bar and sees Gabe. "Wasn't he sitting there earlier?"

I shrug. "Yeah." Best to say as little as possible about that.

Badger gives Gabe a good stare-down, then retreats to his office.

I slide down the bar to Gabe. "Sorry I'm stuck. You going to head to the hotel?"

"Nah. I'm happy to wait as long as it's okay that I'm here."

My belly warms over. He has to be dead exhausted, but he wants to stay with me.

When we finally head to the hotel, I think I'm too tired for us to do much. Gabe has to be, too. He did a heap of traveling today.

But once we're locked in the room by ourselves, we find the energy.

It may have been only two days apart, but it was actually two good-byes ago.

And we're more than ready to say hello.

Chapter 30

GABE

Tillie drives us downtown the next morning. The coffee shop is on a street of businesses meant to cater to office workers. But this is a weekend.

Still, there are young couples in athletic wear walking their dogs. Shoppers peer in storefront windows.

And there's definitely a bustling interest in coffee.

The coffee shop we've seen in Anita's pictures has an outdoor space in front, surrounded by a metal fence to keep passersby from weaving through the tables.

It takes a couple of circles around several blocks before we find a parking spot.

"Do you have a strategy?" Tillie asks as we head up the sidewalk. "Like maybe sitting inside near the window so you can watch both areas? Or hide behind a newspaper?" She bumps her elbow into mine with a grin. "Or I have these."

She pulls a set of fake eyeglasses with a nose and mustache from her purse. "Put this on."

Even with the stress I'm under, the sight of the old-fashioned disguise makes me laugh.

"I can't believe you got this." I stick it on my face as we walk, getting a good titter out of two kids following their harried mother.

But the family reminds me of what we're doing, and I pull them off. "Thanks for lightening the mood."

She tucks the glasses back in her bag. "I have crosswords, silly magazines, a book of dad jokes, and a horror novel queued up on my library account. If you're not up for laughter, we can do a read-aloud of the scariest scenes and terrify our table neighbors."

"You really planned for this."

"Of course! We might be here for hours." She wraps an arm around mine. "And I get to gaze upon your impressive male beauty."

We turn the corner, and the metal rail comes into view. My step slows automatically.

"You've got this," Tillie says. "No matter what, you get to bang this girl at the end."

"I think I'd rather go back and do that now."

"No chickening out."

"I am happy to gobble all day long."

"That's a turkey."

"Right." My head goes light as I see a woman sitting at a table. I come to a complete stop.

Tillie turns to look. "You think that's her?"

"Surely it can't be that easy."

"Your mom did her research. Her croissant pictures tend to be at an outdoor table. It's half past nine. The probability is actually pretty high."

"We have to get closer to be sure." My voice breaks halfway through the sentence.

"Tell me what you plan to say to her."

I draw in a shaky breath. "Are you Anita Clemens?"

"That sounds good. You ready?"

"Yeah."

We walk to the gate. I fumble with it for a second, and Tillie reaches across me to open it. I keep looking at the woman. Is it her? It's the right hair, darker than mine, braided over one shoulder. She wears a hat, pale straw with a navy-blue polka-dot ribbon.

She's talking on her phone while she spreads a hand over a glossy magazine. She hasn't looked up, but her jaw is right. It fits the woman I saw in the picture. She's slight, but not thin. A navy cardigan covers a white shirt. Khaki pants.

I think I should feel something. Like I should know, all the way down, that this is the woman who gave birth to me.

We step inside the gate. She's five tables away.

"You okay?" Tillie asks.

I can't respond. I don't know.

Tillie pulls me forward. I try not to resist, but I don't move.

"Do you need a moment?"

"What if it's not her?"

"Then we sit somewhere and wait."

Right.

The idea that it's not Anita helps me take a step.

But we've passed only one table when the woman looks up and sees me.

And drops her phone.

It clatters to the sidewalk.

The woman presses her hand to her chest.

We move closer. I'm supposed to ask her if she's Anita, but she seems to recognize me.

"You can't be Donahue," she says. "So you must be Gabriel."

I have no idea what she means, but I stop walking now that she's said my name. There are similarities. The way our eyes slant the same way in the corners. The shape of her upper lip.

When nobody speaks, Tillie bends down to pick up Anita's phone.

"It doesn't look harmed. Call is still on, though." She passes it to Anita.

Anita doesn't look away from me as she lifts the phone. "Mattie, I'll have to call you back. My past just caught up to me." She ends the call and sets the phone on the table.

I clear my throat. I want to sound strong and unaffected, even though I'm anything but. "Then I guess you're Anita Clemens."

She nods. "And you're Gabriel. Or were. Did they keep the name I gave you?"

"Yes. I go by Gabe."

"Gabe Clemens?"

"No. I took my mother's name. Or, she gave it to me. When she adopted me."

Anita nods. She gestures to the table. "Sit down. Of course."

Tillie quickly arranges two more chairs on the opposite side. "Should I stay or go?"

"Stay," I say. "I'd like you to be here."

"Is this your . . ." Anita trails off.

"Girlfriend," Tillie says. "I'm Tillie James. I live here in Atlanta."

Anita glances at her with a small smile, then turns back to me. "Do you, Gabe? Live in Atlanta?"

Is there hope in her voice? Or concern?

"No. I still live on La Jarra."

She nods. "It's a beautiful place. Did you do one of those DNA tests? When they became popular, I knew it meant you might find your birth family. I have a distant uncle named Arthur who did it and emailed everyone the results."

"No. My mom kept tabs on you in case I ever wanted to meet you."

She folds her hands together on her lap. "And now you do."

"Yeah. It's been . . . There are some question marks."

"Of course." She looks beyond me, out onto the quiet street. "I've practiced what I would say a few times, especially since Arthur

195

entered the genetic database, but I find now that I'm here, it's all quite wrong."

When I don't answer, Tillie speaks up. "I don't think there needs to be any speeches. Maybe just sit with this a bit."

Anita smiles at Tillie. "You're very wise."

The server appears. "You have more! Can I get you some coffee? Tea? We have fresh buttered croissants."

I can't even come up with my order, but Tillie has it. "Two coffees. Mine with as much cream as seems reasonable. Gabe likes his black with one sugar cube."

"How cute," she says. "Just like . . ." She pauses. "His mom! I see it. Or an aunt, maybe?"

Both my gaze and Anita's shift to her cup. We take our coffee the same way.

"Thank you," Tillie says, and the girl bounces off.

"I've heard of things like this," Anita says. "Genetic predispositions. I guess we just proved it." She lifts her cup, but it rattles on the saucer, so she sets it down again.

We're both nervous.

"How did you know it was me?" I ask.

"You're the spitting image of your father." She smiles, but it doesn't hold, and her eyes are bright with emotion.

"That's Donahue, then? My father?"

"Yes."

After this, we sit and hold the silence. The coffee arrives, and I stir it idly.

Finally, Anita says, "I suppose you've come to find out why a mother would leave her newborn in the hospital of a foreign country and fly away."

I clear my throat. "I know some of the story. That you were already pregnant when you arrived on a seasonal work permit. You were a server.

You made a lot of . . . connections with people there, but nothing would stick. That you tried to nurse and take care of me, but then you bolted."

Anita draws in a shaky breath. "That's quite a lot of information you have."

"It was a big deal at the time. Your name comes up around me way more than you might think."

"I suppose not many foreigners give birth and run away." She tries again to lift her cup, and this time gets past the rattle to take a sip.

Tillie watches us both. I'm glad she's not from La Jarra. Her view of Anita isn't discolored by decades of rumor.

"I've made many mistakes in my life," Anita says. "Having you wasn't one of them. But the reality of you in my arms, in a country where I had no friends, no family, no help, was something else."

"You couldn't take me with you?"

The cup rattles so hard as she sets it down, I'm sure it will crack. She draws another long breath. "I think maybe I should start at the beginning."

Chapter 31

ANITA

November 1994

I met Donahue Fitzgerald at a concert in Savannah, Georgia. I was nineteen, rebellious, and had just moved from the oppressive home of my mother and stepfather. I was sick of listening to fights and crying and wanted to be free.

I answered a want ad—we still had those in the nineties—and found a roommate, Miranda. She was wild. Totally crazy. Her boyfriend was a drummer in a band, and I had an instant social life.

I got a fake ID and more than once got kicked out of a bar for dancing on the tables. This is not something I did before Miranda and her crowd. I would never have had the confidence. But we acted crazy, and the friends I made ate it up.

I got spotted by the manager of a gentleman's club, and not the kind where businessmen sip brandy. He offered me a job, and when I saw the earning potential of that line of work, I jumped on it. It was the best act of rebellion I could think of against my horrible parents. I hoped they learned about it and lost their minds.

One night after work, Miranda told me her boyfriend, Arsenal, was doing a pop-up concert on the rooftop of a building in downtown Savannah, not far from our place.

I had my stripping outfit on under my coat when I met them there. The coat was missing two buttons, so every time the wind blew, you could see my fishnets and the tiny red vinyl skirt.

Most of the working girls were sensible and left the club in sweats unless they were doing a backdoor endgame with a customer. But I liked the feeling of dressing like that. My stepfather would have killed me. I loved the idea that I was wearing it out into the regular world. I felt powerful in it. I was in control.

When we got to the concert, there were hundreds of people drunk and high up there. I wonder how nobody fell over the edge. I slammed shots and danced, showing off my stripper clothes. Someone set up a plank of wood on cinder blocks and put me on it.

I was noticed that night and had my pick of boys. But one stuck out to me. I'd never seen him before. He had a dirty-blond shag that went wild when he played invisible drums to the music. He was way into it, arms flying, but when he spotted me, he stopped cold and immediately headed my way.

He leaped right onto that makeshift platform and danced with me. I was way interested. I half undressed him right there in front of everybody, and he let me.

I'd never met anyone as intense as him. Finally, I had met my match.

We jumped right into everything, hooking up in the stairwell next to the elevator shaft before we even knew each other's names.

We became an item. But Donahue couldn't hold a band. He was always late to rehearsals, too likely to blow off a gig. By the time I met him, nobody was giving him a shot other than to substitute for a night.

But he could drum. He had tremendous talent.

I figured out a couple of months in that if I was going to be with him, I'd be footing all the bills. Miranda started staying at Arsenal's all the time, so it wasn't any big thing for him to sleep with me. He came to the club most nights to watch me strip.

He was the one to hear about getting a work visa to La Jarra. We could do any old job, he said. He could wait tables until he found an island band. It would be a fresh start. He wanted to be a rock star in paradise.

I was shocked to find out there weren't any strip clubs on the island, so I'd have to wait tables or work at a hotel, but I liked the idea. Maybe we had a shot at being regular people. I was turning twenty soon, so it felt like a new beginning for us both.

We applied for jobs to get the work permits, and I got my boss to say I was a cocktail waitress. I wasn't anything special on the pole, so it was no great loss to him.

And we got in. I ponied up the cash for the flights. We went on a real bender those last nights in Savannah. Drunk every night. Donahue did harder stuff, but I generally avoided it. We said goodbye to everyone in a big way.

Then the morning we were supposed to leave, he was just . . . gone. We didn't have cell phones then. I ran all over town looking for him. Got our flights delayed by a day.

But I couldn't find him.

Miranda had cut our lease loose, and I'd already sold the furniture or chucked it. I really had no choice but to go. I didn't show up for my new job right away. I was destroyed. Utterly wrecked. So feeling sick, not wanting to get out of bed—all the signs that might have told me I was pregnant—went right past me in the midst of that heartbreak.

And no wonder it happened. The way we partied. Half the time I didn't take my pills properly because I hadn't come home for two days. I'd thrown up more than one dose after a night of binge drinking.

What was done was done.

When I settled into what I was dealing with, I panicked. I showed up for work and begged to be kept on. I couldn't afford to go home and find Donahue. I got hold of Miranda a few times, but all she told me was that he wasn't going to the usual pop-ups or parties. I didn't tell her about my condition.

I was stuck. So I tried to replace him. I went out with anybody who would go. I used all my stripper skills to hook them, but nobody really trusted me. Still, I kept trying. I slept with dozens of men. As soon as one cooled off, I found another. It's no wonder people still talk about me.

Then it got obvious that I was pregnant. I had no friends. Nobody trusted their boyfriends or husbands around me. I hadn't discerned, not really. Anybody I thought could help me out, I'd burned through.

I was lucky my boss at the restaurant was a bit of a loner. If he got wind of my antics, he didn't say anything to me about it. Of course, none of my coworkers would have much to do with me. I'd screwed all the guys at the restaurant, and the women hated me.

It was a long, terrible pregnancy. My doctor was kind, though. And a few nurses. Sometimes my appointments were the only good parts of my month.

Then you came. I didn't have anyone to help, but a nice volunteer sat with me. She made me a CD of songs, and we played them over and over again. Madonna. Spice Girls. TLC. I think of that night you were born whenever I hear "Waterfalls."

I named you Gabriel, but when they brought me the paperwork to fill out with your father and all that, I fell apart. I couldn't stay in La Jarra. I had no help. I couldn't afford childcare working at a restaurant. I did better stripping, but I was a mom now and there wasn't a club, anyway.

Nursing you wasn't working, and the lactation consultant who came in knew exactly who I was. She was awful, but then I'd done her dirty by lap-dancing for her fiancé.

I had to leave. But where would I go?

There wasn't much I knew how to do.

The only real way I knew how to survive wasn't available to me on the island, but it didn't matter. It's not like I could have found midnight day care.

I saw no way out.

So I left. I walked out of the hospital and went straight to the airport and got on the next plane I could. I didn't even pack anything. I just went.

La Jarra was paradise. I was leaving you in the most beautiful place I'd ever seen. It was the only gift I could give you.

My story isn't pretty. I wasn't a good person. But now you know.

Chapter 32

GABE

Our coffee grows cold. Tillie has scooted close, her leg pressed against mine.

"So where is Donahue now?" My voice sounds like it's scraping over wood.

The creases around Anita's eyes have deepened since she told her story. "I don't know. He never got on Facebook. He doesn't turn up in searches. I never saw him again. Maybe if you do the DNA test, you can find more family on his side. But he never knew you existed."

"You didn't hire someone to track him down?"

"I was totally broke when I came back to Georgia. I couldn't have done that then, and by the time I did have my life somewhat in order, too much time had passed for it to have made any difference."

"Did you look me up?"

"There wasn't the internet then."

"There is now." I don't really mean to grill her, but I want the answers, and I'm not sure how much longer I can sit here. I feel on fire, like her words are acid flung at my open skin. Everything everyone said about her is true. This is where I came from.

If we drink our coffee the same way, how much else do we have in common?

And even if I take after Donahue, he's no better. Worse, actually.

Coming here was a mistake. Now they are both the devil I know.

Anita's gaze flicks between me and Tillie. I'm not sure what she's looking for, but if it's absolution, I doubt either one of us has it. "I have occasionally put the name 'Gabriel Clemens' into a search. There's a famous dart player. But he's certainly not you."

My voice is hard and sharp, like a rock sharpening a knife. "I never had Clemens as a name. Mom told the social worker with my case that she was next of kin, a cousin far removed. She was the only one who claimed to know you, and they didn't have a placement for me, so they gave me to her. I got lucky."

Anita sits forward, her eyes bright for the first time since she started her story. "Was she the one who sat with me? What is her name?"

"Taralyn," I say.

"Yes! Taralyn! It is beyond my brightest hope that she would have taken you. She was there when you took your first breath."

I bite back a retort that it could have been anyone. Or no one. That she had left a mess for others.

But I don't. There's no point in it. My anger now wouldn't change who she used to be or what she did.

"Do I have any brothers or sisters?"

Anita shakes her head. "No. I never married. I met a few nice men along the way, but they never felt like enough. And the reckless ones I wanted to go after . . ." She runs her finger over the rim of the cup. "I learned my lesson on that."

It's quiet a moment, and then Tillie asks, "So what do you do now?"

Anita smiles. "I'm a librarian." She flips over the magazine to show the cover to *Librarian Today*. "I like working with the microfilm, the crumbling old books, and the research wing. No one knows my history. I've never told a soul. But I preserve history for others."

"So, you got on your feet?" I ask.

"It took some doing. My belly didn't go back to normal after you, so I couldn't strip. No one would take me. Probably a good thing. I got a job in a gift shop with a used-book section. The elderly woman who ran it was probably the first real mother figure I ever had. She got me hooked on reading and eventually helped me apply to go to junior college. She was so proud I got my MLA and found a job with books. She felt like she left her mark on the world. With me. Imagine that."

Her eyes brim with tears. "I know I don't have the right to ask, but how are you? You're twenty-eight. What is your life like aside from this lovely young woman?"

I don't want to answer. I don't want to tell her anything. But Tillie squeezes my hand, and I remember I'm not doing this for Anita. I'm doing it for her. And me. For us.

"I run a hut on the beach that serves drinks to tourists. I lease it, but it's mine to run. I'm saving for whatever's next."

She smiles, seeming unaware of my feelings or else glossing over them, and the corners of her eyes smudge from her wet eyeliner. "And how is Taralyn?"

"She sells candles in the tourist market. She was the director of a conservation firm, but she retired a few years ago and mainly does her crafts now."

"I remember that. She was quite a bit older than me. And was she married?"

"No. She says I'm the only man for her."

Sadness flashes across Anita's face. "So, no father. But she was a great mom?"

"The best."

Anita nods. "You've turned out so beautifully. I'm so grateful you came to find me."

I have no idea where to take this next. I wasn't prepared for the anger, the fire, the pain. I want to escape it. I turn to Tillie.

"You ready to go?" she asks.

"I think so." We stand up.

Anita rises with us. "I work at the Central Library if you ever want to find me. Or online."

I'm not sure what I want other than to get away and think. "Okay."

She nods, tearing up again as if she might get it now, that I'm not interested, that there was no absolution, no reason to leave me other than mistakes, panic, and fear. "Thank you for letting me see you." She steps forward for an embrace.

I hesitate a moment. It feels wrong to hug this stranger. To give her what my mother earned all the years she raised me. I stiffen, but then Tillie meets my gaze. She's emotional. She's feeling something. And she knows where I'm at. She's been in this place. Worse, even. She faced it day after day, the closed door of her father's room, the misery ignored.

So I take a step toward Anita and let her wrap her arms around my shoulders.

When she's close, there's something about her that isn't foreign at all. Her hair tickles my cheek. Her heart slams against my chest. I once knew these things about her. Somewhere, deep in the recesses of my subconscious memory, I felt that hair. I heard that heartbeat. It was the first sound I knew.

We hold on longer and more tightly than I think we will.

She has a hard time smiling when we part. "Good luck, Gabe. I wish you both well."

Tillie takes my hand as we walk away. I don't look back.

"You did it," she says. "How do you feel?"

"I was mad."

"That's fair. She left you."

"Then shocked that all the rumors were true."

She nods. "Those were hard things to learn about your mother."

"Birth mother."

Tillie squeezes my hand. "Right."

"Do you think she regrets leaving me behind?"

"Yes. I do. It's affected her all her life. Today was hard on you, but I think it was pure misery for her, even though she did get to see you."

I stare up into the clear blue sky as if the clouds will arrange themselves into answers. "Should I have stayed away?"

"No. I think it's good to face your mistakes. And she did. She told you everything."

She had.

We head back to Tillie's car, but once we're inside, we keep sitting. "There's a great park along the water not far from here," she says. "Would a walk help?"

"Yeah. That sounds good."

"It's no beachfront, but it's nice."

She drives us down several streets, but my gaze stays unfocused out the window. Donahue Fitzgerald. The man who doesn't know I exist. I don't feel any urge to look him up. If Anita can't find him, I doubt I could, either. If he partied as hard as Anita said, he's probably dead by now, anyway.

We park along a street lined with trees. There are winding walkways and benches in the shade.

When I step out of the car, Tillie takes my hand. I feel like I'm walking in a fog, but she's the one clear figure.

"Will you do the DNA test?" she asks.

"I don't know. Maybe someday."

"Are you going to see her again?"

"I'm not sure of that, either."

Tillie pulls me closer to her, and we stroll down the light-drenched path, past sunbathers on towels on the grassy hill, beyond a bridge that arches over the water, and around this big open space in the city where she lives.

Tillie squeezes my fingers. "You're still struggling with something. We talked about how the meeting probably affected Anita, but what about you?"

I try to put it into words. "I feel like I've walked through fire."

"And got a hug at the end. Or was that part of the fire?"

"No, I think the hug actually put out the flames. I recognized her somehow. She felt . . . true."

"I wouldn't expect a miracle after a single meeting."

We follow a path past a playscape where happy kids run and shout, their mothers watching from park benches.

I had that. Mom took me to the park. I had playdates and friends. Everyone knew I was adopted, but she made it not matter, even if we didn't look alike, even if there was no nuclear family, just us.

It was a good childhood. The right one. A real gift.

I don't have to include Anita in my life, but I have that choice now.

She's not my mother and never will be. But she's proven herself today. She owned up to her mistakes. Anita had a hard start and made big mistakes. But she broke a cycle. I will never know what she felt she had to do to get out of her home and find a way to survive. She recognized she was attracted to people who would hurt her and chose a different life.

These are lessons worth sharing, worth passing on.

One day, maybe, I will have kids. I will have to teach them. So will Mom.

And they could probably use all the grandmothers they can get.

Tillie's stomach rumbles, and we both laugh.

"You think you could pause your gorgeously intense ruminations long enough to grab some lunch?" Tillie asks.

"I can."

"Good. It's my turn to show you a city. It's all right here." She gestures to the park with its pathways and trees.

Atlanta is earthy and green. It feels more solid, more grounded than the sandy beach and endless ocean surrounding La Jarra. This place holds on to both its past and its present. It can't simply wash it away with the waves.

"How about we start with a picnic?" I ask.

"Perfect!" She turns us around to head a different direction. "There's a great sandwich shop near the park. We can bring it back here."

And just like that, the biggest moment of my life is behind me.

Chapter 33

TILLIE

Gabe spends a week in Atlanta. We see all the sights during the day before I go to work. Some nights he spends the whole shift with me, helping out behind the bar when Badger's not around.

Other nights he checks in with his mom and the friends running the bar.

They're struggling to keep things afloat. He's regretting not shuttering it or hiring a real bartender, if he could have found one. With more time, he might have trained Morrie and Anya how to make proper cocktails, but even the condo complex manager has called to ask about what's happening to his beach hut.

He's needed in La Jarra.

We shove all that aside as we take drives through Atlanta and spend languid hours in the hotel bed. We also avoid talking about what will happen after he leaves. Dwelling on the future will ruin the magic, so we keep our sense of island time even while taking in the city.

I manage to get off early for Gabe's last night in Georgia. We walk through Olympic Park to see the fountain light show. I've never gone since moving here, and it seems fitting to take in a tourist attraction with him at my side.

The night is warm and the foot traffic light as we wander the grounds of the old Olympic Village from the 1996 games. The fountains serve as a splash pad for kids during the day, although Lila has never driven Rosie this far to play in it.

We approach the area right as a new cycle of the light show begins. Water shoots into the air from hundreds of spouts, lit in different colors. "Chariots of Fire" plays from hidden speakers, and the water arcs in time to the beat.

People around us hold up cell phones to capture the spectacle, but I settle my back against Gabe's chest. I already know from my beach trip that no video can capture what this moment feels like, and I want to sink into the experience with my full attention.

The music winds through the trees and fills the open space. The breeze lifts my hair off my shoulders, and Gabe's arms tighten around me. I feel cocooned by him, safe and happy.

We watch, our gazes lifted, as the show goes on. I suspend all thoughts of tomorrow, and Gabe getting on a plane back to La Jarra, and what can possibly happen after that. I might not ever see him again. I certainly can't afford to fly there. And how often can he realistically come here?

I refocus on the lights and music. It's a perfect night, and I won't ruin it with imperfect thoughts. He's mine in this moment, and that has to be enough. Our two weeks together turned into three. How many people get 50 percent more happiness than they thought they would?

When the fountains stop flowing and the music ends, we walk hand in hand down the sidewalks, past the Coca-Cola Center, the concert venues, and along the side streets.

"It would never be possible to hold the Olympics somewhere like La Jarra," Gabe says, staring up at the towering shells of the two closest arenas.

"Too small an island?"

"I guess we might have enough hotel rooms, but there simply isn't enough open land to put huge buildings like this. It's like a city unto itself."

When we make it to a street, we stop to eat at a greasy-spoon diner a block off the main plaza. It's hard to force myself to swallow. This goodbye feels a thousand times harder than the one on the island.

We take our time heading back to the car, although once we reach it, I race across town to get us to his hotel. We won't make the same mistake as before and not savor every moment before he leaves for the airport.

We curl together on the bed, his body fitted around mine, his finger trailing down my shoulder. This is when he finally brings up our future. "You know, visitors can stay up to six months on the island. You couldn't work, but you could be there."

I instantly think of Lila and Rosie. "I can't just leave."

"Because of your sister?"

"I watch Rosie while Lila's at work. Her job at the pizza parlor isn't near enough to pay for day care. We've looked and looked. She can't do it without me."

He nods, his chin bumping against my head. "I can look into giving up the bar. Maybe I can sublease it. I definitely can't leave Morrie and Anya in charge."

I sit up at that. "You can't give up your bar! I won't let you! And why would you leave an island paradise for Atlanta?"

"For you."

"But your mom. Your friends."

"What if we moved all three of you to La Jarra?"

"And abandon Ensley? And Garrett? And how would we pay for ourselves? Rely on you? I can't do that. Lila would definitely never do that. We're used to making our own way."

"I could hire you. I have paperwork on my end to do showing I tried to fill the job locally, but it should work out. Labor like ours is hard to come by."

I turn to face him. "But then Lila and Rosie are relying on my job. What if . . ." I don't want to say it. It's not the right thing to say.

But apparently, he knows. "What if we don't work out?"

I nod. "Ensley had the same issue with Drew. She realized working for him wasn't smart. She tried at first and they had a big fight and then he fired her. She didn't return to helping out at his veterinary clinic until they were engaged."

He draws in a breath, and I quickly sit up. "Now don't go proposing."

He holds up his hands. "I wasn't going to!"

"You weren't?" I smack him with a pillow. "Why not?"

"Because I knew you would hit me with the nearest object!"

"Good thing it wasn't a vase!" I smack him again.

"Hey!" He tries to pin me down, but I squirm away from him. "But a telephone will do!" I reach for the side table.

"Oh no you don't." He picks me up and tosses me back to the center of the bed.

Then he's on top of me, all his warm skin pressed against mine.

And for some reason, this is the moment the dam breaks. The tears start coming and they refuse to stop.

He pulls my head to his chest, his hands in my hair. "Tillie, it's all right. We'll figure it out."

But will we? My options are to work for him or to marry him. Neither makes sense for someone I've known three weeks, especially not with a sister and niece in tow. And Lila doesn't even want me to be with Gabe. This can never work. Never, ever.

"This trip was supposed to fix this," I tell him. "I thought you would meet Anita and somehow it would all magically fall into place."

"Maybe I did, too."

"So it was for nothing. You coming here didn't change anything." Tears fall fast and furious down my face.

He kisses my wet eyelids, brushing away the tears on my cheeks. "I'm glad I met my birth mother. I'm glad you convinced me. That mattered. You got me to do something I could never face before."

"I did. And I'm proud of you."

"Another week with you wasn't nothing. It's been everything."

I nod and grasp the back of his head, bringing his mouth to mine. And we go back to where we were, our bodies in sync, a frenzy of mouths and fingers and connection.

Tomorrow will have to take care of itself.

Then all the days that follow.

Chapter 34

GABE

Mom waits for me at the gate in La Jarra. She takes one look at me and pulls me in for a hug.

I let her, filling all my senses with home. The lilting, musical cadence of the island dialects cuts through the general noise. The smell of sun and sea air clings to everyone's clothes. The tourists chatter with their nervous energy, and the locals take their bags to taxis, happy with their shopping finds.

But it's not the same as when I left. Life here feels different without Tillie.

Mom drives me to her house, filling the quiet with idle chatter. "And then the entire bachelorette party decides to buy every one of my *Fuck ordinary* candles. I spent all day yesterday making more."

When I fail to respond with so much as a grunt to the last part, she reaches out to squeeze my hand. "Tell me about Anita. I got your texts, but I want to hear about her in your own voice."

She parks in front of the peach wood-slat house where I grew up. I duck out of her car and wait until we're inside to start talking.

I set my backpack on the coffee table. "She expected I would show eventually. Her uncle did a DNA test, and she figured it was only a matter of time until her abandoned son came looking for her."

Mom opens kitchen cabinets as I settle in a straight-backed chair at the table I've eaten at since I could hold a spoon. "That's interesting. Are you going to do the test to find your father?"

"I don't think so. He never knew Anita was pregnant."

"Right." Mom takes down a loaf of bread and opens the end. "So you're absolving him?"

"No. But there's no point finding him. He abandoned her after she upended her life to come here based on his idea. I doubt he'd have been father material."

"That must have been quite a blow for her to come here alone only to discover she's pregnant."

"It was. She had no family to rely on, at least none she wanted. But she was probably never going to be a permanent resident. She was only seasonal. Based on what she said about how locals felt about her, plus what you've told me, I'm not sure anyone would have sponsored her for a long-term work permit."

"Probably not. We did talk about that in the hospital." She pulls a stick of butter and a block of white cheddar from the fridge. Grilled cheese. She knows my comfort food. She is the source. Unlike Anita, who chose to know nothing.

No, that's not true. She did look later. She just didn't know how to find me without the right name.

"Did anything she say resonate with you? Make you pause? Maybe you're still thinking about it?" Mom asks.

"I don't get the sense that she loved me. Only that she didn't know how to take care of me. She was stuck with no one to help her."

Mom lays a slice of bread in the pan. "I was there, Gabe. The way she looked at you was no different than any mother in that maternity ward looked at her child. She suffered with her decision. And she's had to live with it."

This is more than Mom has said before about Anita. My whole life she's surrounded me with her love and told me I was a miracle given to her by a woman who wasn't able to care for me.

But not that it had been a hard decision.

Mom layers cheese and bread. "All of this happened for a reason. You met Tillie to convince you to see Anita, and for Anita, in turn, to give you the most important advice of your life."

"Not to abandon your kid?"

Mom turns. "To know that if you willingly give up something you love, you can survive it, but you will carry the feeling with you all your life."

My heart thunders to my shoes. She means Tillie.

But there is no way out of this. Tillie and I went over it again and again. The feeling of being licked by fire comes over me again. This is too much. I want my old way. The island way. Aimless. Easy. I press the heels of my hands into my eyes to rub away these concerns.

The aroma of toast and melted cheese brings me a sense of calm. That's why Mom makes candles. Smells are the real powerhouse in memory and emotion. When she mixes scents into her wax, she's hoping to bring about the feelings that will push the action. Fuck anger. Fuck misery. Fuck feeling stuck.

We don't say anything else until Mom sits across from me and slides the plate and a glass of swanky across the table. "Your favorite."

I nod. Funny how not hungry I felt all the way home, and now that she's put this food in front of me, I'm ready to devour it.

Maybe Anya's right. She's a little bit health nut and a whole lot witchy.

"I think you should hang on to Anita's information," she says. "Do something light. Maybe send her a Christmas card each year. Hold the line open, but not necessarily move unless you feel ready."

That's good advice. "All right."

"And what about Tillie?"

I'm halfway through the sandwich, but that brings me to a halt. I set it down. "She won't leave her sister and niece. I could bring them all here, hire her, and get her a work permit, but she's worried about putting that level of strain on us from the beginning."

"She can be a visitor for six months."

"But without a work permit, she'd really be stuck with me. And Lila doesn't trust me. There's just no way."

Mom rests her chin on her hands, her elbows on the table. She must have dyed her roots while I was gone because her tumbling hair is unbrokenly black. "And you're not moving there?"

"I could. I don't know. She doesn't want me to give up the bar. She was pretty adamant about it. She feels La Jarra is perfect compared to the city."

Mom fiddles with the fringe on the orange placemats. "Then you two said your goodbyes?"

"Basically."

"Will you be okay?"

I shrug and force myself to eat a few more bites.

"I don't believe for a minute that you went through all this with Tillie and Anita for nothing," she says. "When the world is moving with this much purpose, the earth itself will break open, and an opportunity will peek through the crack. Keep your spirit ready, Gabe. Watch for the shift."

I sip my swanky and stare out the sunny window over the sink. Mom always says things like that. But in this case, we knew what we were getting into, and it ended the only way it could.

Chapter 35

TILLIE

Gabe's departure kicks off the bluest period of my life I've ever known. Everything feels dull and desaturated, like every day is so overcast that you never see the sun.

I'm sure the one-two punch of both separating from this amazing man I met and leaving a paradise island to return to my mediocre life put me over the edge.

Not to mention losing the daily presence of my oldest sister, who took taking care of us younger siblings very seriously far longer than would have been expected.

Ensley stops by about a week after Gabe goes home. Lila has finally cracked the code on the pizza sauce at the restaurant where she works and insists on making it for us.

She puts Rosie to bed and we have a late dinner, arguing amiably over the validity of pineapple as a pizza topping, throwing more cheese on than necessary, and adding and removing black olives from various sections behind each other's backs.

But eventually, two small pizzas go into the oven. We discuss what to drink, and Ensley asks if I have the ingredients for a swanky panky.

And that's it. I burst into tears.

We end up at the banged-up kitchen table, me sitting down and my two sisters fussing over me. Lila presses a tissue into my hand while Ensley tucks my hair behind my ears to keep it out of my face.

"How did you two leave it?" Ensley asks.

"The only two choices were for him to be my boss or to get married!" The end comes out as a wail, and I hide behind the tissue. "And I can't exactly leave Lila and Rosie! And you and Drew! And Garrett!"

Lila slides a glass of water onto the table in front of me. "Take some slow sips," she says.

I grasp the cup, but the ice rattles as I bring it to my mouth.

"Have you been talking to him?" Ensley asks. "Are you sure it's over?"

"Sh-sh-sure, we text." I sound four years old. "But he's t-t-two flights away. And I can't afford to go. And I hate my job. And I'm stuck and I can't do anything."

My vision blurs as I spot Ensley sending an alarmed look over my head at Lila. "Has she been like this since he left?"

"No," Lila says. "I thought they were sticking to their vacation-fling decision. Nothing serious. Take it easy."

"D-d-don't talk about me like I'm not here! I could always hear you whispering. Even when we were kids! It's scary when you talk about m-m-me!"

Ensley drags a chair close to me and sits down, leaning in. "We don't want you to be scared, Tillie. We're here. We've got you."

Lila closes in on the other side. "It's all right."

"Is it, though?" I want to pull myself together, but I can't. I feel like I'm falling headfirst into a swimming pool, but there's no water to stop me from smashing into the concrete floor.

Ensley sighs. "We tried to tell you."

"Stop it!" I cry. "You're the one who ran to Drew over a couple of texts and a night in a shed!"

She has the sense to get quiet over that. I won't say a word to Lila about Dodge. That's too low a blow.

219

"You'll get past this," Lila says. "I got past bigger things."

This jolts me out of tears. It's true. Lila lost Dodge, not that he was any great catch, and not that she had a choice, but the consequences were bigger because she was pregnant. And now she needs me to help with Rosie. And Ensley needs her chance at happiness.

And none of this works unless we stick together. It's how we always got by. It's how we'll continue to do it.

"I love you guys," I choke out, and they close in tighter, a sister hug that has to be enough. It's always been enough. It will have to get me through.

They hang on to me until the smell of smoke wafts in from the kitchen behind us.

"Oh no!" Lila cries, leaping up and rushing to the next room.

The shock of it knocks me out of my tears. We follow her as she opens the oven door. Rolls of smoke pour out.

"Don't let the fire alarm go off and wake the baby!" Lila cries.

Ensley drags a chair to the smoke detector and stands on tiptoe to rip out the batteries right as the first beep sounds.

I hurry to the window in the dining room and throw it open.

Lila uses a dish towel to push the smoke toward the window.

"Good God," Ensley says as she climbs back down. "We can't even make pizza without a disaster."

"Shut up," Lila snaps. "We were helping Tillie."

I wave my hand in front of my face, eyes smarting from the smoke. "Don't blame me! I'm just the baby!"

Ensley calls for pizza delivery while Lila and I slide the blackened pizzas into the trash. We flap towels at the smoke until it dissipates.

When we're finally seated with the open pizza box, an extralarge half veggie supreme, olives only on one quarter, and half ham and pineapple, Lila says, "Are we good? Tillie, are you better now?"

I'm not, but I know the drill. Don't bother saying you're hungry if there isn't anything in the fridge. Don't complain about an outgrown pair of shoes if there's no way to replace them.

"I'm good."

But we all know I'm not. We eat pizza in silence until we hear Rosie's cry. I jump up from my chair. "I'll get her."

I rush out of the kitchen to Lila's room. Rosie is standing in her crib in the corner. "Tuhtuh," she says, and lifts her chubby arms.

Her tiny body is heavy as I lift her to my shoulder. "Tuhtuh's here." I shift from foot to foot as I rock her. "I'll always be right here."

It's the vow I made, the one all of us made. To help each other. It's why Ensley and I moved to Atlanta in the first place, when Dodge left Lila pregnant and poor. We need each other.

Gabe has his life.

This is mine.

I shouldn't have fallen for him, but it's clear that I did. Now I have to be like Anita and let him go. Like her, I will survive it.

I rock Rosie so long that she falls asleep on my chest. Only when Lila comes to place her back in her crib do I realize how much time has passed.

"Ensley's going home," Lila whispers. "Go say bye."

I do, and hug her before heading to my own rumpled bed. There's a text from Gabe on my phone.

Gabe: Sold ten swanky pankies tonight. Mendo has changed his story. There's no longer a mermaid. Just two lovers on a beach. Miss you.

I type out miss you, too, and let the tears fall again. When did I become a crier? I never have been before. This was a fling. A few weeks of fun. Not worth crying over.

But I decide to roll with it.

Tomorrow I'll be tough Tillie again, tossing gross men out of my bar and working long hours in my best boots without complaint.

But for tonight, I'll be me. Sad Tillie. Uncertain Tillie.

A Tillie who wishes she could be in paradise.

~

The weeks go by the same way they did before Ensley's wedding. Lila to work, me watching Rosie. Lila comes home. I go to the bar.

Despite our impossible situation, Gabe and I continue to text. Morrie and Anya have decided they will never be good at cocktails, but Morrie's been hosting karaoke nights at the hut, and Anya helps take orders when it gets busy. I do have a legacy there, after all. They have more business, more locals, and more fun.

I'm glad. Something good came out of our three weeks.

I'm working at Badger's bar when I get a text from Gabe that almost makes me drop a bottle of whiskey.

Gabe: There's a tropical storm headed our way. Don't worry if you can't get hold of me for a few days. If it hits, power and cell towers go first. We'll be all right. The island's built for this.

My body flashes hot. I back away from the bar and push through to the kitchen, frantically texting him back.

Me: Please let me know as much as you can. Will Mendo and his boat be safe?

Gabe: They'll take measures. And I will.

Me: When will it hit?

Gabe: If it doesn't turn, sometime tomorrow. But it could turn.

Me: I hope it turns.

Badger spots me texting. "What the hell are you doing, girl? Get back out there! This isn't break time."

"I don't get any break time," I shoot back at him.

"That's how I know it ain't your break."

Whatever. I pull up a weather app and switch it from Georgia to La Jarra. And I see it, a pulsing pinwheel, all the potential landfalls marked with dotted lines. Tropical Storm Calinda.

Don't hit La Jarra, I tell it. *Stay away, Calinda.*

When the crowd thins, I tell Badger I'm leaving. I really don't care if he fires me. I listen to weather reports as I drive home, frustrated that they only talk about a potential Florida landfall but nothing about the islands.

As soon as I tiptoe into the dark house, Lila and Rosie sound asleep, I drape myself over the bed with my phone.

It's after midnight for Gabe. Did he close his hut early? He'd be done by now, regardless.

I'm texting him.

Me: Updates? I'm watching the storm.

Gabe: Then you know as much as we do. Everyone's prepping. I have to head to Mendo's to help. I'll be in touch.

Me: Be safe.

I sleep fitfully, and each time I wake, I check Calinda's path. I find a La Jarra storm site that sends updates and recommendations for how to prepare via text. I sign up for alerts, and they immediately start coming.

24 hours to landfall.

Lock all storm shutters, if you have them.

Board windows.

Place sand bags around your perimeter and any low-lying areas.

Collect supplies, including flashlights, blankets, dry clothes, water, and food.

Charge all electrical devices.

Check your generator.

Prepare to evacuate for shelters.

A link to a list of them pops up.

At dawn, with Calinda still heading their way and expected to upgrade to a hurricane, La Jarra officials begin evacuating hospitals and nursing homes via planes. They send out an alert to citizens to prepare for flooding on the roadways.

I think of how close we were to being there when this happened, and of all the tourists there now. Are the turtles okay? Do the stingrays know how to get food on their own if the boats don't show up to feed them?

And Gabe's hut. How much wind can it withstand? It's certainly not hurricane-worthy.

When Lila and Rosie get up, I hurry out to the living room. I can't manage my fear alone.

"There's a storm headed to the island."

Lila sucks in a breath. "Oh no."

"It could turn."

She sets Rosie in her high chair. "Will it?"

"I don't know."

Lila spreads Cheerios on Rosie's tray and draws me into a hug. "Are you doing okay?"

"Gabe doesn't seem worried. He says the island is built for it."

"They would have to be."

"He said cell phone towers would eventually go down."

"When did you last hear from him?"

"About four hours ago."

"Let me get the laptop." Lila hurries to her room. Our only computer is a duct-taped machine that's a hand-me-down from Ensley, but it will get on the internet.

She opens it on the coffee table, and we bring up the Weather Channel. It's better to see it on a big screen. As soon as we type in *La Jarra*, a video pops up with weather forecasters talking about the various paths of the storm. Cuba's on alert. Florida is no longer in the path.

Their excitement over a newsworthy weather event makes me so mad that it's hard not to flip the laptop over. But of course, we can't do that. It's all we've got. I grip the edge of the chair instead.

Rosie gets rowdy, so we move her to the living room, where she can toddle in circles around the coffee table, babbling in a singsong voice. It's a happy sound. My anxiety drops a notch.

"It hasn't hit yet," Lila says, following the line of the storm with her finger. "But it looks like it's going to."

My phone rings with an actual call. It's Gabe.

I snatch it up.

He sounds tired. "Sorry I missed your texts. We had to shore up Mendo's house. That area might flood."

"Is your apartment safe? Your mother's house?"

"Yeah. Those are on higher ground. Our big concern will be a storm surge on the beaches. The hotels are well constructed. But the piers and docks, those will get hit. They're closing some roads."

"Where are you?"

"At Mom's. I don't care about anything at the apartment."

"Are all the planes gone? I saw they were evacuating people."

Lila leans over my shoulder. "Don't even think about going there."

I shush her.

"I'm not sure. But it could be a long time before passenger planes fly. The priority will be supplies. But we get hit a lot here. Flooding from the storm is the primary problem. Power might go out for a day or two. We all have generators. But cell service and internet will almost certainly go."

"I'm so worried, Gabe."

"Calinda isn't even a hurricane yet, and it's not clear if she'll get there. We'll be okay. I promise."

"Don't promise what you can't control!" I grip the phone so tight my fingers ache.

"I can promise you on this one."

"Okay."

"I'll keep in touch. Mom wants to bring in all the potted plants. They're her babies."

I manage a small laugh. "Okay."

"I'll be fine, Tillie. I promise."

"Okay, Gabe. Talk to you later."

The call ends.

"See, he's fine," Lila says. "So no flying there."

I shake my head. "Multiple barriers to that. One, planes are busy evacuating people. Two, I can't afford a ticket. Three, I'm not out of my mind."

"Right, it's way too dangerous."

"I honestly don't care about that." I sit up straight and face my sister. "I'd rather be in danger with him than safe without him."

"Tillie! You were with him three weeks! It's in the past. Leave him in the past."

I stare at her. "What is wrong with you? I already told you I wasn't going. Why do you hate him so much? You've never liked him. You made me lose that last night with him. For what?"

"You didn't lose anything! He came here anyway!"

"Is this about Dodge? Are you mad because Gabe is so wonderful when Dodge was so awful?"

"No!"

"Then what is it?"

She picks up Rosie and heads for the kitchen, but I follow her. "Lila! What has gotten into you?"

She whirls around. "Ensley has Drew! You have Gabe! All I have are my terrible choices! I work at a dirty, awful pizza joint! I can't afford to pay my own bills! And you—you're going to leave me for him. I just know it! Then what will I do?"

Rosie's face puckers. She shoves her face into Lila's chest.

I work hard to keep my voice calm and even. "I would never abandon you and Rosie. There was no conversation between me and Gabe that didn't involve both of you. We realized it couldn't work, so I let him go."

"How am I supposed to live with that?" Lila's voice is high-pitched, but even in her upset, she pats Rosie's back to keep her calm. "I can't ask you to sacrifice anything else for me!"

I squeeze my hands into fists. "I can't win with you! If I stay, you can't live with your guilt. If I go, you fall apart. What do you want to happen here?"

We're both stopped by a plaintive siren sound from my phone. It's the alert.

Landfall expected in four hours. Storm status: Upgraded to Category 1 Hurricane.

"Still want to be with him?" Lila asks, her voice almost a sob. "At risk of dying?"

"I do, actually." I press my hand to my mouth, and think about it again. "I really do. If there is a storm to be endured, I'd rather endure it with him than avoid it and not be with him."

Lila takes a step back. "Really?"

"Really." I start pacing. "Gabe is in a dangerous storm. I want to be there and weather it with him." I turn to face Lila. "It doesn't matter that it was only three weeks!"

She presses Rosie to her shoulder. "You're sure?"

"I'm sure." I pick up my phone to text Gabe one more message.

Me: Whenever there is danger, I want to face it with you. Danger worries me less than going through it without you.

My heart pounds against my chest for every second that passes by without a reply. Was that too much? Should I have kept that feeling to myself?

No. If that's the last thing I get to say to him before his cell towers go down, then that's what needs to be said. It was the right thing, even if it was too much for him. Even if that's not what he wants.

But then a message comes through.

Gabe: I feel the same. If there's something to endure, I want to do it with you.

Lila peers at the screen. "So, that's it?"

I shrug. "I can't do anything about it. But I had to say it."

She nods and heads back to her room. I watch the storm all the rest of the day. It skirts the beaches of La Jarra midafternoon. The video footage is terrifying.

Giant waves swamp the beaches where we walked. Docks fly through the air and disintegrate into pieces. Boats smash together like children's toys.

And I get no more messages from Gabe.

Chapter 36

Gabe

Mendo kicks the remains of a shed that used to be on the other side of the marina parking lot. "Well, that's a mess."

I stand beside him and blow out a long stream of air. He's right. The walkway out to the slips is destroyed. "I guess you won't be owing any dock fees."

"I better not."

Several boats are smashed together. Mendo's isn't among them. He drove his boat to the opposite side of the island the moment it was clear where Calinda was going to land. His brother is guarding it, anchored near the swamp.

"You're going to be one of the few working tour boats for a while." I smack him on the back.

"Yeah, with no way to load passengers."

"This dock will be back up in no time. It's too critical, like the cruise port."

"Still need building supplies." Mendo looks up in the sky. "And power. Don't forget that little detail."

He's right. Most of the homes have generators, but they can only power so much. We haven't had phone service since the storm hit. I haven't been able to assure Tillie I'm all right.

But the news is surely reporting that there have been no human casualties of the storm. Not here. Hopefully that will keep her calm.

"You ready to go check out your hut?" Mendo asks.

"Yeah."

With so many trees down, the roads are impassable by car. I took my motorcycle out this morning to see how far I could get. I found Mendo trying to reach the dock on his sister's pink bicycle and picked him up.

We take our time riding through town and down the highway to the condos. It isn't too bad out here. The flooding is limited to the usual spots, and I manage to navigate the debris. The crews will get that cleared in no time.

But small, unsecured constructions have not fared well. Like the shed at the marina, there are wrecked outbuildings and chicken coops everywhere.

I pull into the condo complex. A few trees are down, and everything is dirty from the storm. But otherwise, it's relatively unharmed. I park in a spot meant for residents. I don't think they're going to give me grief about it today.

We've just started our trek down the path when Sarah from the leasing office rushes to catch up to me. "Gabe! Hey!"

I stop. "Everything okay?" I ask her.

She looks between me and Mendo. "Yeah, sure. I live on-site and we just upgraded the generators here, so there's been minimal disruption. Nobody even lost their fridge goods." She flashes a quick smile. "But Orson told me to tell you to forward your business insurance to him, and we'll help handle the claim."

My gut tightens. "What claim?"

"To the contents of the hut. I assume you had inventory, a register, plus some appliances, right?"

What does she mean? I'm anxious to walk to the beach. "So it was damaged?"

"Oh." Her expression falters. "You haven't been out there yet."

"Shit," Mendo mutters.

"I'll get back to you," I tell Sarah, and start striding quickly through the complex.

A crew is already cutting up trees that have fallen in the path. We skirt one and then we're at the sand.

And I stop in my tracks, momentarily confused. Did I take the wrong path?

I move farther out on the sand.

No. This was the right one.

But the sand is completely unbroken here. No footprints. No chairs. No debris.

Just pure, smooth beachfront.

"What the hell?" Mendo asks. "Shouldn't your hut be, like, right here?"

I try to answer him, but my voice is as lost as the bar I once tended.

Mendo moves to where the hut stood. "How did it just . . . fly away? Wasn't there concrete or joists or anything?"

There wasn't. It was a plain wood construction sitting on the ground. Every so often we'd have to pack in sand to keep it level.

And it flew into nothing.

Sarah catches up to us. "We found a few bottles in one of the courtyards," she says. "And the blackboard. It's remarkably unharmed. It's in the office."

I lift my hands to my head, elbows outstretched. So that's it. I won't ever be able to convince Tillie to come here and work with me. I don't even have a job myself.

I don't have a bar. I don't have anything.

"You'll get insurance money, right?" Mendo asks.

I nod. I will get a check. Not a big one. It will only be for the contents of the hut. The fridges. The register. The dishwasher. Maybe some of the inventory.

I turn to Sarah. "I guess they don't have a timeline for when they'll rebuild?"

Her gaze darts away. "I, uh, don't think they plan to. Dorian will call you. The bar was never something he wanted. It was a legacy structure from before he bought the complex."

"Well, damn," Mendo says.

I don't look her way.

Because that's it.

I'm definitely starting over.

Chapter 37

Tillie

It's three days before I hear from Gabe. Three long, horrible days.

Then the call comes.

I'm on shift at Badger's, but I walk straight out of the bar and into the night. I couldn't care less if nobody gets a drink tonight. Badger's there. He can pull beer.

"What's happening? Where are you? Is everyone okay?"

His voice is smooth and unconcerned. "Hey, slow down. We're all right."

I sit on the curb. "You have power?"

"Mom does. My apartment is still out."

"But you're okay?"

"No casualties on the island. Just a lot of rain and downed trees. The marina is toast, but Mendo moved his boat."

"Oh, good." I close my eyes, trying to catch my breath. "It's been horrible, not knowing anything."

"I was hoping you were keeping tabs and saw nobody was hurt."

"I did, but it's hard to trust the information coming out as being complete."

"I get that. Are you okay?"

"I walked out of Badger's. He might fire me. It would probably be a good thing if he did."

"He can't run that place without you."

"Oh, I don't know. He managed for two weeks when I was with you." That seems so long ago.

"I do have a bit of sad news."

My stomach clenches. "What is it?"

"The hut's gone. It wasn't anchored, and loose things didn't fare well."

I'm glad I'm sitting down, because my head spins. "Like, *gone* gone?"

"Gone gone. No trace of anything other than a few random bottles that landed in the courtyards. The fridges might turn up, but they may be at the bottom of the ocean."

"Oh no."

"Oh, wait. The new menu board survived. I have that." He laughs a little.

"Oh, Gabe. When will they rebuild?"

"They're not. Turns out they'd rather not have alcohol sales on premises."

I clutch my phone. "What are you going to do?"

"I wanted to talk to you before I decided."

The words are out before I can think them through. "Please don't say you're coming here."

"You don't want me to?"

I clutch at my phone. "You can't leave the island for this place. I watched you here. It's too landlocked, too many buildings. You need that open sky. The ocean."

"Tillie, it's where you are."

"And I want you to be where I am, but . . . I can't ask you to give up that wonderful place for the life I live here."

"I figured that's how you would feel. And as soon as news of the hut got around, people made offers. Experienced bartenders are really needed here. One of the big resorts is opening a trendy new bar and needs a full slate of employees. It was in the works before the storm, but I didn't think much about it until this."

Relief thunders through me. Picturing him working with me at Badger's grim bar is all wrong. "Will the opening be delayed?"

"No. The resorts are already cleared and functioning. The cruise port will resume operations by next week, and the airport is reopening the schedule. Other than the marina, we'll be fully back to business within two weeks."

"And you'll go work at this hotel?"

"Yes. I know the resort manager, Clay. We worked together back in the day. He took me aside yesterday when he spotted me and Mendo at the marina office. He heard about my hut. He said I could run the new bar and bring on anyone I trusted as staff. Morrie's going to come work for me. He liked running events at the hut."

A group of regulars passes by, tilting their heads to watch me sitting on the curb. I wave them into the bar.

"When will that start?"

"Soon, I'm guessing. I'll probably do the interviewing for him since he's overseeing the renovation. It'll be operational later this month."

"That's a lot. Your hut. Your life. It's a big change."

"Did you start looking for a new job yet?" he asks.

My heart hammers. "No. I'm the worst about staying put, even when it sucks. We all were. Change is scary."

"Sometimes you don't have a choice."

"Right. When your hut decides to run off with a gal named Calinda."

He laughs brusquely.

We're quiet a moment, and then he says, "I could get you a job at the new bar. Lila too, although she might like something else at the hotel. When we were stuck in the dark at Mom's house, she mentioned she might like to look after a toddler, if that helped."

That's a big deal. "Really?"

"Yes. I know Lila hates me, but—"

"She doesn't. We talked about it. She's just scared. She's been through a lot."

"Her ex definitely couldn't give her any trouble all the way in La Jarra."

"Where would we live?"

"Mom has an extra bedroom. And there are apartments. I could even move back in with her and let you two have mine. I think we could figure that part out."

"Is this the right thing?" I clutch at the concrete curb.

"It solves some of the problems. You wouldn't work for me, technically. Clay would be your boss. If we broke up, you would still have a job."

A car passes by, its headlights momentarily blinding me before it moves on.

"Tillie?"

"You think this is a sure thing?"

"You can at least apply. Clay will sponsor the work permits. There's no way he'll have enough staff locally. If anything goes wrong, you can always go home. Or if you love it here, we could work opposite shifts. I can't imagine—"

I interrupt him. "Yes."

"Yes?"

"Yes. I'll apply. And I'll talk to Lila. We'll see what happens. Okay?"

I can hear the smile in his voice. "Okay! I'll get you the paperwork. It's going to take a while. Even without the storm, these things take some time."

"I understand."

"Tillie, it's going to work. I'm sure of it."

"How long would we get to be there?"

"At least the seasonal permit, which is eight months. But we'll probably go for the full nine years. After eight years, you can apply to stay, with or without me being involved."

"Unless we get married."

He laughs. "Unless we get married."

"And then I could stay and work, too?"

"Well, I'd expect you to remain barefoot and pregnant—"

"Gabe!"

He laughs. "Yes, you could stay and work, too."

"Okay. Let me try."

"I love you, Tillie. I know it's fast, but after not getting to talk to you for three days, I wished more than anything I'd have said it."

My throat is so tight I can barely swallow. "I think I love you, too, Gabe. And if not, then I can always just have sex with you until something better comes along."

He laughs so loud I have to pull my phone away from my ear.

"Consolation prize accepted. I should go. I need to call a fair number of people now that service is back. I wanted to talk to you first."

"Thank you. Bye, Gabe. I think I love you."

"Bye, Tillie. I know I love you."

I hold the phone in my hand.

My life has changed.

Totally.

All the way.

But now, my sister.

I glance back at the bar. Badger hasn't come for me yet.

I dial her number. It's late, but she should still be up. Rosie is long past her bedtime.

Her voice is a question. "Why is my sister calling when a text will do?"

"Hey."

"Hey. You okay?"

"Gabe called."

237

"Oh. He's okay, then?"

"His hut is gone."

"What?"

"The hurricane took it."

"Oh, Tillie. It was such a cute place."

"It was."

"What is he going to do?"

"A new fancy hotel bar is opening up, and his friend is making him the manager. He's going to be running it and hiring the staff."

She's quiet a moment. "And he wants you to come work there, too."

"There's a job for you, too. We thought of you. He's willing to give his apartment to us, and his mom will even watch Rosie!"

"That—that's a lot."

"I love him, Lila."

"Are you sure?"

"Totally sure."

She blows out a breath into the phone. "Well, we weren't going to tell you, in case you got your hopes up."

I go still. "Hopes up for what? Who is 'we'?"

"Me and Ensley. She called her old boss, the one from Alabama."

"What for?"

"They're trying to get me an entry-level position at the bank. If I get it, I can afford day care for Rosie. I won't need your money or your babysitting. I'll be on my own two feet."

"When did you do that?"

"The day of the hurricane. I saw it. I saw what he was to you. I didn't believe it before. But I did then."

"Lila—I'm not trying to cut you out."

"I know. I know you're not. But I have to find a way to make it on my own. It's time, Tillie. It's time we all grew up."

Tears threaten. "I don't want to. I thought we'd always be together."

"We will. Just not in the same house. I'm okay with it. I had to live without you before, remember? When I moved in with Dodge? We can do this. We can have the magic, all of us. You with Gabe. Ensley with Drew. And me with Rosie. None of us will ever be alone."

"When will you find out?"

"Any day now. So do it, Tillie. Get your work permit. Go to the island. Just make sure you always have a space for us to visit."

"I will."

The door to the bar slams open. Badger stands there, drying his hands on a towel. "Get in here before I drag you back."

"Gotta go," I whisper to Lila, and end the call. Then I laugh and stand on my tiptoes to kiss his cheek. "You're a real Georgia peach, Badger."

"Shut up and get to work."

His roughness doesn't bother me at all. I dash behind the bar, and nobody, not the sad regulars or the obnoxious drunks or the dirty old men, can bring me down.

By the time the days get short and the shadows grow long, I won't be putting up with them here in Badger's bar any longer.

I'll be in paradise.

With Gabe.

I have to believe it.

I know what his mother's candle would say.

Fuck doubt.

Chapter 38

GABE

Six months later

"Don't forget to lock the register!" Tillie calls as she frantically unloads the last set of glasses into the racks over the bar.

"Done!" I double-check that the cash drawer is secure and power down the electronics. Then I reach up to flip off the red and green lights decorating the carved poles at either end of the long burnished-wood counter.

Despite the crazy crowd only a half an hour ago, the tables are empty.

"You ready for your first Christmas Boat Parade?" I ask Tillie, who swaps out her bar boots for tennis shoes.

"I'm so excited. Thank goodness Clay agreed we should shut down the bar so we can go."

"It's practically a national event. Of course he'd shut it down."

She ties her laces, and I grasp both of her hands to lift her from the chair. We look around a moment, something we often do after a shift, when the bustling, busy crowd is gone and the room belongs to only the two of us.

It's our home away from home, the one we share. Work still isn't work with Tillie. I'm starting to realize it never will be.

She squeezes my hand. "My first La Jarra holidays! I'm super pumped about Boxing Day. It's like two Christmases." She slides a tote bag over her shoulder.

"And the second Christmas is a beach party."

She squeals.

Christmas is two weeks away yet, but the Christmas Boat Parade is one of the big events of the holidays. There might not be snow on the island, and it's not going to get cold, either. But we have our own ways of celebrating the season.

We head out the side door and lock it, skirting the piles of pure-white banked sand that are decorated with tiny pine trees and tinsel. It's the closest thing we have to a white Christmas in La Jarra.

I take the bag from Tillie as we hurry toward the bay. The shopping district is a mass of people walking between stores and pausing to look at the goods displayed in outdoor stalls.

"The tree isn't lit yet!" Tillie cries. "Hurry!"

We head toward the canal, keeping our eye on the tree. Music from the live band on the big stage gets louder as we leave behind the shops and arrive at the walkway along the water.

Suddenly everyone is counting down. "Ten, nine, eight . . ."

"It's like New Year's!" Tillie says.

On the one, the giant tree at the end of the canal lights up. A great cheer rises like a wave over the water.

"I got to see it!" Tillie kisses my cheek. "I thought for sure we'd be too late by the time we shut down."

"I'm glad we made it." My phone buzzes with a text from Anya. "They're wondering where we are," I tell Tillie. "Let's move."

We squeeze past tourists and locals lining up along the rail to see the parade. Finally, we make it down to the dock.

"There's Mendo's boat!" I pull Tillie to the left.

Anya stands near the front, waving in her Mrs. Claus swimsuit complete with a Santa hat. "Come on board!"

Mendo takes Tillie's hand as she steps off the dock to the boat. When she's safely on, he turns away.

"Hey!" I call. "Where's my gentlemanly assistance?"

"I'm making off with your woman!" Mendo calls back.

I hop over the gap and rush up behind them, pulling Tillie to me. "Same old tricks."

Mendo tugs on his ball cap. "Can't blame a guy for trying!"

We wander to the back of the boat, where everyone's waiting for the parade to start. Morrie's there, and Chuck, and all of Mendo's family.

His mother, Kia, passes me a bowl of jerk chicken over rice. "Happy Christmas season, my love." She kisses both of my cheeks, then turns to Tillie. "Happy Christmas."

Food is also foisted upon Tillie. I set the bag on the floor, and we slide onto a bench.

"You missed the tree lighting," says twelve-year-old Violetta, shaking her braids at me. She's gone full Christmas in a red and green sundress.

"We saw it," Tillie says. "We were almost here."

Anya scoots Violetta over to sit next to us.

"I love your suit!" Tillie says.

"Isn't it great?" She shakes the red top so that the jingle bells ring.

I'm relieved Anya and Tillie have hit it off so well. When Tillie first moved here, she stayed with me, but we quickly decided we should have some space while we were still in the early stages of dating.

She and Anya got an apartment together, and they've become fast friends. Tillie's still trying to get her to see Morrie in a different light, but no luck so far.

"It's the first boat," Violetta cries. She stands up to point. "Look! Look!"

A small yacht completely covered in white lights arrives in the canal. After a few moments, all the lights turn red.

"Whoa!" Violetta says, and runs to the other side of the boat to her mother. "Did you see that?"

Mendo takes the opportunity to steal her spot. "Maybe I should ditch you all and decorate my boat next year."

"Yes!" Violetta cries. "I can be the Christmas Queen!"

His mother fixes a strap on Violetta's dress. "It takes a lot of power to light a boat. You'll need a bigger generator."

Mendo nods, his face shifting from red to green as the lights on the first boat change again. "Yeah. Gotta sell more tours first."

I wrap an arm around Tillie's waist. "It's nice, right?"

"I love it," she says. "It's like the Disney electric light parade but on the water."

"I've never been to Disney."

She leans into me. "Me neither. But I've seen videos!"

"Do you want to go to Disney?"

"I can save it for when I have kids."

I draw her close. "Kids, huh?"

"Don't get any crazy ideas." She elbows me in the ribs.

I lean in close to her ear. "You give me all the crazy ideas."

Mendo smacks us both on the tops of our heads. "Don't get any ideas on my boat. I know you two."

"What does that mean?" Violetta asks. She's sneaked up behind him.

"Nothing. It means nothing. Oh, look, it's the crab boat. They've got more than last year." He points out over the water.

Another vessel has arrived. It's flat-bottomed and filled with characters outlined with light. One is a mermaid, and she is surrounded by crabs.

"We've come full circle," Tillie says. "The mermaid sunrise and the reason we met."

"It'll be months before the crabs are breeding again, and that's twice you've brought up reproduction in the last five minutes," I say.

"What's reproduction?" Violetta asks.

"And . . . time to move the child. Mom has dessert." Mendo steers Violetta to the table where the food is laid out.

The boats come faster, the next with a lighted tree so tall it rivals the one in the bay. It's quickly followed by another with a loudspeaker system, the entire hull covered in lights that blink in time with the music.

"Have you given any thought to what we talked about for the Georgia trip?" Tillie asks.

I rest my chin on her shoulder. We're heading to Atlanta to celebrate a late Christmas with her brother and sisters. Tillie wants me to reach out to Anita and have coffee again.

"Are you going to visit your dad?" I ask.

"Unfair question. That's a three-hour drive. I have to see how it fits in."

"I think if I visit Anita, you should at least consider going to see him."

She's quiet and I know she's thinking about the old house, walking in it again, and maybe her father not even talking to her. The sisters occasionally try. Ensley and Tillie made a pilgrimage a couple of years ago in hopes of getting him to meet his first grandchild, but he didn't so much as open the door. They're not sure he ever saw the wedding invitation they sent.

It's asking a lot for her to try again.

"Okay," she says. "But you're going with me."

"Deal." She went with me to see Anita the first time. It's only fair.

Plus, I want to know where she grew up, what spaces she filled. I've known Tillie for half a year, but there is so much still to discover. Her hometown will be a great next step.

The boats motor around the bay in their bright glory. Mom texts me. She's hanging out with her friends tonight. Did you see the crab one? Make Mendo do it next year!

"Yo, Mendo, my mom agrees you have to do up the boat next year. We could split the cost."

He turns. "What would you need a big generator for?"

"I don't know!"

But then it all hits me in one flash of insight. Another hut. A new bar. One I control. Not rented. Bigger, maybe a repurposed shack.

I remember something else. On the beach near the restaurant where I took Tillie for our first brunch, there's a house, tucked in underbrush. It's been for sale for a while, because it's tiny and nobody wants to live that close to public parking.

But if I could buy it and get it rezoned as commercial . . . my head starts spinning and I miss the last few boats.

The fireworks that end the parade bring me out of my thoughts. Tillie squeezes my leg. "You're lost in thought."

"I am."

"Anything good?"

I see the years ahead finally, bright and clear. Converting the house to a hut. Opening one side to the ocean. Building a wooden deck that connects to the beach.

And Tillie working with me.

I have to stop myself from starting right then, asking Mom to mention it to her Realtor friend. Calling the permit office.

"Yeah," I finally say. "Real good."

"Does it include me?"

I kiss the top of her head. "Tillie James, everything good includes you."

I won't tell her yet. I'll make some calls. Run some numbers. Look at my savings.

But maybe by the time we're in Georgia, I'll know. And we can announce the plan to her family. Everyone will be happy for us. Drew and Ensley, settled into their new house with a menagerie of pets. Lila and Rosie, who also got a new apartment near Rosie's day care and the bank where Lila has been working since before Tillie left Atlanta. Even Anita, if I decide to see her, and tell her, and let her in a little bit more.

And possibly, if everything goes right, the next time the crabs race across the beaches to scare tourists, the future we're planning together will be our own.

Epilogue

TILLIE

The four of us stand in the center of the renovated house. Me. Gabe. Anya. Morrie.

It's five minutes until we officially open his new bar for the first time.

Gabe seems ridiculously nervous for something that will be quite simple.

When the clock strikes noon, we will open all the floor-to-ceiling shutters to the ocean side of the room. We kept only the kitchen and bathrooms enclosed, knocking out all the other walls to create a big open space.

The ocean breeze will filter in, and the people waiting out there, quite a few of them based on the noise levels, will get to come in and order drinks.

Every detail is perfect. The interior is turquoise with red accents. A huge mural has been painted on the back wall, a reflection of the beach view on the opposite side, only draped with fishnet and dotted with beautiful metal art of all the varieties of crabs you can find on the island. The artist somehow made even the black land crab seem a little less hellish.

Above it is the name we chose together: the Swanky Panky.

There are two rows of low wood tables with cane chairs on the open side. Behind them are three long high tables with stools, suitable for seating larger groups. The varied heights ensure that everyone in the bar can see the ocean.

The counter of the bar fills the side wall, all wood and cane and bamboo to match the decor. The mirrored backsplash reflects the entire establishment, although the glass shelves are filled with bottles of liquor to make every drink we can imagine.

Mendo's mom, Kia, pushes through the swinging doors from the kitchen. "I have enough red conch chowder for two hundred," she says. "Let me know the minute you think we need another batch."

"Will do," Gabe says, but his voice isn't quite normal. He's rattled, for sure.

It was an important decision to us to serve food at the bar. It won't be a full restaurant, but every day of the week, we will serve a different dish, sold until it runs out.

And we agreed that the one thing we will never serve is crab. It's almost time for their migration again, and I'm honestly looking forward to a moonlight watch to witness them scuttling over the sand to drop their eggs. Everything will have come full circle.

The far-right shutter opens a few inches and Mendo's face appears. "We've got a rowdy crowd out here. You'll be ready in three minutes?"

Gabe nods. He turns to Morrie. "Is the sound system up and running?"

Morrie tosses his wireless microphone in the air and neatly catches it in his palm. He's dressed in a bright blue-and-red outfit. "I'm ready to rock 'n' roll."

Anya drapes her arm around my waist. "This is the perfect day. It's just . . . the perfect day." She's oddly emotional.

"It is," I say, curious about the both of them, Gabe and Anya. Maybe opening ceremonies have more emotional pull on the island than I'm used to.

The five of us will staff the new bar. Kia will cook. Gabe and I will mix drinks and handle tables as needed. Morrie will serve as runner, event coordinator, and easygoing bouncer. Anya will wait tables with us until we determine if we need to hire additional waitstaff.

We each stand in our designated spots. The tall blue wood-slat shutters run floor to ceiling, and we each have one to throw wide. Morrie flips on his mike. He holds up his hands, his five fingers spread.

Then four. Three. Two.

We all open our shutters. A cheer rises from the crowd. I'm momentarily stunned. That's a lot of people.

Kia murmurs, "I better make more chowder."

She tries to step back, but Anya holds out her hand. "You have enough."

Morrie steps forward first. "Welcome, everyone, to the opening of the Swanky Panky! Let's introduce the crew to your favorite new nightlife spot on La Jarra."

He gestures to Kia.

She murmurs, "Good Lord," before stepping out.

"Mama Kia is going to be making a new island dish every day for you guys to sample. Don't delay, because when her dish of the day is gone, it's gone. And you do not want to miss it. Today she has made red conch stew!"

A big cheer rises up, and Kia waves, then bolts to the kitchen. She really doesn't like to be in front of a crowd.

Morrie turns to Anya. "Now let's hear it for our next crew member!"

Anya hops forward with a big wave. Her braids swing as she turns around to show off the blue-and-red Swanky Panky apron. She pulls off her blue Swanky Panky hat and tosses it into the crowd. There's a clamor for it, and the winner raises it in his fist.

"There's plenty more of those!" Morrie says. "We'll be giving out a hundred of them today, or if you want to make sure you get one, they are for sale behind the bar."

He wraps an arm around Anya. "This lovely lady is Anya. La Jarra born and raised, she will take care of you as you try all the classic drinks from Gabe's old hut plus a whole menu of new ones."

Anya bounces and waves, and a cheer goes up as well as a chorus of whistles.

Anya squints at the crowd and points as if to warn them to mind their manners.

Morrie holds out his arms to quiet our guests. "I'm Morrie. I'll be the master of ceremonies each and every evening at the bar. And if any of you are acting like fools, I'm the one who will carry you out and toss you on your can." He mimics Anya's point and squint.

Another laugh rumbles through the crowd.

"Most important of all, I bring you Gabe and Tillie. The bar is their brainchild. After Hurricane Calinda took down Gabe's old hut, they came up with the beautiful place that you see here. Let's give it up for the man and woman of the hour, Gabe Landers and Tillie James."

The noise rolls at us in a rising roar. I glance over at Gabe. He somehow looks even more anxious than he did before.

I reach out to squeeze his hand, but I keep a smile on my face. Maybe he's worried we can't handle so many customers. Does he think they'll get unruly because there will be a wait?

Morrie heads our direction. "Our fearless leader has a few words to say before we officially open our doors."

I didn't realize Gabe was going to speak. But it makes sense. Morrie walks the mike over to him. My gut tightens when I see Gabe's hand shake as he takes it.

This is not the Gabe I know. I've worked with him for almost a year at the hotel bar. He's never nervous.

"Hey, everyone," Gabe says.

I look out to see if I can get a rough count on the crowd. Along the front are Mendo and the rest of the friends I've gotten to know better since first meeting them at the diner so long ago.

Then I spot Gabe's mom. She strides forward as if she's late. Strange. But then I see who she has with her.

Anita.

Anita's here.

Is this a surprise for Gabe? Does he know?

I turn to him quickly, but his gaze is right on his mother and Anita. He gives them a nod. So he knew she was coming.

Maybe that's why he's nervous.

My stomach settles. Of course. We saw Anita over Christmas, both when we first arrived in Atlanta, and again after our failed visit to Alabama to try to see my dad. He hadn't opened the door to his bedroom, which was his usual response. Gabe still enjoyed seeing our old house, the pictures on the walls, and what few keepsakes we had from our childhood.

But as far as Anita, both of those visits went remarkably well, and the two of them have exchanged several emails since.

But it's different having her here. It must be hard for her, too. She hasn't been to the island since she took off twenty-nine years ago.

Maybe Gabe's worried about what his friends and the other island-ers might say about her when they figure out who she is. The rumors didn't die in all that time, and her presence will most certainly stoke the fire again.

Yeah, that totally explains his anxiety.

He waves to the crowd. "Hello, everyone, and thanks for coming. I'm going to ask you all to indulge me in a little personal business."

Personal business? Surely he won't bring Anita up here.

Actually, maybe that's perfect. If he shows huge support for her, they can't talk badly about her.

But he takes my hand and turns me to face him.

The minute I meet his nervous gaze, I understand what this is all about. My throat goes completely tight, and my belly flips.

When he gets down on one knee, the crowd goes crazy, the whole beach erupting in cheers and screams.

Gabe tries to say something into the mike, but there's no way to hear him.

We wait for a moment, surrounded by noise, smiling sheepishly at each other, until Anya grabs the mike and wolf whistles into it. The sound is so piercing that it quiets the crowd.

She passes the mike to Gabe.

He draws in a deep breath, but he looks significantly less nervous now that the moment is here. "A lot of you know how I met Tillie. She was a tourist."

The crowd gives a long "Awww," before Anya slices her arm through the air to cut them off.

"She was only supposed to be here for two weeks. But in those two weeks, we figured out something important. We couldn't live without each other."

Someone in the crowd yells, "And sex on the beach!"

Gabe laughs. "She definitely knew all about those." But before they can get rowdy again, he adds, "Because she is a bartender like me."

His hand is warm in mine. I watch the breeze lift his sandy hair, the pale lines around his eyes revealed when his face gets serious.

"We decided that separating was not something we could do, and after Hurricane Calinda took down my bar, we decided to both go work in the heart of the resorts. Our boss, Clay, was good enough to sponsor Tillie for a work permit."

He turns to look at the building behind him. "I knew that if I was going to open another beach bar, the only way I wanted to do it would be with her by my side. So today I am sealing the deal with a question and a promise."

He pulls a tiny velvet box out of the pocket of his blue shorts.

"Tillie, I promise to always keep you interested. To always have fun. To always honor the traditions you bring to this island as well as

251

the ones we will create together. And I promise to love you. Whether we live here, in the States, or wherever life might take us, my home is where you are."

The crowd is so quiet that I can hear the waves pounding the sand behind them.

Gabe draws in another breath. "Now for my question." He keeps his gaze on me, but when he asks, everyone knows what he's going to say, so it's not just Gabe who says the words. It's everyone.

"Will you marry me?"

The words fade out as everyone quickly quiets again to hear my answer.

I lean into his mike. "Yes, Gabe. Yes, I will."

I hold my hand out as the cheers of the crowd crescendo to their loudest yet. He slips the ring, a perfect clear diamond on a silver band, on my finger.

He stands, lowering the mike to his side. We both glance out at his mothers—the one who brought him into the world and the one who raised him. They are holding each other's hands, eyes glistening with tears.

He let Anita come to this. He let her be a part of something so important. Not just the opening of his bar, but his promise to me. Maybe she did lose him, like I almost did. But just knowing her changed him. Changed us. We made our decisions better because of what we learned from hers.

As he leans down to kiss me in a gesture that is as familiar as my own heartbeat, I realize family is so much more than the ways it's always been defined.

It's formed by the people who are with you for the journey. Maybe, like Anita and my mom, they're along for only a tiny part of the ride. Or, like Gabe's mom and my sisters, they've been here every step of the way.

But for the next stage, I'll be with Gabe.

And our paradise will be wherever we are.

EXCERPT FROM

THE WEDDING CONFESSION

Chapter 1

ENSLEY

I can't believe what I'm seeing.

I've heard about situations like this at weddings.

In viral videos. Social media rants.

But this is the first time I've seen one right in front of me.

I glance over at my best friend, Ronnie. She's the bride, dressed in a beautiful but simple knee-length sheath.

Her mother's dress.

The mother who died only two years ago, before Ronnie's engagement.

The wedding was supposed to be a small event at the park where Ronnie's mom used to push her on the swings. She wanted to honor this amazing woman who had been a mother figure to all of us in the bridal party.

Well, the original bridal party.

Now there's ten bridesmaids and ten groomsmen. A country club. A swing band. And a seated dinner for four hundred.

This wedding got hijacked.

And now this.

The guilty party is the person right in front of me. Her arrival has left all the bridesmaids in shocked silence, piled up in the corner like a bushel of peaches in our strapless, puffy dresses that flatter no one.

Ronnie lets out a whimper. I know that sound. She's trying to control herself to avoid an outburst.

I can't believe it. I just can't.

The center of the attention is Felicia, Ronnie's new stepmother.

We don't know what came over Ronnie's dad when he married her. But Felicia is a firestorm. She commandeered their lives, using those big pouty lips to convince Ronnie's dad to sell their thirty-year family home for a McMansion near this country club.

Felicia is a trustee of the club, and once Ronnie announced her engagement, Felicia insisted the wedding should mirror their *elevated station*, whatever that means.

I felt helpless during the last few months, watching Ronnie's charming dream wedding unravel.

But not today.

Not with this.

Because Felicia has entered the room, not in the stately blue dress we thought she was wearing as stepmother of the bride.

But in a full-length beaded white gown. She even has baby's breath in her hair and a tiny white veil over her eyes. All that's missing is a bouquet.

Next to her, Ronnie looks like a flower girl.

She's been in the room a full minute, and no one has spoken.

"Well?" Felicia asks. "What do you think? It's the dress I always wanted to wear to an affair like this."

I see how it is. Felicia married Ronnie's father in a weekend getaway to Vegas that probably involved vodka and edibles, and she's making up for everything she missed.

Ronnie tries to get a few words out. I can tell how much it's killing her to say something nice. "It's a lot."

Felicia strikes a pose, fanning out her dagger nails. "Of course it is. An original Vera Wang. I would have nothing less for my dear new daughter's wedding."

Does she really think she's doing Ronnie a favor here?

"I like Vera Wang," Ronnie stammers. Her dress was off the rack at Dillard's. In 1991. "Where's Dad?"

Felicia examines a nail. "Your father's leg is bothering him. It's why I changed. I was going to save this gown for the reception, but it seems, my dear, that I'm walking you down the aisle!"

"What?" The word explodes out of me before I can stop myself.

Felicia gives me a sidelong glance. "You should be happy for us, Ensley." She says my name is if it leaves a nasty taste in her mouth.

I step close to Ronnie. "You want me to do something real ugly?" I whisper.

Ronnie leans close. "Remember your positivity training. You're all sunshine now."

Right. I can't afford therapy, so Ronnie paid for us to get training to cultivate the sunshine demeanor I've always wanted since moving past my difficult childhood. "I'm *positive* that I should do something ugly."

For the first time since her stepmother invaded the dressing room, Ronnie cracks a smile.

I glance back at the rest of the bridesmaids. Ronnie's older sister is serving as the maid of honor, but she's watching us in astonishment like the rest of the puff-dressed observers. Aren't we supposed to have Ronnie's back?

Ronnie and I have been best friends since we were children. She was there when my mom died when I was five. And I was there when she lost hers. There is no tighter bond than that.

I have to do something about this stupid dress and prevent Felicia from ruining Ronnie's entrance.

I glance around the room, searching for something that will help. I spot the fireplace tools. Is violence the answer?

No. I might get blood on my dress.

And then I see it. The perfect solution.

I hope someone is videoing it, because I'm about to be a viral sensation.

I can see the caption: *Perfect bridesmaid saves wedding.*

It's a tray filled with crystal goblets. Champagne. White wine.

And *red.*

I keep my voice casual as I walk over to the tray. "Felicia, may I offer you a glass of wine?"

Felicia smirks, her lurid lips glossy. She thinks she's won me over. "Champagne, please."

Ronnie watches me with concern as I pick up a glass of champagne for her stepmother, then choose wine for myself.

Red, of course.

Ronnie's eyes go saucer wide as she watches the next few seconds unfold. I think it's one of my finest moments.

I step closer, the glasses held out in front.

I trip, stumbling over nothing.

Then I toss both glasses straight at Felicia's pristine bodice. The wine soaks her, staining the white satin before the goblets crash to the floor and shatter.

"What have you done?" Felicia tries to step out of the way, but she's far, far too late. She looks like a zombie bride after a snack.

"I guess you'll have to wear the blue dress after all," I say. "Sorry."

I glance back at Ronnie. She mouths, *Thank you.*

See, I told you I'd save the day. I might aspire to be sunshine, but I can *burn.*

Except—the moment isn't over.

Felicia's face turns redder than her stained bodice. She makes two fists like a toddler refusing to go to bed and lets out a terrifying shriek.

The wedding planner bursts into the room. "Oh my God, what is it?"

"Call security!" Felicia yells. "Call them right now or you'll never work another wedding again!"

The poor woman nearly drops her phone. "What happened?" Then she sees the front of the dress. "Oh."

"Get security now!"

The woman scampers off.

Felicia turns to me. "You did that on purpose. I want you out of here."

"I'm here for Ronnie, and I'm not leaving," I say.

Her eyes narrow, and the pure evil aimed at me almost makes me shiver.

An oversize man in a brown uniform races into the room. "What's wrong?"

"Her," Felicia says. "Jeremy, get her out of here."

Uh-oh. She's on a first-name basis with the security guard.

"No!" Ronnie cries. "She's my best friend!"

"Take her in the hall," Felicia says. "She doesn't belong here."

The guard hesitates a moment, but Felicia's voice gets more strident. "Jeremy! Take her in the hall!"

That's actually a good idea. Ronnie's seen enough. "I've got this," I tell her. "Don't worry."

And before the big lug can put his hand on me, I walk ahead of him into the gold-wallpapered corridor, my puffy peach skirt swaying around my knees with my swagger.

Felicia closes the door to the bridal chamber and faces the hall. "This woman intentionally ruined my dress," she says to Jeremy.

"I tripped," I say. "I'm a bridesmaid."

Jeremy looks back and forth between us, taking in the ruined dress. "If she just tripped—"

"Jeremy," Felicia snarls. "I need her gone. I'm a trustee here. You should listen to me when I say she's a threat to our club."

Jeremy sighs. "Let's go." He reaches for my arm.

"No!" I spin aside. "I'm not leaving my friend!"

"Don't let her make a fuss!" Felicia hisses. "Take her the back way out!"

I wave my arms so Jeremy can't grab hold. "That woman is crazy! I tripped!" But I'm not entirely convincing. I *did* do it on purpose.

"Just follow me," Jeremy says. "It will be all right. Let's cool off."

He doesn't seem like he's going to actually throw me out, his face more annoyed than angry. He starts down the hall.

I hesitate, but Felicia says, "Go!"

All right. I'll go. We have some time before the wedding anyway.

When we're sufficiently far from Felicia, the guard says quietly, "Look, Felicia's been around this club a long time, and this isn't her first fit. She'll get over it. Just take a walk, let her calm down, and we'll let you return in half an hour."

"Half an hour!" I reach for my phone, then remember it was confiscated by the wedding planner. All of ours were, so that they wouldn't accidentally make noise during the ceremony. "The wedding is in fifteen minutes!"

"Whatever," the guy says. "Don't come back for fifteen minutes."

"Fine."

We continue down the hall. "Where are you taking me?" I ask.

"Out the back. You can walk on the golf course. Sit on a bench. I don't care. Just stay away from here for a little while."

I blow out a long, annoyed breath. I'm supposed to be sipping wine and hanging out with my best friend. Damn Felicia and her white dress.

A roar of male laughter bursts from an open door ahead. It must be the men's dressing room. I plan to peek in as we pass, but before we make it there, a groomsman steps out. "I'll make sure Ronnie hasn't sent a spy," he calls back into the room.

I almost smile. Ronnie did threaten surveillance if she thought they were drinking too much before the ceremony.

Based on the laughter, she was right to worry.

He glances the other way first, but when he looks toward us, my breath catches. It's Drew Daniels, and he's gorgeous in a tux. Like, unbelievably delicious.

I knew him well growing up. He and my older brother, Garrett, played football together, and I often sat in the window mooning over Drew as they practiced in the yard.

Seeing him dressed like this reminds me of all the fantasies twelve-year-old me used to dream up about Drew and prom and our very own wedding one day. Dashed, of course, because he was sixteen to my twelve and thought I was a twerp.

Unfortunately, today's bridal party lineup does not have him escorting me, so we haven't so much as shaken hands. But from the flutters in my belly, that girlhood crush is far from over.

Drew takes in the guard, then me, his face darkening. "What's going on here?"

I hate to admit anything. I almost say I'm the spy, but end up with the truth. "Felicia kicked me out," I say. "I have to go wander around while she cools off."

"Where?"

Jeremy speaks up. "Just out on the green."

"What did you do?"

I hate that he's finally talking to me, and it's about this. "I got wine on Felicia's dress."

"That would definitely get her riled." He falls into step beside us. "But I don't like them escorting you out of here. What if they lock you out?"

I glance up at the guard. "He assures me that I'll be able to get back in."

Drew's beautiful lips press into a firm line. "I think I should come along to make sure."

My heart swells. Drew has no idea how often I imagined him saving me whenever I got into tough spots as a kid. His family might not come from money, but they had a beautiful brick house, two parents, and the sort of home life I longed for. I always knew he would sweep me away from the dark, sad, dirty house with no mother and a father who rarely spoke to any of us after she died. My father still doesn't.

And here he is. Drew. It's hero time.

We enter the bowels of the club. The offices are dark on a Saturday night. At the end of the hall, we turn into a large room filled with rows of stacked chairs. There's a huge set of double doors on the back wall, which I assume is where deliveries are made. We seem to be heading for that.

This seems weird. There should be dozens of random exits to a sprawling building like this. Alarm bells start to ring. "My punishment is only for fifteen minutes, though, right?"

"Sure," Jeremy says.

Drew must also start to feel concern, because he says, "So you're sure we can walk around for a while, and then she can come back in?"

The guard smiles again. "Sure."

He unlocks one of the double doors and opens it to the cool night air. Outside is a concrete ledge that juts over a pit. Just as I figured, this is where deliveries arrive.

Jeremy angles me toward the door. "Go on now."

"But—"

"Out you go." He gives me a hefty push.

I stumble forward onto the concrete ledge. There isn't much space before the sharp drop where trucks pull up.

"Watch that!" Drew shouts.

I hear nothing else. My heel snaps, caught in the ridge between the concrete and the metal edge of the loading dock. I wave my arms, trying to sidestep and move toward the stairs I see to the right.

But I'm off balance. I can't find my footing on the broken heel.

I tilt forward to stare into the concrete hole.

Then, like a big ol' peach careening off a grocery store display, I start to fall.

ABOUT THE AUTHOR

JJ Knight is a *USA Today* bestselling author of romantic comedy and sports romance. She's a fierce mama bear for all the humans under her care: biological, adopted, and those in need of mom hugs. Her books portray characters who learn to push through hardship to find love and belly laughs.

Follow her on TikTok: https://www.tiktok.com/@jjknight.author

Find her on Goodreads: https://www.goodreads.com/author/show/7827726.J_J_Knight

Like her on Facebook: https://www.facebook.com/jjknightauthor

Visit her website: http://www.jjknight.com